Alw—
joy and ...
all the best

The Boy with Golden Eyes

Marjorie Young

iUniverse, Inc.
New York   Bloomington

The Boy With Golden Eyes

*This is a work of fiction. All of the characters, names, incidents,
organizations, and dialogue in this novel are either the products
of the author's imagination or are used fictitiously.*

iUniverse books may be ordered through booksellers or by contacting:

iUniverse
1663 Liberty Drive
Bloomington, IN 47403
www.iuniverse.com
1-800-Authors (1-800-288-4677)

*Because of the dynamic nature of the Internet, any Web addresses or links contained in this
book may have changed since publication and may no longer be valid. The views expressed
in this work are solely those of the author and do not necessarily reflect the views of the
publisher, and the publisher hereby disclaims any responsibility for them.*

ISBN: 978-1-4502-3477-1 (pbk)
ISBN: 978-1-4502-3489-4 (cloth)
ISBN: 978-1-4502-3490-0 (ebook)

Library of Congress Control Number: 2010929442

Printed in the United States of America

iUniverse rev. date: 7/26/10

Acknowledgments

It truly did take a village to nurture this book.

Eternal thanks to Dilip and Carole Hiralal for making my dreams come true.

Deepest gratitude to Ann Butler, Manfred Wolf, Helen Chamberland, and Michael Wolf for their endless patience and help.

Many others gave support and encouragement, including: Rika Wakayama, Mimi Young, Anne Dinning, Glenn Young, Leslie Schneider, Shannon Buckner, and Barbara Goulter.

And a very special thank you to Lucie Wolf for making my Lira come alive.

I love you all!

To Sammy – the 'real' Rupert and my inspiration. I love you.

Chapter One

Thus day, without warning, Rupert's life would change forever. For as long as he could remember, he had forever lived deep in the forest with his grandparents. This was most strange because he never had met anyone else. His father had died before his birth and his mother soon after. His grandparents never permitted him to leave the wood, yet always refused to speak of the world outside.

Rupert was extraordinarily smart and curious. By the age of two, he'd discovered his grandparents' books and soon taught himself to read. By age five or six, he'd read everything in the little cottage. But then, new books would appear.

Rupert understood the mystery, but only in part. Every few months, his grandfather would vanish in the middle of the night. Yet his grandmother would offer no explanation. He'd return within two weeks' time; again while Rupert slept. So the boy would awaken to find his grandfather home bearing new books as well as food, and other necessities.

Thus Rupert concluded there must be some town, or at least a village, about a week's journey away. But his grandfather would refuse to reveal where he'd gotten the supplies, or how he'd managed to transport his heavy load through the forest. The little family possessed neither horse nor cart, nor were there any roads that Rupert had ever discovered. When the boy begged for an answer to this puzzle, the cryptic reply would be, "It's not difficult if you put your mind to it." However, that told him less than nothing.

Of course, having read many books, Rupert was aware that most people didn't live as he did. They dwelt in small towns, great cities...or even castles or fortresses. He knew many kingdoms existed with different languages and customs. And how Rupert longed to experience these fascinating possibilities himself; to see the world - or at least the village he suspected was tantalizingly close! But when he questioned his grandparents, they merely sighed and sent him off to play.

Rupert did love the forest. Having no human playmates, he was friends with almost all the animals and trusted them, knowing they would never be untruthful or evasive as he suspected his human companions often were.

He had special whistles to summon his comrades; one for the wolves, another for the rabbits and so on; though he could also communicate with the power of his unspoken thoughts. The boy somehow possessed an instinctive understanding of the woodland creatures, and was always most grateful for their company.

His most beloved companion was a glorious red fox he called Kara. Fellow orphans, they shared a special communion which brought them both joy. Rupert managed to spend a portion of almost every day with her, and they were among his happiest moments.

The only exception to this fellowship was the bears. Though powerful and majestic, the boy sensed they preferred their own kind and would not welcome his intrusion into their world.

He had also received knowledge of the wild things that grew in the forest, having been taught to prepare healing remedies from many plants and trees. Rupert enjoyed this instruction, because so often his kin were taciturn and remote.

One day a most violent storm arrived, and Rupert was ordered indoors. The tempest continued for four days, and the confinement was making him restless indeed. He glared resentfully at his grandfather calmly sorting dried herbs at the small table by the fireside; his grandmother placidly kneading bread nearby. *They* seemed content to remain endlessly indoors. Perhaps that was because they were old, he thought. But as for Rupert, he felt imprisoned.

Finally the unprecedented rain and wind ceased, and he immediately begged permission to go out. His grandparents turned toward him in unison, sharing a quiet, unsettling stare. Finally, his grandfather spoke. "Yes, it is time. And so, fare thee well, boy." A puzzled Rupert then regarded his grandmother, who gave him a small, enigmatic smile. "Off with you then, and don't forget...keep a clear head."

Rupert hesitated at their strange demeanor, and then shrugged. He turned and dashed out, thinking only that he was at last free and longing for his beloved Kara. While the storm raged, he'd envisioned her safe in a small cave she'd once shown him.

He raced in that direction for almost two miles, blissfully inhaling the marvelous scents of the moisture-laden trees, entranced by the melody of their branches swaying in the still-powerful breeze. Finally coming to a halt, laughing with delight at his mud-spattered tunic and leggings, he called out silently to Kara. Before long, the glorious sight of his fox friend speeding towards him greeted his eyes, and in another instant, she had leapt into his outstretched arms.

It was a fine reunion, and Rupert was relieved to know his friend survived the storm without incident. She rubbed her beautiful soft face against his again and again until he at last placed her back upon the soggy earth. He took off at a trot, knowing she would keep apace. The boy hardly had a destination, but simply wished to exert himself after a confinement longer than he'd ever known.

It was some time later that he found himself at a part of the forest normally avoided; a small clearing with one gigantic oak at its center. Surrounding it, at some distance, were half a dozen smaller trees. There had always been something eerie and unsettling about this place to Rupert, as all the branches of the circling trees grew away from the huge oak.

But this day, what the boy saw made him stare in disbelief. For now he observed that all six of those trees had their branches pointing *towards* the one towering at their center.

"How could this be?" he wondered aloud to Kara, most bewildered. Perhaps it was a result of the storm? Yet something else was occurring; a strange sensation drawing him to that very oak like a powerful magnet pulling at the center of his being.

With caution yet tremendous curiosity, Rupert moved forward, helpless to resist. Kara moved cautiously by his side, sensing something was afoot. He circled slowly round the mighty tree, and then stared amazed at what he beheld: the edge of a wooden box protruding from the earth. How long it had been concealed there, he could not imagine. For decades? Centuries? An irresistible power had brought him to its side. Rupert was convinced that he was surely meant to make this discovery. Somehow he had been born for this moment.

Falling to his knees, Rupert began to frantically dig at the drenched earth to free the box from its tomb. Kara, using sharp claws, eagerly lent aid. The boy's thoughts were wild, for surely he'd uncovered a treasure! His grandparents must be very poor to live as they did. What if the box was filled with riches? They could live in a beautiful home in a marvelous city! And even have horses to ride and partake of the chocolates and cakes he'd read of and dreamed about.

Progress was too slow for the frenzied lad. Looking about, he found a sharp stone and grabbing it up began to pound at the rotting wood. A jagged opening was soon created. Then, in a slow-motion and dream-like moment that would change his life forever, Rupert reached in and drew out a sword.

It was magnificent - a scabbard of gold covered with rubies and sapphires. It felt very heavy in Rupert's ten-year-old grasp. In disbelief, he drew the blade. It gleamed inexplicably, despite its long burial.

The boy was overcome with an alien emotion, an overwhelming connection to this resplendent object. Rupert knew with certainty that exhilarating triumph and overwhelming sorrow were somehow attached to it. Gripping it fiercely as his heart pounded, he fought back tears whose source he could not name.

After a long while, he gently kissed the sword and lay it down upon his cloak to protect it from the wet earth. He then turned eagerly back to the box and again reached in.

This time, a fabulous necklace emerged: a gorgeous red ruby of enormous size surrounded by a circle of sparkling diamonds on a long chain of heavy silver. It was indeed dazzling and Rupert had seen nothing like it. He felt the same emotional tie as he had towards the sword, and examined it reverently for a long moment before laying it carefully upon his cloak as well.

There was yet another article awaiting Rupert's discovery. He pulled it out, at first uncertain as to what it might be. It was a beautifully carved large silver oval with a hand grip, three sapphires forming a triangle upon it. Intrigued, he turned it over to suddenly realize that the object was a looking glass!

He had never seen his own reflection and what he beheld startled him greatly. His face was of astonishing beauty, with striking and harmonious features rarely to be seen. His hair was thick, black, lustrous, and wavy, falling to his shoulders, his complexion deeply tanned. But Rupert, having never encountered other children, had no one to compare himself to, and vanity was not in his nature.

No, what astonished him were his eyes! Framed by bold black brows, surrounded by bristling black lashes, they were extremely large, and of an amazing, blazing golden color. They almost seemed to glow like beacons of light.

His thoughts raced to his grandparents' eyes; they were brown, ordinary, normal. The boy sensed that his own must be special - in a manner he could not truly fathom. So the treasure was not the only mystery he'd uncovered that day.

Rupert had never been as amazed, astonished, or overwhelmed in all his life. He must fly to his grandparents and tell them immediately. Why, now they might be rich and live so very differently. A thousand alluring prospects raced through his thoughts. Perhaps he might be properly educated, have friends, and travel the world!

Gathering the sword, necklace, and mirror in his cloak, the boy raced toward the cottage, Kara at his side. He tried to envision his family's reaction when he displayed his find. They'd lived in the forest all their lives and yet never knew of this treasure themselves. How proud of him they'd be! Or such was Rupert's hope. They could be most unpredictable. But this was too great a secret to keep. It was astounding!

As the boy approached home he bid Kara farewell; his grandmother never permitted his friends inside. The fox departed, but drawing nearer, Rupert became wary and slowed to a halt. The forest hares and squirrels that usually greeted his return were nowhere to be seen. The familiar sounds: his grandfather planting in the garden or chopping wood; his grandmother cooking or washing in the stream…nothing of that reached his sharp ears.

Rupert grew most uneasy. Something was surely amiss. As he advanced toward the cottage, treasures under his arm, his apprehensions grew. He called out to his grandparents. But for the first time in his life, no answer came. In disbelief, the boy pushed open the cottage door. He called out yet again; but only an eerie silence greeted him.

The boy with golden eyes stood stock still in the doorway of the only home he'd ever known. At that moment Rupert knew the truth. It struck him like a terrible blow. His grandparents were gone. *They weren't ever coming back!*

Chapter Two

Rupert stood frozen at the cottage threshold. The knowledge that his grandparents were gone forever made him tremble with bewilderment. It was a long moment before he could force himself inside. Cautiously, the boy placed his treasures by the fire and looked about. He could not bring himself to call out again, for he knew there would be no answer.

The lad attempted to calm himself, to think. Perhaps they were merely out gathering herbs or the like? But no, something deep within his soul declared this was untrue. Though he could not explain it, realization struck that finding the long-concealed treasure had caused his grandparents to depart.

Had they mysteriously disappeared like spirits in tales of old? Or had they taken up their possessions and willingly abandoned him? Neither possibility made sense. But he was faced with the undeniable truth that he was ten years old and truly alone.

Rupert examined the dwelling. As far as he could judge, nothing was missing. His grandparents' few belongings remained untouched. A friendly fire burned as the kettle above it boiled. The enticing scent of freshly baked bread perfumed the surroundings. Yet the haunting image of his kin vanishing into thin air remained. It was all most incomprehensible.

Dusk was approaching and the boy realized he had not eaten since dawn. He shakily made himself a cup of hot tea, then tore off a chunk of fresh bread, and spread it lavishly with honey; something his grandmother had frowned upon.

Rupert sat by the fire to eat. It proved exceedingly difficult: a painful knot dwelled in his stomach. When he attempted to sip the tea, one teardrop plopped into the cup.

The boy roused himself from this sign of weakness. After all, his grandparents had abandoned him without a second thought. He must strive to forget them, before pain overwhelmed him. But he felt lonely as never before.

Rupert arose with a start. Surely his animal companions had not deserted him! He rushed to the door and whistled for his rabbit friends. Within moments, four brown forest hares appeared, though not without confusion, as they had never been summoned at night. But this night seemed to be different. And so, after a moment's hesitation, into the cottage they came. Rupert embraced each in turn, and gave them carrots from his grandmother's small garden.

And then he called out to his beloved Kara. She arrived with little delay, and she too was welcomed indoors for the first time, maintaining a respectful distance from the hares. The boy explained matters with his thoughts. Kara did her best to comfort her companion, for which Rupert was most grateful. And at last, he remembered the treasures.

Dashing to the fireside, he unwrapped his cloak. The sword, necklace, and mirror had not vanished as he'd half-feared. For this day had been so overwhelmingly strange he could hardly imagine what bizarre event might next occur.

Joy and energy again coursed through his being, sorrow for the moment forgotten. The treasure was very real and he took each amazing object up one by one, his heart racing almost unbearably. "They must belong to royalty," he breathed to Kara, for whom else might possess such wonders. He knew he could never sell them, as he'd briefly imagined, for he now wished never to part with them.

Examining each gorgeous article in turn, he could not resist peering at his reflection once again. Yes, those astounding golden eyes still shone back at him, filling his being with wild hope and much uncertainty. Intuition still proclaimed that his grandparents' betrayal must be connected to the treasure's discovery. It was a bewildering yet tantalizing mystery.

Then, another thought struck him with great force: *He was free!* At long last he could leave the forest, see the world! He would depart at once, for there remained no reason to stay.

Rupert turned to Kara, explaining his decision. The forest was her home, and he had no right to believe she'd willingly abandon it. But to his joy, she consented to accompany her friend, at least for a time. And that was all he could wish for.

Exhaustion from this unforgettable day suddenly overwhelmed him. He curled by the fire, Kara on one side, his treasures on the other, the forest hares grouped at his feet. It was only moments before a deep sleep overtook him. Strangely, no dreams of his grandparents haunted him through the night. And Rupert was no longer afraid.

He awoke before dawn as was his custom, alert, alive, and filled with a powerful vigor. True, the day before had been no dream. There was no sign of his grandparents' return. Yes, they were truly gone forever.

However, this grim reality did not appear as dark in the light of the morning. He embraced his freedom as a magnificent gift. He must depart away! He, who loved books so much, felt he'd come to the end of one chapter - that of the forest and his grandparents - and was to begin again with the unknown.

His animal companions bounded outdoors to gather their breakfast as he prepared his own; a huge portion of porridge into which he tossed large quantities of dried fruit, nuts, and honey. That done, he looked about, wondering what he might wish to take with him on his sublime journey. With startling clarity, Rupert realized there was little he wished to bring. Everything here belonged to his old life. From this day, his existence would begin anew.

Rupert took up his knapsack, tossing in one change of clothing, all the remaining bread, a jar of honey, nuts, dried fruit, and a flagon of water. He then looked to his treasures. Yes, the looking-glass and the necklace would fit nicely into his pack; but what of the sword?

Above the fireplace hung his grandfather's rusted weapon. Somewhere there must be a belt to hold it. Rupert rummaged through the small trunk holding his grandfather's meager belongings and soon found what he sought. It was too large, but the boy fashioned the belt so the fabulous treasure-sword could hang down his back. Wearing his cloak, it might hopefully be hidden from sight.

Prepared at last, Rupert stepped outside. His rabbit friends were watchfully waiting. Tears sprang to his eyes as he realized he must part from them, perhaps forever. And he had dozens of other friends: deer, wolves, comrades large and small that he loved. He would not summon them, for he could not bear the thought of so many painful farewells. Kneeling, he embraced each of the beautiful brown hares, and told of his departure. He bid them a painful adieu then looked hastily about for Kara. She awaited not many yards distant.

He took one step back into the cottage. Rupert surveyed its interior, his golden eyes sweeping over each object, realizing with absolute clarity that his life had been cleft in two. This, his only home, was irrevocably part of his past. His future was all that mattered now - his thrilling, unimaginable future.

As he stepped out again, Kara raced to his side. Rupert grinned down at her, euphoria filling his being. He had no idea where to go; only a vague hope to discover where his grandfather had journeyed on his mysterious absences. But where that might be, Rupert could not guess.

The exhilaration of new-found freedom rang through his heart. He would encounter other people, see places yet unknown! Laughing aloud, he reached down and took up a large stick, tossing it gleefully into the air. When it fell to his feet, it pointed north. Very well, to the north he would go.

Rupert set out into the forest, concealed treasure upon his back, Kara by his side. As if awakening from an endless dream, he felt truly alive for the very first time. And whatever awaited, he was ready!

Chapter Three

Rupert journeyed through the forest for hours. Or more precisely, he ran, skipped, and leapt through the wood, Kara at his side, feeling elated beyond measure. The thought flowed through him again and again: "I'm free!" For the very first time he might go wherever and do whatever he wished, with no stern-faced elders to deny him.

Sundown took him by surprise. Infused with energy, he could easily have traveled through the night; however that would have been unwise. Finding a spot by a stream, Kara left to gather her own dinner as he pulled bread from his knapsack and consumed a great hunk, dripping with honey. Rupert boldly dipped his fingers into the jar and licked them greedily. He laughed as the sweet substance dribbled down his chin, and laughed again when an inquisitive squirrel came to investigate, sniffing at the boy's honey-covered face.

After downing a handful of nuts and some water, the boy settled in for the night. It was his first time to sleep outdoors; his grandparents had never permitted that either, though they had instructed him in the mysteries of the heavens and how to find his way with their guidance. Now he lay upon his back, leaves crunching beneath him, looking up through the waving branches to the myriad stars. What a glorious night! The moon had not yet risen, and he was thrilled and dazzled by the 'River Of Heaven' as he knew the night sky was called in a far-off land he'd once read of. Finally, he drifted to sleep as Kara kept watch.

Rupert awoke eager and rested well before dawn, and after another hasty repast, set off. The weather had changed, and soon a steady drizzle began. He could have taken shelter, but would permit no delay in this journey to a new life.

The youthful traveler knew well the ways of the forest, and again made rapid progress. Bedded down for the second night, he'd yet to discover signs of human habitation although constantly on the alert. But he was not concerned; if it took a year to find civilization, he would not complain.

That evening, he reverently examined his treasures. Perhaps the mirror was most fascinating. How strange to go one's entire life in ignorance of one's appearance. But that was not unusual; looking-glasses were rare indeed and only the very rich might be supposed to possess one.

Rupert wondered again and again at the sight of his strange, luminous eyes. He had a dark premonition they might attract undue notice when finally encountering strangers, and every instinct cried out for caution.

He traveled on for the next three days. After consuming all the bread, there remained nuts, berries, and roots to eat, and water to drink. However, fatigue was setting in, and a touch of loneliness as well. He adored Kara, and the spirited fox was truly a fine companion. But Rupert longed for human contact and hoped to soon encounter it.

That wish was granted the very next day. Rupert had begun his march before dawn, and now the sun was overhead. He drew to a halt at a startling sound new to his experience. It was clearly some sort of creature - but what? The high-pitched whinny was none too distant, accompanied by the echo of hammering hooves. A moment later, something else reached his ears - human laughter. The boy gasped. He crept forward, taking care to remain out of sight. The forest gave way to a clearing, and Rupert stood in wonder at what he beheld.

Rupert recognized the beast now, having seen so many drawings in books. It was a horse, a magnificent horse, light golden-brown with a dazzlingly long flowing white mane and tail, so astonishingly powerful, graceful, and superb. It raced across the meadow, glory in every movement. And atop the horse was another breathtaking vision.

It was a girl, a very small girl! How could someone so tiny manage to ride such a gigantic steed? She used neither saddle nor bridle, but clung to the horse's mane. Girl and stallion seemed as one. With utter joy she cried, "Go, Majesty faster...fly, fly!" And he responded most willingly.

Rupert had never seen such an amazing sight. The girl - the first he'd ever encountered - so vivid and free and beautiful! She had very long, wildly curling flaxen hair, almost as white as the horse's mane. It flew out behind her like the banner of a proud princess. How astonishing that the first beings he should encounter were these two: horse and rider, so wondrous to behold.

The mighty steed raced closer and then slowed cautiously. The girl, curious, searched for what her horse had discovered, and spotted Rupert half hidden by tree and shadow. The towering stallion reared up on his hind legs. His rider remained astride, impressing Rupert all the more. Knowing he'd been discovered, the boy emerged from the shadows in some confusion, suddenly overwhelmed by shyness.

The lass spoke. "Hello," she said. Laughing at receiving no reply, she repeated her greeting. "It's very rude not to say 'hello' back," she chided.

Rupert stepped forward. "I'm so sorry! I hope I didn't startle your horse," - the first words ever uttered to anyone but his grandparents. No wonder Rupert felt so very awkward.

"Nothing would scare Majesty," she assured him. She regarded the strange boy with avid curiosity. She could not but notice he was staring at her and her horse in a most peculiar fashion. "What's wrong? You look as though you've never seen a horse before."

Rupert's laughter rang out. She didn't know how very true that was! "Yes, indeed, I've never seen a horse before...or a girl for that matter."

"Why, that's the silliest thing I've ever heard. How is that possible?"

"It's because I've lived all my life in the forest with my grandparents. I've never met anyone else - until now."

The bewildered girl gazed at him, wondering at this fantastic statement. At last she slid down and approached Rupert's side.

"Well, if that's true, I'm happy to be the first to meet you! My name is Lira...what's yours?"

"I'm Rupert. I'm ten years old."

"I'm seven...well in three months' time."

Rupert stared. It may indeed have been rude, but he could not tear his eyes from her. She was astonishing, with masses of tumbling silver-gilt curls and bold eyes like flaming dark-blue sapphires. Her cheeks and lips were deepest rose, her complexion soft and fair. Her knee-length dress was of rough blue material, tattered in several places. She was barefoot, her feet and legs covered with mud. Yet her smile was radiant. From her garb, he suspected she must be poor. But how could a poor girl possess such a magnificent creature?

"May I examine your horse? He's glorious," begged Rupert when he reluctantly turned his eyes from Lira.

"His name is Majesty. And you're right, he is the most beautiful and wonderful horse in the world!"

Rupert approached cautiously, sending a message that his intentions were friendly. And then he dared touch Majesty's face, feeling the breath go in and out of those huge nostrils. Majesty lowered his head, calm as a king receiving tribute.

"Is he difficult to ride? Do you ever fall off?" Rupert demanded, his awkwardness forgotten.

"Never," Lira exclaimed. "Majesty and I are good friends and I trust him completely."

Rupert comprehended that he was encountering an utterly new experience; opening a new chapter in his book of life. His nervousness was rapidly departing as he reveled in the moment

But then Lira declared it was time to return home; she must help her grandfather prepare their noon repast and finish her chores. "Please do come along," she urged Rupert.

How he longed to accept! But he remembered the treasure, knowing his first duty was to protect it. How foolish to suppose he could safely carry it about. Yet the boy fervently wished to see Lira's home and meet her grandfather.

Rupert stated that he must first inform his animal companion Kara, who awaited in the forest. Lira wished to invite her too, but learning Kara was a fox, thought better of it, as a fox might attack their chickens. Rupert was momentarily enchanted at the thought of chickens, but remembered to focus on concealing the treasure.

Lira pointed with an outstretched arm back over her shoulder. "Our farm is about a mile in that direction. Come as soon as you can, promise?"

Rupert did so, and watched as Majesty knelt down, permitting Lira to climb upon his back. And then, in a flash, the commanding steed was galloping off in the direction of home.

Rupert made his way to where Kara waited, greeting her with a dazed smile. After describing the encounter, he explained the need for concealment of his treasures. With Kara's aid, he searched for more than an hour, and at last found a hollow log, very ordinary in appearance, which was precisely what he sought. It was a good two miles from the clearing where he'd seen Lira and Majesty. Nothing surrounded it but thick forest, and there was no sign that woodcutters or anyone else might frequent the place.

He cleaned out the hollow space and reverently placed the treasures within, wrapped in his cloak. Rupert then stuffed either end with leaves and sticks, confident he could easily find this spot again, but that no one else would. Kara promised to stand guard until his return.

After embracing his companion, Rupert stood and took a deep breath. He brushed and straightened his simple attire of tunic and leggings as best he could. Rupert was truly to visit Lira's home and encounter her grandfather. He half-feared this was merely an enchanting dream.

Chapter Four

A startled Rupert realized that sunset was upon him; had it really taken so long to choose his hiding place? He quickened his pace and at length reached the clearing where he'd seen the magical sight of Lira and Majesty. Racing across the meadow, he soon discovered the farm from a hilltop - a most inviting sight. At least twice the size of the cottage where he'd grown up, the dwelling was made of wood with a thick thatched roof. A corral stood to one side, where Majesty was grazing lazily. In the back was some sort of barn. Smoke puffed from the chimney, as if in welcome.

Rupert galloped down the hillside and found himself at the cottage door. Filled with trepidation and the greatest curiosity, he took a deep breath, and gave one hesitant knock.

After a brief pause, the door swung open. The man who greeted him could not possibly be Lira's grandfather; *he was so young*! He had shoulder length, light blond hair which glinted of gold, the same color as his narrow moustache. The fellow was very tall and lean, dressed in simple, somewhat shabby garb. But his handsome features were alive with intelligence and his light blue eyes gleamed with something akin to astonishment; he seemed as taken aback by Rupert's appearance as the boy with his. There existed an air of lively warmth in his demeanor, yet Rupert intuited this man had known much sorrow. Enthralled, Rupert had forgotten to speak.

"Well, hello there, young sir. And what can I do for you today?" His words were light, but his clear blue eyes gleamed with intense curiosity.

"Is this where Lira lives?" Rupert was finally able to blurt out.

"Why, yes indeed. I suppose you must be young Rupert. We'd been expecting you since noon, and here it is supper time. I'd begun to think you a creature of mere fantasy!"

"Oh, no!" Rupert exclaimed. "It was all quite true! Do forgive my delay..." Rupert paused in confusion. After all, he could hardly reveal the cause had been concealment of his treasure.

"No excuses required; do come in." This man's smile appeared warmly genuine. His own grandfather had always seemed so cool, so remote. Yet Rupert could not help but notice this fellow's gaze of fascination as he regarded his guest. Could his golden eyes be the cause?

Rupert stepped slowly inside. The cottage was simple but inviting. The chairs were covered with cloths of red, blue, and yellow. Wild flowers were in a metal vase upon the tabletop, and wooden carvings of animals lined the mantle above the fireplace. Best of all, Rupert saw books. So many books! The shelves were filled with them. Rupert was entranced, and then remembered his manners. He turned towards his host again as the back door opened and Lira entered bearing a small basket.

"Lira, your friend has arrived at last. I see you spoke true after all."

Lira raced towards Rupert with delight. "I'm so glad you found us. We're always very glad of company, as guests are so rare nowadays. This is my grandfather, Liam."

"Lira, go add the herbs to the stew. I believe young Rupert must be famished. You will join us?" asked Liam.

Rupert accepted with alacrity. The house was filled with delicious smells, and Rupert was indeed very hungry. Within minutes, they were seated round the small table. Rupert felt surprisingly at ease though eating with strangers for the first time.

The repast was delicious - some sort of vegetable stew. The dark bread was freshly baked and fragrant, but before he could partake,

Lira urged him to put butter upon it. Gingerly, Rupert applied the sweet-smelling substance, new to his experience, and then took a big bite. His mouth watered with delight, his eyes growing round with surprise. Lira and her grandfather laughed warmly.

Rupert's hosts were content to limit themselves to a few friendly remarks, realizing their guest was quite ravenous. Finally, when Rupert's appetite seemed satisfied, they permitted themselves to inquire from whence he'd come and why he was alone.

The ordeal was an awkward one for Rupert. After all, he could hardly mention the treasure, and felt ill-at-ease discussing his grandparents' abrupt disappearance. So the boy simply stated that he'd lived all his life with his kin in the forest, never seeing anyone else, till the day he'd returned to find his grandparents gone.

Lira and her grandfather exchanged glances. Such a strange story! And Rupert had the feeling that Liam was less than convinced of being told the whole tale. Rupert blushed to think he *was* lying in a way. But he couldn't think of anything else to say.

"So," said Liam, "you've lived isolated all your life? Very odd indeed!"

Rupert could only agree. "Truly odd as I now discover; though between my animal friends and my books, I was for the most part content."

"Books!" Lira cried. "You know how to read, then?"

"Yes, of course, since I was very little. We had lots of books, and when I'd read them all, my grandfather would bring back more. Every few months, he'd depart in the middle of the night, returning in about two weeks' time. I knew there must be a village not far off; that's what I've been searching for. Perhaps there I might learn news of my grandfather."

"There's a village not many miles distant," exclaimed Lira. "Sundays are market day; perhaps we might go and seek out the bookseller."

Rupert was overjoyed that he'd been traveling in the right direction after all. But Liam appeared more interested in Rupert's reading ability.

"So you can read, young sir? I'm very glad to hear it. You see, my many books have been going to waste. My eyesight has begun to fail in recent days. Oh, I can see well enough for most matters, but I'm no longer able to read, and thus have been unable to teach my granddaughter."

"So Lira can't read?" Rupert was shocked.

"Well, there are no schools anymore, of course; only for the very rich, and girls are seldom allowed," Lira explained as if this were common knowledge.

This was news to Rupert, who recalled that his grandmother could read quite well. How could that be? Wasn't she just a simple woman who'd lived in the forest?

They continued to sit by the fire and eagerly converse. Rupert felt at his ease and far more at home than with his own family. He found himself offering to teach Lira to read and volunteered to read aloud to them every night. His new friends greeted this plan with alacrity.

And it seemed a happy plan to Rupert, knowing it would be dangerous to wander here and there, fearing for his treasures, never knowing whom to trust. Perhaps it would be advisable to remain for just a little while, visit the village, and search out news of his kin.

And how wonderful to introduce Lira to reading! And perhaps she'd teach him to ride Majesty in return. Liam could certainly use help around the farm and Rupert was young and strong. Yes, he could remain for a time.

Finally, Rupert began to inquire of Lira and Liam's family. He felt he might ask anything, and they'd reply truthfully.

Lira explained that her mother died of a fever when she was but a year old. Her father was gone too, but not of sickness.

Liam took up the story with a dark look in his penetrating blue eyes. "Lira's father is my own son Daniel; a good and courageous young man. Our kinsmen were barons long ago, owning a large estate and enjoying a most fulfilling existence serving the royal family for hundreds of years. The kings of that line were strong, wise, and peaceful, and all had prospered.

"But then, terrible times arose. A marauder of unknown origin had threatened war, but at the last moment, requested a meeting with our good King Marco. His Majesty agreed, always open to any peaceful resolution. But Marco was deceived. Upon attending the peace talks, accompanied by his three royal children, the villainous Zorin invited them to a feast, and there poisoned them all; murdering them and eventually the rest of the royal line.

"With that, the devil Zorin invaded. The citizens resisted, but with their beloved sovereign slaughtered, none remained to lead them. The people were vanquished and ever since, Zorin, and now his son Ryker, have decimated the land.

"All loyal to King Marco were punished. Our family was stripped of most of its possessions; nothing remains but this small farm. This horror occurred when I was but a boy. And now, justice, hope, and peace are but a distant memory.

"Nothing remains of that valiant royal family," Liam finished with a profound sigh. "The good people of this kingdom continue to suffer. Wars, plagues, they come like unwelcome guests. Young men are forced against their will to serve a bloody usurper. That was indeed the fate of my dear son. We have heard nary a word from him in five dreadful years, and often fear he has perished in the wars or of a fever."

"Well," Lira whispered, "maybe he'll come back. And maybe the legends are true that another king with golden eyes will return!"

Rupert, who had been attending in rapt fascination, gasped aloud. "*Golden eyes!* What did you say about golden eyes?!"

"Why," replied Liam, returning Rupert's stare with a piercing look of his own, "our monarchs for countless generations have had golden eyes. No other possessed them -'tis indeed a mystery. But father to son, king to prince...all golden-eyed!"

Rupert stared in wonder. *He* possessed golden eyes! Could he conceivably be part of this royal family? But no, they had vanished long ago. Yet now, he was stunned to see Lira and Liam did not apprehend the truth. How could they fail to notice what he'd beheld so clearly in that mirror? He turned to Lira. Her grandfather's vision was failing; but what about her?

Rupert struggled for a neutral tone. "Please do tell me, Lira. What is the color of my eyes? For you see, I've never beheld my own reflection." Of course, he said nothing of his looking-glass.

Lira was amused. "So sorry to disappoint you," she said with a smile. "Your eyes are beautiful indeed, but very dark - almost as dark as your hair."

Rupert attempted to conceal his great confusion. How could this be? The boy's mind stumbled; perhaps his eyes were only golden while in his forest home? Or perhaps the mirror contained magic and…

Liam interrupted his wild thoughts. "You appear disappointed, young Rupert! Hearing my tale of the Golden-Eyed Kings, perhaps you wished to be one of them? Beware, for that would be perilous indeed. A golden-eyed lad would be arrested on the spot and turned over to King Ryker! And the penalty would certainly be death. So rejoice in your life-saving dark orbs."

Rupert was overwhelmed with bewilderment. If having golden eyes made one the usurper king's foe, he was grateful that they no longer appeared that hue, at least for now.

But he knew what he'd beheld in his reflection! It must certainly be connected to the tragic saga of the lost royal family. Now he had even more secrets to keep. And many more mysteries to solve.

Chapter Five

The next days were amazing ones for Rupert; perhaps the happiest ever known. Lira and Liam continued to treat him with astonishing openness and warmth. And each day brought new experiences that filled him with wonder.

After a restless night wondering why his golden eyes had apparently turned dark, he was awakened before dawn by Liam gently shaking his shoulder. He could hear Lira's giggles, already by the cottage door, torch in hand. Rupert was handed his own torch and the three made their way to the barn.

There, he was introduced to the goat, cow, and chickens, all creatures never before beheld. Majesty also slept in the barn and whinnied in salutation. The two children went to stroke his great head for a morning greeting.

Rupert felt powerfully drawn to the splendid beast. Of course, the steed was the very first he'd ever seen. But there seemed to be more to the connection than that. However, there was no time to ponder, for Lira informed him that the cow and goat must be milked and he had to learn how to do it.

Rupert was delighted and fascinated. Two more different creatures would be difficult to imagine. They had no objection to his close scrutiny. And Rupert, the greatest of animal lovers, absorbed every detail.

Lira perched on a little stool next to the cow called Lulu, and showed him how to proceed. Rupert observed with admiration the tiny girl's nimble fingers. He was eager to test his own skills, but the results were less successful. Apparently, it was more complicated than it appeared. All three of them soon dissolved in laughter, which continued as Rupert made equally clumsy attempts to milk Iris, the goat. But he soon caught on. Liam instructed Lira to gather eggs, and she headed back to the cottage to prepare their morning repast.

Rupert could have spent half the morning eyeing the chickens: strange fowl that could hardly fly and made such amusing, clucking sounds. He was used to the soaring, singing birds of the forest, gliding with grace above the treetops.

Liam, his light eyes gleaming in amusement, informed Rupert that their work had indeed just begun. Now came cleaning out the stalls of all the animals and replacing the muck with clean hay. It was a hard and odorous task, but Rupert was delighted to participate. "I'm helping Liam," he thought with pride. His own grandfather seldom desired his assistance. The boy basked in being of use and in receiving praise for his efforts.

At last it was time for breakfast, and Rupert was famished. Back in the cottage, Lira had prepared steaming bowls of porridge, along with bread, butter, and tea. Porridge proved quite delicious with butter added to it. Rupert ate several helpings, and then felt ashamed of his hearty appetite. But neither Liam nor Lira seemed to mind. He felt accepted, just as he was.

After breakfast, Liam announced the time had come for Lira's reading lessons. Delighted, she embraced her grandfather. Rupert, with a twinge, realized he'd never witnessed, or indeed even experienced, such a display.

Rupert requested pen, ink, and paper. He and Lira were soon seated side by side. Liam made himself busy sorting spices and herbs by the fire, so he might observe. Rupert didn't mind. He carefully wrote out the letters of the alphabet for Lira, teaching their names and pronunciation. He had her copy them as he wrote, instructing her in writing as well as reading from the start.

Lira was on fire with enthusiasm. Her sapphire eyes blazed as if lit from within and her pink cheeks glowed. Rupert was amazed at how bright she was; memorizing everything immediately. By the time he'd written the complete alphabet, she could repeat it back to him and draw most of the letters without error.

Rupert was moved by her joy. "Do try to spell your name," he urged his pupil. Lira wrote it out with great care, whooped with delight, hugged Rupert with all her might and planted a kiss upon his cheek. Rupert awkwardly accepted the embrace.

The girl ran to her grandfather and into his arms. For Lira to read and write was something they'd always dreamed of; now the vast world of knowledge was at last open to her.

"This is indeed a happy day. Your father would be very proud," Liam told a glowing Lira.

The lesson continued. The eager pupil learned to spell her grandfather's name, Rupert's, Majesty's, and those of her parents. Tomorrow, he'd teach her to read and write simple sentences.

"Why," he thought to himself, "she'll be reading books in no time at all." Her mind was like a thirsty sponge, absorbing everything presented to it.

However, the lesson drew to a close, for there were many chores awaiting. While Lira worked in the garden, Rupert and Liam chopped firewood. There were fences to mend, tools to sharpen, and animals to look after. The tasks were endless.

Rupert reveled in it all. The noon meal, when they finally paused for it, was a simple affair of bread and a strong goat cheese new to Rupert's experience. There were apples for dessert; he polished off two, and was encouraged to take more in his pocket for later.

Then it was time to exercise Majesty, a task that Lira considered pure joy. "Every day I take him to the meadow where you first met us," Lira explained. There the stallion was allowed the violent exercise he craved.

"Today, you must learn to ride Majesty," Liam declared to Rupert, who responded with heartfelt joy.

"Thank you so much!" Rupert exclaimed as the two children raced out. Liam watched them lead the steed away, greatly perplexed and intrigued.

The idea of learning to ride thrilled Rupert's soul. After all, he'd only experienced walking on his own two feet. The boy recalled the previous day's never- to-be-forgotten image of girl and beast, now forever a symbol of beauty and freedom in his mind. And how he longed to sample that freedom himself!

Lira was eager to become Rupert's teacher. "It's all very simple," she declared. "Just trust Majesty, feel a part of him."

It sounded easy enough, but Rupert was less confident than he appeared. When they reached the open field, Lira had Majesty kneel down and invited Rupert to climb up behind her.

Before he could hesitate, Rupert found himself sitting astride the golden stallion, arms about Lira's waist. Lira asked Majesty to walk, and Rupert churned with excitement. How different the world looked from high atop this towering creature! What a strange sensation to be in motion without his feet touching the ground.

Majesty sped to a trot. Apprehension filled Rupert as their pace quickened, but Lira, feeling his tension, reminded him to relax, and soon he could and did. Feeling no fear, Rupert wished to go faster and faster, and sensing this, Lira urged Majesty on. Almost immediately, the steed was racing across the meadow, the two riders shouting with joy.

Before long, Lira brought Majesty to a halt, and slid down. "Rupert, you must ride on your own!"

The now fearless lad did not hesitate. Rupert grabbed Majesty's silken white mane, urging him forward with voice and thought. The stallion instantly obliged, taking off at a gallop. All trepidation flew away, and the boy felt invincible!

Of a sudden, Rupert had an extraordinary experience. Images of combat flashed before his astonished eyes; visions of arrows flying, swords clanging, horses charging, and banners flying. But were these images true, or products of fancy? From the past, or from the future? Rupert could not know, yet he felt lost in the wonder of the moment. How he wished he were carrying his secret treasure-sword that he might brandish it high above his head! In exhilaration, he shouted out a war cry. The boy could hear Lira's laughter from across the meadow.

At last, the girl waved him to a halt. It was time for Majesty to run free. Reluctantly, Rupert dismounted. "You were amazing! Are you certain you've never ridden before?" exclaimed Lira. He'd taken to this task as effortlessly as she'd learned to read. Rupert only laughed.

They both settled on a nearby log as Majesty frolicked. What a beautiful sight that was! After a long pause, Rupert turned to his friend. "Please, tell me about your astounding horse." Something inside him now burned to know the truth.

Lira was happy to oblige. "Majesty came to us in a very strange way," she began with excitement. "One night a few weeks ago, I had a terrible nightmare about my father. He was locked in a dungeon, hungry and sick. When I awoke, Grandfather Liam was at my side.

"I feared to describe the terrible dream, not wishing to worry Grandfather, but I told him all. He tried to comfort me, saying he'd had dreams too of late that his son would come home. And that we'd all three be united and a family again at last.

"It was most difficult to believe those soothing words," Lira continued. "But my grandfather said in his most recent dream just two nights before, my father had promised to provide a sign of his return, and of peace returning to the kingdom as well."

Lira turned to Rupert in growing eagerness, speaking in a rush. "It was not two days later that we awoke to hear a horse whinnying by the cottage door. We dashed out to discover an exceedingly beautiful stallion, and no rider in sight.

"We were amazed. None of our neighbors owned such a beast. Of course, the wicked King Ryker has soldiers everywhere; but they would never possess such a mount. He must belong to royalty.

"Grandfather Liam and I approached the towering creature. He welcomed our attentions, and seemed content to remain. Grandfather built a corral, and warned me not to mention his existence unless his owner might appear.

"But as the days went by, no one came. I noticed that Grandfather regarded the stallion with much emotion. Finally, he took me upon his knee and explained that this beautiful horse, which I had named Majesty, was the symbol of the hope he'd predicted.

"Grandfather Liam explained that as a boy, he'd seen the noble King Marco on many occasions: at his castle, parading through town, or riding off to battle. And he'd never forget King Marco's horse, the fabulous Rico."

Lira continued joyfully. "Rico was a huge golden stallion with a gleaming silky long white mane and tail. He appeared as strong, beautiful, and valiant as the king himself. And Majesty looked exactly like him...they could be twins!

"Of course," Lira continued, "Rico was never seen again after King Marco's murder at the hands of that nasty Zorin. But the moment my grandfather discovered Majesty, he felt convinced of a connection to our late liege. This was the sign my father had promised to my grandfather in his dream: that darkness would be lifted from the land and that his dear son might return at last!"

Rupert attended spell-bound to Lira's words. Could this magical horse *truly* be a link to King Marco...or the return of the Golden-Eyed Kings? He wondered at the visions of bravery and battle he'd witnessed while atop Majesty. Was *he* to be riding Majesty into combat someday, heralding the resurrection of the lost royal family?

Was it mere coincidence that the twin of King Marco's great horse had found Lira and Liam at the same time Rupert unearthed a royal treasure? Leading to the discovery of his golden eyes? After which, somehow, he'd been led to their door?

What could it all mean? Deep in his heart, Rupert believed that Majesty had delivered a profound message this day. He and the stallion were linked; destined for a yet unknown role in returning this kingdom to its former glory. And the boy prayed it meant that Lira's father and Liam's son would return as well.

For the first time in his existence, Rupert became aware of something or someone guiding his path, leading him to a new destiny. He could not know its identity; but he was determined to discover it. And not to fail at any cost!

Chapter Six

For the first time in Rupert's life, sleep proved elusive. He could not overcome the feeling that he had embarked upon on a mysterious mission somehow connected with the saga of the Golden-Eyed Kings, and his mind was filled with restlessness.

The boy experienced a powerful energy coursing through his being. Yet, the undeniable fact remained that he was but ten years old, and could not possibly possess the wisdom to address his many questions; or even, in truth, what questions to ask.

He longed to confide in Liam. His family had long served the Golden-Eyed Kings, and on several occasions had actually met the last of the noble line, King Marco. Surely, Liam was a treasure- trove of information concerning their history.

Yet Rupert hesitated. He loved Liam and little Lira as his own blood. But something in his heart warned against trusting them with all his secrets; the secret of the treasure, the fact that he might have golden eyes, that Majesty had shown him unsettling visions, the sudden eerie feeling that something or someone was now directing his path. He could hardly comprehend how completely his life had altered. He'd gone from a boy living isolated from the world to someone who might have a role to play in the kingdom's destiny!

Rupert daily thought of his treasures, lying hidden in the forest. His heart felt foreboding concerning their fate. It was difficult to control the urge to dash into the forest to check on their safety. The boy knew Kara would guard them as best she could. But what if someone had stolen them away? Rupert's heart contracted in horror at the thought. They had now ceased to be mere treasure, but rather symbols of the Golden-Eyed Kings and their tragic, lost kingdom. How they had come to be buried in that obscure corner of the forest remained a mystery. But it was another puzzle the boy vowed to resolve.

Rupert also missed his precious fox friend deeply and was frustrated he could not somehow visit her in stealth. All day long he was with Liam or Lira. He hesitated to ask for time apart, fearful that Lira would insist on accompanying him. The moon would be full in a few days' time, and Rupert determined to then try to leave undetected, for he dared not use a torch to light the way.

Once the decision was made, Rupert gave a sigh. It seemed he'd gone from a child's thoughts to adult concerns. But his life had changed, and there was nothing to be done but face that fact. Moreover, despite his challenges, the boy was tremendously excited about the bewildering turn his life had taken. There was so much to enjoy every moment, and so much to anticipate. Why, tomorrow morning they were going to the village market. An entire village filled with crowds of people and new sights! And perhaps he'd discover the bookseller, who might know of his grandfather.

But in truth, Rupert wondered if he honestly wished to find his grandparents again, for he'd rather remain with his new friends. And since his grandparents had deserted him, the lad suspected they might not even desire his return.

He finally fell into an exhausted slumber, only to have Liam shake him awake well before dawn. They had to arise even earlier than usual this day, as the village was over five miles distant. It was necessary to arrive, attend to their business, and return before dark.

Rupert leapt up with sleepy-eyed enthusiasm. He quickly joined Liam and Lira in the barn, breezed through his chores, and then the morning repast. He had endless curiosity concerning the village, but Liam advised against high expectations.

"Years ago, the market had been a wonderful thing. Many hundreds of people lived in the settlement, and many more came for market day. There were acrobats, jugglers, actors, puppet shows, and magicians galore to enliven the proceedings. Every sort of food, clothing, trinket, animal...just about everything one could imagine was on display. The people wore their best bright colors and it had been very festive indeed.

"However," Liam continued, "those happy days have vanished forever. With the slaughter of the true royal family, fear rules the land. King Ryker's soldiers are everywhere, surveying the people for the slightest word or deed against their evil master. So many have perished of hunger and illness, been thrown into prison, or dragged unwillingly into the army, that the population has fallen by at least half.

"Now an atmosphere of anxiety prevails, as citizens merely hope to trade their goods for items they desperately need. Instead of a land of plenty, this is now a land of want. Rupert, you must not expect much in the way of merry-making," Liam warned.

Despite the sober lecture, the fact remained that Rupert had never been to any village before, and had never been with more than two people at the same time. So what lay ahead was still an adventure. He was taken aback, however, when Liam and Lira appeared ready to depart wearing dark cloaks that covered them from head to foot. It was a shame to Rupert that Lira, who was as beautiful as a little flower, should be so concealed that the world could not admire her glowing face. But Liam had another cloak for Rupert, and soon he was as hidden as they. It was explained that it didn't do to draw attention to oneself, as the king's soldiers and spies were everywhere.

They set off on foot, Liam pushing a little cart before them. It carried fruit and vegetables they hoped to trade for grain. Rupert understood that they couldn't ride Majesty, for his very existence must remain hidden lest the guards confiscate him.

Of course, Rupert never minded walking. He and Lira frolicked along the road, laughing and dashing about, and Lira taught him some lively songs. However, when encountering other travelers, they kept heads down and remained silent. It saddened Rupert that the citizens lived in such isolation and fear.

The path to the village was a winding, uphill walk, so progress was slow, but eventually they reached their goal. Rupert's spirits had been so very high, but the dark mood that greeted him made him take a breath.

There were fewer than two hundred people in all, he observed, and most were attired in dark cloaks. Instead of bands of musicians as in the old days, there was but one lone plaintive fiddler at the entrance to the village; a sickly beggar hoping passersby would toss him a few coins. Rupert wanted to weep at the sight.

The boy saw yet sadder sights as they walked on. Hungry women and children sat upon the ground, hoping to sell or trade their meager wares. Liam whispered that their fathers and sons had most likely perished or been forced into service. So many were now left on their own to survive. Here and there, a few ragged youngsters ran about, but for the most part the mood was somber and subdued.

Fear was in the air, and Rupert himself felt a stab of foreboding when he witnessed King Ryker's men for the first time, covered from head to foot in black armor, long swords strapped to their waists. Carrying forbidding spears, and mounted on horseback, they looked formidable indeed - almost inhuman. Rupert could now comprehend very well Liam's warning against attracting their notice.

Still, this was Rupert's first time in a village. There was so much to see...wilting piles of produce, clothing and trinkets, and even animals for sale. Scrawny wild dogs ran about...his first sight of such creatures. Liam warned they were not to be trusted. Rupert had no fear of any animal, but kept his distance for Lira's sake. Abruptly, Rupert longed for a dog of his own. With one as his companion, surely he'd never be alone again, come what may!

The boy remembered he'd come in search of the bookseller. Liam guided him to where he normally set up his stall. But this day he was not to be seen. Instead, there were a dozen or more bedraggled citizens, mostly women and children, milling about.

Rupert overheard their conversation. It seemed they were waiting for the bookseller; he could be hired to read and write letters for the villagers, because these days most were illiterate. Many had sons or husbands in the army, or daughters married to men who lived far off, and this was their only means of contact. Several women had tears in their eyes; if the bookseller did not appear, they could neither read messages received, nor reply to them.

Rupert was moved and impulsively, if not wisely, spoke up. "If you please, I can read and write, and would be most happy to be of service."

There was an astonished gasp from the crowd as well as from Liam and Lira. The villagers were shocked not only to find a literate boy in these sorry times, but that he'd dare to make himself so conspicuous.

Rupert was unnerved as he gazed up at Liam's silent, disapproving face. Still, he would not refrain from aiding these poor souls.

"Forgive me," he announced, "I have no paper, pen, or ink. But if you could provide them, I'll be happy to be of assistance."

After a moment's hesitation, some of those who waited produced what he'd requested. Within moments, Rupert was seated cross-legged upon the ground, and an orderly line had been formed. He began reading letters aloud and composing responses to faraway places. Most of the missives were so sad! Young Rupert was receiving a quick education in local conditions. People wrote of hunger, sickness, and longing for missing loved ones. It was often necessary to report the death of a family member.

Rupert felt a passionate longing to aid these people, hardly noticing that the villagers were staring in wide-eyed wonder at his bravery and clear sympathy for their plight. His most unusual dark coloring and outstanding looks could also not escape the notice of those who might peer beneath his hood. A murmur ran through the throng, as they wondered who this strange boy might be.

Liam found himself in a quandary. How he longed to grab Rupert and drag him away from curious eyes! But doing so would only make him the more conspicuous. Liam believed there was something fascinating and mysterious about Rupert from the moment he'd laid eyes upon him. Somehow Liam felt compelled to shelter the lad and keep him from harm. But here Rupert was, attracting a crowd the very first time he'd entered the village!

Now what was to be done? Liam did not know. He recognized that Rupert was an innocent. The lad knew nothing of the world, having lived isolated all his life. Liam blamed himself. He should have warned the boy more severely, but had not wished to spoil Rupert's anticipation at being out in the world for the first time.

Rupert was kept busy for a long while. Finally, the last letter was written. Many wept their thanks, and attempted to press money into his hands, as he adamantly refused. But they insisted. Rupert finally compromised by keeping only a small portion of what was offered.

Rupert was delighted to have a few coins in his pocket - the first money he'd ever possessed. Liam wished to depart for home at once, but Rupert pleaded for time. He had not yet explored the market and greatly desired to make some purchases. In truth, he longed to buy gifts for his dear friends.

Rupert took Lira by the hand, and asked what she'd like. The happy girl desired hair ribbons, and Rupert was pleased to oblige. They found the ribbon seller, and he insisted she choose as many as she liked, and soon Lira had ribbons of blue, green, and red. She knew better than to try them on, having promised to always to keep her face concealed.

Joyfully, Lira ran to tell her grandfather, who had gone to trade his fruits and vegetables for oats and flour. A moment later, Rupert spied a necklace with red and blue stones. He'd get it for Lira as a surprise! He found he had enough coins for the purchase. Continuing his exploration, the boy spotted something that thrilled him - a magnifying glass! Perhaps with its aid, Liam could read once more. Inquiring of the price, Rupert found it more than he could pay. He sighed in disappointment, and reluctantly placed it back upon the display.

"Why, you're the lad who was writing those letters," said the gaunt elderly fellow. Rupert admitted it was so. After hesitating a moment, the merchant declared it would be a pleasure to present the glass as a gift. Rupert, startled, insisted on paying all the money he had left. But the man refused. "You've done so much for so many today. You're a very special young lad, and I'm mighty pleased to be of service to you," he whispered, taking care not to be overheard.

The frail stranger wrapped the magnifying glass in paper, slipped it into the pocket of Rupert's cloak, and sent him swiftly on his way. Rupert realized many citizens were furtively pointing him out; that he was the subject of many a hushed conversation.

He knew Liam must be most anxious to depart. Rupert spotted him across the green with Lira. He moved to join them when a lady enveloped in a flowing dark cloak approached.

"Please, young sir, I need your help with a letter."

Rupert attempted to decline, but she begged him, declaring it would only take a moment. He could not see her face, but her voice was so insistent that he could hardly refuse. Rupert sat down on the ground as she handed over pen, paper, and ink.

"Here is what I wish you to write," she began. "But first, please look at me."

Rupert, startled by her request, involuntarily glanced deep into the face that was hidden from view. The boy could tell nothing of her age or appearance.

The lady gently reached out to touch his waving black hair. Rupert felt a strange energy flow between them, and, as when astride Majesty, the boy suddenly saw a vision; this time of riding not into battle, but instead through a crowd cheering in jubilation! A sea of hands reached out, and voices shouted for the Golden-Eyed King. But again, he could not see the face of the rider, or determine whether this was a vision from the future or the past.

Rupert gasped in astonishment. The lady remained silent and calm. He felt somehow she could witness what was in his mind's eye. After a long moment, she spoke again.

"Here, write these words please: 'Dear Friends, I do believe our longing is near an end. Someone with golden eyes is back from the dead. He is even now in our midst. Our prayers have been answered!'"

Rupert looked swiftly into her still-concealed face. Who was she? Was she speaking of *him*? The boy leapt to his feet before completing his task, almost dizzy with astonishment. Could she know his secret?

The lady placed a basket before him. "Please accept this as payment. But you must not open it until you return home. *Promise me!*"

A stunned Rupert nodded wordlessly. Bending to retrieve the basket, he could feel the weight of whatever was inside. He was dazed and confused, confounded and intrigued. But when Rupert stood up again the woman abruptly vanished before his eyes!

Chapter Seven

Rupert stood frozen in place. How could this mysterious lady be there one moment and gone the next? He whirled about to see if he could spot her retreating figure. But it was difficult to tell one person from another when almost everyone wore long cloaks and hoods.

Rupert struggled for calm while gazing about to assess if anyone had witnessed what had occurred. Liam was staring at him from across the village green. For a timeless moment, the boy was at a loss, and remained holding the unopened basket to his beating heart.

Without warning, Rupert felt an iron grip turning him about. He found himself facing two of King Ryker's guards. Clad in black armor, they looked strange, even terrifying. Rupert was addressed in an ice-cold voice.

"Here, boy, let's just see what you're hiding in that basket!"

Rupert involuntarily attempted a step backwards, but the soldier's steely hold prevented him. And out of the corner of his eye, he observed Liam rushing to his aid.

Rupert felt eerily calm; though fearing the outcome should Liam interfere with the guards. Without hesitation, Rupert attempted to communicate with his friend, just as he'd always done with his animal companions, warning him back. He must have succeeded, because Rupert, stealing another glance in his direction, observed Liam slowing to a halt while yet some distance away.

"Why sir," Rupert inquired respectfully to the guard, "what is amiss with my basket that you wish to examine it? And do forgive my puzzlement. This is my first visit to this village, and I'm yet quite ignorant of the customs here."

The crowd that had begun to gather gave a collective gasp. How could the boy dare address those fearsome guards? Any other villager would have silently handed over the basket, while trembling in fear.

The soldier lifted up his visor, exposing a pair of cold, pale-blue eyes. He reached down and roughly yanked back Rupert's hood, revealing his face clearly for the first time. Again, there was a murmur from the crowd, marveling at the boy's beauty. Most citizens were sickly and pale, but Rupert exhibited a marvelous inner glow and a very rare perfection of feature. Moreover, his dark hair, eyes, and complexion were an extreme rarity. He looked like someone in a picture book.

"Allow me to see who dares speak back to the king's guard," growled the blue-eyed fellow. "And don't look all innocent-eyed at me! I saw that lady hand you the basket and disappear like some magician. Hand over that letter."

Before Rupert could react, the guard snatched up the paper, still lying where he'd dropped it. But Rupert sighed in relief, for he'd been too startled by her words to continue writing after she'd mentioned the Golden-Eyed Kings.

Rupert's adversary read aloud: "Dear Friends, I do believe our waiting is nearing an end..." He looked down at Rupert. "What did she mean by that, boy?"

"I assure you, I know not," he replied calmly. "She was a complete stranger, after all. Having no money to pay, the lady gave me the basket instead. I picked it up, but she'd left already."

"'Left' is it? I'd say disappeared in an instant!"

Rupert peered at the guard wide-eyed. "Really?" he exclaimed. "How I wish I'd seen that!"

There was a smattering of laughter through the crowd and the guardsman felt the little brat was making a fool of him. He snatched up the basket. The second guard lifted his own visor and regarded

Rupert for a long moment. This fellow had dark green eyes that somehow comforted the boy, though his heart pounded with worry over what might lay concealed within the hamper.

The green-eyed soldier spoke. "Come, Ned, this lad isn't worth our time. It's the woman we want, but she's gone now. Give the boy back his payment."

But Ned would not be easily deterred. The crowd seemed to hold its collective breath as he opened the basket. Only the two soldiers could see the contents. They both peered in and burst into snide laughter.

The young man with green eyes addressed a determinedly calm Rupert. "So that's your payment, eh? It'll cost you far more than it's worth!"

They snickered again, and the green-eyed fellow handed the woven container back to Rupert. "Good luck with that. And now I urge you to be on your way."

"Why, thank you sir," replied Rupert. "I'm happy to be of service. As happy as you are, I'm sure, to serve such a noble king!"

Again, his words were fine and proper, but something in his tone made the blue-eyed soldier want to strike the insolent child. In fact, he raised his arm to do so when the other fellow interfered.

"Oh leave him be, Ned. He's just a lad who doesn't know our ways. He'll learn soon enough, I'll warrant you."

The grim-faced Ned gave Rupert a mighty shove that knocked him backwards to the ground. The stunned boy managed to hold on to the basket, however.

Liam and Lira began to race towards him, but again, Rupert sent them a mental message to remain calm. Most unexpectedly, however, some of the citizens began to speak up...something they hadn't dared in decades.

A hesitant voice was heard to say, "For pity's sake, leave the boy be!" Another exclaimed, "He's done nothing wrong"...while another prayed, "Bless that sweet-faced child!"

The guards were greatly taken aback. There were several hundred villagers present, but fewer than a dozen guards. They'd hardly required large numbers to subdue the populace, which had long been too cowed to even speak before the soldiers.

But this day was different, and the king's men knew this boy was the center of it all. They wondered far more about him than they did the disappearing woman. And despite being pushed violently to the ground, the boy continued to look up at them with calm, dark eyes. His gaze seemed to penetrate their being. The effect was most disquieting.

The guard with green eyes reached down and helped Rupert to his feet. "Get on with you." Rupert smiled in a way that made the fellow feel a strange desire to bow down before the lad. He was greatly perplexed. "By the way, what is your name?"

"My name is Rupert," he replied softly, and the villagers whispered his name to one another, like a word carried by the wind. "What is yours?"

"I'm the king's guard, Morley."

But Ned had lost patience. "Never mind our names...we'll be watching *you* should you dare to come again. For that matter, wherever you may be, we'll be watching. Now all of you depart away. The market is over for this day!"

The citizens reluctantly began to scatter, but all had eyes upon the young stranger. The two guards mounted their horses, glaring down at the crowd. Rupert stood staring back at the men, frozen to the spot. And then, Liam and Lira were at his side.

"How brave you are!" exclaimed the girl. "Why, you're braver than all the villagers put together!"

Rupert dismissed such claims with a brief laugh. He gazed into Liam's eyes, which were aglow with fascination, pride, and alarm.

"I longed to come between you and the guards, but you begged me to hold back; and so I refrained against my better judgment. But, I see I would have only increased the danger. However, we must depart at once, for darkness will soon be upon us."

The three headed out toward the road leading from the village. Liam pushed his cart, now filled with supplies. He invited Rupert to place the basket upon it, but was refused. The boy also declined

Lira's entreaties to open it, explaining that the lady had requested he wait until returning home, and he planned to keep his promise.

They hadn't gone far when the sun began to set. It was a beautiful sight, but Rupert observed that Liam was far from at ease. There were many dangers in the dark, from robbers and wolves, to the king's men.

But within moments, several dozen villagers had joined them on the way. Without saying a word, the citizens trailed behind, acting as protectors to Rupert, Lira, and her grandfather. It was their way of thanking the boy for helping with the letter writing, but even more, for standing up to the guards. No one had done so in living memory...not without being struck down on the spot.

How this captivating lad had managed the courage and calm, they could not fathom. He'd even inspired a few of their number to speak up. And now Rupert inspired the citizens to stand together instead of going their usual separate ways, to provide the boy and his family with a measure of safety. And how much stronger they felt when joined together than when isolated and apart.

They traveled the five miles back to the path that led to Liam's farm. There the three of them turned, and the rest continued silently on their way. But all concerned believed that day something had awoken in their hearts that had too long been allowed to slumber. Something very much like hope and courage.

The three arrived safely home. The moment they set foot in the door, Rupert lay the basket down and with Lira crowding next to him, opened it. Inside was a puppy...a very large sleeping puppy. Lira laughed with delight, and Rupert was pleased indeed. When he'd seen the wild dogs at the village, he'd wished for a dog of his own, and behold, his wish was granted!

As Rupert reached inside the basket, the puppy awoke and began to happily lick Rupert's face. He was a golden yellow color with a black muzzle and ears. His paws were huge, perhaps an indication of his future size.

Rupert, admittedly delighted with the pup, still felt a measure of disappointment. The mysterious lady had spoken of the Golden-Eyed Kings, and he anticipated what was concealed would be connected with that. He experienced some confusion; that is, until he looked up into Liam's face.

"Why, that's a Mastiff puppy," the tall man exclaimed. "They were the guardians of the late royal family. Every Golden-Eyed King possessed one!"

"But, why didn't the soldiers mention that? They merely laughed!" wondered Rupert, again amazed at the golden-eyed connection after all.

Liam shook his head. "I suppose they didn't know. After all, our true kings are long gone. Ryker's men merely thought it a good joke that the dog would eat you out of house and home."

Rupert promised to earn money reading and writing letters to pay for the puppy's food. And Lira promised to sell things she grew in the garden. But Liam's expression appeared distant and thoughtful.

Rupert encouraged Lira to play with the pup. He'd remembered the magnifying glass and Lira's necklace still in his cloak pocket, and wished to conceal them so they might be a surprise...perhaps on their next birthdays. He picked up the basket, intending to put it away along with the cloak.

"By the way," Rupert inquired innocently, "when are your birthdays? I was just wondering."

"Mine is the 13th day of the ninth month" replied Lira with a giggle, as the puppy was licking her nose "And Grandfather Liam's is the 18th day of the tenth month. When is yours?"

"Oh, mine is the 3rd day of the tenth month," replied Rupert absently.

He chanced to glance down into the basket where the pup had been wrapped in a blanket. Something caught his eye. Within the folds lay a glowing object. It was a ring; a very large and heavy ring of shining gold, a huge red ruby at its center.

The wild beating in his chest made him dizzy. This ring certainly belonged to a king! Before he could reach for it, he heard the words of Liam, though they seemed to come from far away.

"Your birthday is the 3rd day of the tenth month? Why, that is the birthday of so many of the Golden-Eyed Ones: King Marco, his father and grandfather as well! Even the ancient founder of the line, King Theodore! By some strange fate, so many were born on that very day!"

Rupert looked up to see Lira and Liam regarding him with some amazement. And he felt that the time of concealing the truth must be drawing to an end.

Chapter Eight

There was a long pause after Liam's startling announcement that the birthdays of so many of the Golden-Eyed Kings and Rupert's own were one and the same. It was, in a way, the moment that Rupert had been waiting for; an opportunity to open his heart and pour out his secrets. But something deep within urged silence. Liam was regarding him, his forthright, wonderfully clear blue eyes searching Rupert's for a true response. But after a pause, the older man turned away. Perhaps, he reminded himself, there was nothing for Rupert to reveal.

So many striking signs had pointed towards Rupert being a most extraordinary child. His rare dark coloring and fineness of feature brought up memories of a long-lost glorious queen. But he could hardly have a direct connection to the Golden-Eyed Kings. After all, his eyes were deepest brown, and that should settle the matter. But Liam's heart instinctively knew this boy was a keeper of secrets. Confidences, however, could not be forced.

Rupert felt burdened by guilt. He wondered why he could not reveal all to the two people he trusted and loved. But some force that was a part of him yet also something more, demanded restraint. His secrets were a most hazardous burden. And Rupert wondered how much he himself knew of the truth. After all, he knew of the Golden-Eyed Kings...but did he truly have golden eyes? They were there, and then, they were gone.

The awkward silence eventually passed, and Lira, with her instinct for smoothing things over, declared that she was starving hungry, and that the puppy must be as well. She hastened to prepare a meal, wondering aloud what the pup might find appealing.

They had no meat in the house; indeed, they very seldom partook of any, as it was very expensive. But her grandfather suggested eggs, and before long, they were entertained by the pup gobbling up the repast as if he hadn't eaten in a week. They could not help but smile at the sight, and soon the tension had passed. Rupert and Lira sat by the puppy as he also devoured bread and cheese. Fearing there would soon be nothing left, Lira produced cheese and bread for the humans to eat, and all were satisfied before long.

The puppy wished to play, and Rupert, Lira, and Liam were delighted to comply. He was so awkward and adorable with his round body, black face, and giant paws. Liam advised them that Mastiffs could weigh as much as a large man when fully grown. Lira laughed with consternation, adding that the chickens would have to lay eggs at an alarming rate if they were to satisfy him.

Rupert felt great joy at his new companion, though distracted by the ring still concealed in the basket. He felt a blazing excitement, yet regret that he must refrain from sharing his amazing discovery.

So for the moment, he would conceal the ring; but how? He could not yet hope to return to the forest to hide it with the other treasures. Keeping it in the house seemed far from satisfactory. And the boy was seldom alone. When would he even find a few moments to secrete it? For now, it was perhaps wisest to keep it on his person... in his pocket or worn round his neck. But that idea also seemed fraught with danger of discovery.

Meanwhile, Lira insisted the dog have a name, and declared that Rupert must have the honor. But Rupert did not feel up to the task, remaining guilty at the thought of holding back from Liam. Rupert suddenly brightened, insisting that Liam himself must decide.

Regarding Rupert with a twisted smile, Liam suggested 'King'... looking straight into Rupert's eye as he did so.

Rupert blushed and looked down, declaring he didn't really care for that.

"How about "Raja?" the boy then exclaimed, inspiration filling him. Rupert remembered from his reading that in a land very far away, it was the word for "king!"

Liam smiled his approval with shining eyes, and Lira agreed at once. So the puppy, from that moment, was known as Raja.

Finally, it was time for sleep. What an extraordinary day it had been; the visit to the village and all that had occurred. It seemed that this day had contained a hundred hours.

Rupert always preferred to sleep by the fire, Lira and her grandfather in the small room at the back of the cottage. Little Raja, it was clear, wished to remain by his young master's side.

Rupert, with thudding heart, waited a long while until certain that the others were asleep. He lay by the crackling fire, Raja beside him, but curiously, the pup remained awake also. Rupert knew his mission; to take the ring and hide it away. But where? Behind books? Under the table? Beneath the woodpile? Nothing seemed secure. The only course was to conceal it in the forest. But he must await the full moon, which would appear in just a few days. And at last, he would finally see Kara again!

He rose and tiptoed to the basket. He carried it to where the glow from the fire made the contents visible. Raja sniffed at it in curiosity, and Rupert shooed him off. He gingerly pulled back the blanket and, yes, the magnificent jewel was there, its huge red ruby glowing in its fabulous golden setting.

Blood racing, Rupert stealthily lifted it out. It was the first time he actually touched the object. Despite the chill in the room, the ring felt warm. He was sick with anxiety that Liam or Lira might suddenly appear and demand an explanation. But at the same time he was hopelessly entranced, intrigued, and very drawn to the glorious thing.

Tears sprang to his eyes. The great and good King Marco had certainly worn this very ring...and other Golden-Eyed Kings for hundreds of years before him. Rupert realized he should immediately move to conceal it, yet could not resist the lure of trying it on. He knew it would never fit. It was meant for a grown man. And if he wasn't a part of the royal family, he had no business being near it. But the ring had come to him, so perhaps it was permitted?

Holding his breath, Rupert slid it on his finger. He had to hold his hand up, or the ring would have immediately fallen off. He drew his hand close to the fire, to admire the dazzling glow of the ruby and the gold. For a brief instant, the boy pictured himself as one of the Golden-Eyed Kings, leading his people with power and justice and compassion.

But only a short moment later, Rupert began to feel something very different. His head began to pound and his stomach as if hot metal had been poured into it. He keeled over in terrible, agonizing, terrifying pain.

Raja began to whimper, and Rupert, through his suffering, was yet able to fear discovery. He prayed the pain would quickly pass, and for a brief moment it did. But then it returned with a vengeance. He felt both hot and cold, and rivers of sweat began to run down his face and body.

"What is happening to me?" he wondered in despair. "This must mean I was never meant to wear the ring! Or has it a curse upon it?"

His thoughts ran wild, but in his mind flashed images of the mysterious woman with the basket. Perhaps she'd recognized him as a Golden-Eyed One; but perhaps she was their enemy, not the ally that he had presumed her to be. Was there poison of some sort upon the ring?

Rupert became ever more afflicted, as if he was falling into a dark tunnel or well. He began to retch violently; the dinner he'd eaten not long before came back up. But though his belly was soon empty, the horrible heaving continued. Rupert feared losing consciousness. Perhaps he was about to die? But his thought was still of the ring.

He must protect Lira and Grandfather Liam if it was poisoned. In a last gasp of strength, he took the ring from his finger and placed it upon the very bottom of the woodpile by the fire. It was piled high, and he hoped that Liam's custom, of placing new wood on top of the old, would continue. At any rate, there was nothing more he could do. His strength had vanished.

Rupert continued to lie by the fire and retch. He curled into a ball and gripped his stomach in despair. His head ached like nothing in his experience. He felt evil spirits were deep inside beating at him with hammers and axes.

Little Raja whined and ran about in circles. Reluctant to leave his stricken friend, the pup finally raced into the other room, barking and whimpering until Liam and Lira awoke and heard Rupert's moans.

Dashing to his side, the two beheld Rupert in great alarm. They knelt beside him and called his name. The suffering boy could only hold his stomach and moan. When Liam touched his forehead, it seemed to be on fire, his whole body radiating a very strange heat. He ordered Lira to fetch water, and they began to try to cool him down. Lira attempted to make him drink, but though he swallowed a small amount, it was soon retched back up again.

Lira burst into tears. Her mother died of a fever, and she was terrified that this swift strange illness would take her beloved Rupert as well. Liam reminded her sternly there was no time for weeping. He instructed the frantic child as to what herbs to gather to prepare a healing tea.

She ran off to do his bidding, and Liam did his best to clean the floor, and removed Rupert's tunic and leggings to make him more comfortable, at least. He placed the boy near the fire, and continued washing down his patient with cool water, constantly speaking reassuring words, though he did not know whether Rupert could hear.

Rupert appeared almost unrecognizable from the beautiful, vibrant boy he truly was. His skin had taken on a pale, almost greenish pallor, his abundant, lustrous, waving hair lay matted, wet and flat, and his brilliant lively eyes, half open, seemed far away and vacant. Already, his body seemed thinner. Liam had seen many victims of fever, but this seemed different. The sudden onset of symptoms along with stomach pain and retching seemed to indicate poison!

For a moment, he feared for Lira's safety, as they'd all eaten the same dinner. But both he and Lira seemed well enough, as did the pup. Had Rupert eaten anything at the village? He hadn't seen him do so, but could not be certain.

Liam knew great fear. He did not know if his skills were sufficient to heal the boy, or if this being poison, whether any cure was, in fact, possible. But he would do everything in his power. This child felt as dear to his heart as his own missing son.

The night was perhaps the longest in memory for them all. Lira had prepared the herbal tonic, but Rupert never managed to keep it down. He seemed to grow even more ill, if that were possible, and appeared to be drifting away from them. Lira and Liam called his name again and again, but he could never do more than moan in response. The puppy never left Rupert's side, whimpering in fear. Raja seemed to comprehend well the danger that threatened his young master's very existence.

The dawn finally came, and a new day always brings hope. But despite Liam's reassurance, Lira could see he was no better. Rupert's fever and pain continued unabated, and he had fallen into in a coma. This was very different from the peace of a calm sleep. There was something that made Lira feel that he was going far away, to a place where she couldn't follow.

For a very long time, Rupert was aware of nothing but the hideous pain that had invaded his body like some monster from a dreadful tale. He could not think, speak, move. He wished for nothing in this world but that the torment cease. Rupert realized he might very likely die, but was too exhausted to struggle. And truly a part of him welcomed the thought...anything to be at peace!

Yet there was another voice in his heart or head urging him to fight. To not dare let go! He wished to heed that voice, but so little strength remained. How bewildering that one's life and one's own body could change completely in a matter of minutes. Change from being courageous, confident, and curious into a wretched being that would rather die than continue another moment.

But he was too tired to think of anything, really. Behind closed eyes, he saw strange, bright colors, then blackness, the faces of his grandparents, then Liam and Lira and Kara. He saw many beautiful butterflies, and then terrifying beasts pursuing him. His mind whirled round and round until he felt even dizzier and couldn't think anymore. He only wished for rest; for he was now aware that he was just a small boy after all. And what was attacking him seemed a powerful giant.

Rupert's suffering raged for three days. Liam could see him fading, growing thinner and weaker by the moment. He could take no food or drink, and that was the worst sign possible.

It seemed unthinkable that this mysterious and marvelous child, who had turned their lives and even the villagers' lives upside down in such a brief time, could be taken from them. It couldn't happen, yet it seemed that it was so. He did not know if Lira could endure dealing with this new loss, or, in fact, if he could either.

For many hours Rupert had no contact with this world. His mind was in a place of darkness. But of a sudden, he was no longer alone. He opened his eyes and looked about. Lira and Liam were at his side before the fire and little Raja too, but though he could plainly see himself motionless on the blanket, he wasn't really there! He seemed to be floating far above the room.

How extraordinary! The pain had vanished and he felt clear-eyed and euphoric. Perhaps this was death? You just float away! He didn't wish Lira or her grandfather to be sad, but was so relieved that the suffering had ended at last.

Rupert became aware of a bright light behind him. He turned, and saw a lady bathed in golden rays. He did not feel astonished to see this; it appeared quite to be expected. Was this perhaps part of another world?

The glowing apparition reached out to him. He could not see her face clearly, but she seemed to be smiling. She could communicate without words.

"You are not meant for this place yet," she seemed to say. "Why are you here?"

"Is it because I put on the ring?" Rupert inquired. He knew the answer without knowing why.

"Yes, indeed. You were too hasty, as you often are. You experienced the death of King Marco, the Golden-Eyed King poisoned by Zorin.

49

No one imagined you would suffer so. We only supposed you might see a vision of the death, not experience it."

"But, am I a Golden-Eyed King? Was that ring meant for me? There is still so much I don't understand. I don't want to keep making mistakes."

Rupert felt her radiant smile. "*There are no mistakes. Only opportunities to learn!* All shall be revealed in good time. You must learn patience, which is not yet one of your strengths. Your heart will lead you."

Rupert was most unsatisfied. He longed to question her sharply, beginning with her identity, but she turned and began to fade away.

"You must go back now…back to learn so much more."

He called out for her to stay, but she was gone. Rupert instantly felt himself falling, and was once again terribly sick. He longed to weep in despair. He was so tired of battling this agony.

But abruptly, he became aware of something else, something other than pain. There was something rough against his face, rubbing his eyes, forehead, nose, cheeks, and chin, again and again. It would not cease and allow him to return to oblivion. Rupert, realizing there was no escape, moaned aloud and moved his hand feebly to brush it away. He touched something soft and warm and slowly, weakly, opened his eyes.

As if from a distance, Lira and Liam cried out. "He's back!" Lira shouted. "Oh, Rupert, thank you for coming back!"

Rupert saw them through a haze of confusion. Liam, his voice choked with emotion, wept out these words: "We thought you had left us forever, but Raja wouldn't let you go! He kept licking your face and refused to give up. And now you're finally awake!"

Rupert could not truly comprehend what had occurred, but in an instant, he was given broth to drink, and though he swallowed it very slowly and painfully, he managed to keep it down. The nourishment traveled all through his body, bringing back a bit of strength. He attempted to sit, but could not manage to even move a muscle.

But he had returned from his journey. He gazed feebly at the two people and the pup that he loved so very much, and felt grateful beyond measure to be with them once more. For the moment, that was enough.

Chapter Nine

Rupert's recovery was not swift. For two days after he had returned from the brink, he could do nothing more than sleep day and night. Either Liam or Lira was always at his side, along with Raja. Every two hours, their patient was awoken and made to partake of rich vegetable broth. He was far too weak to feed himself, and they patiently helped until he consumed the entire bowl each time. Rupert could not seem to focus on them, or even to speak. But they were happy merely to have him awake and taking nourishment, feeling more confident with each hour that he would be well.

On the third day, there were further signs of improvement. The boy was able to sit up, only for a few minutes at a time, it's true, but that seemed a great accomplishment. He was able to feed himself, and to carry on brief conversations. A bit of color returned to his wan cheeks, and Rupert even managed to reach out and pat faithful Raja.

After another day or two, he was able to partake of bread along with the soup, and continued to drink of the healing teas. It puzzled Rupert to feel so exhausted by doing very little, but Liam explained that such was often the case after so serious an illness.

Rupert felt disconnected to his own body, almost as if he was still watching himself from afar, but this sensation gradually lessened. He became more aware of his surroundings, and able to converse more readily. Liam and Lira now permitted themselves to leave Rupert for brief periods while they attended to the chores that had been neglected for too many days. Of course, Raja kept watch, and could be trusted to alert them if aid was needed.

"Yes, this is surely an amazing pup," Liam assured Rupert when he was up to having a chat. "He saved your life twice already. Once, when he gave the alarm to let us know you had fallen ill. Imagine if we had slept through the night and only found you in the morning. It might have been too late…," he paused, his voice choking with emotion. "And then, again, when we feared you were not returning to us, little Raja kept licking your face, calling you back. How remarkable that he'd know to do that; most remarkable!"

Rupert readily agreed, and managed a smile, a sight so beautiful to Liam that his eyes filled with tears to see it.

"But how long have I been sick? Because "little" Raja looks larger by at least a foot!"

They laughed, for it was true how quickly the pup had grown in so brief a time. Lira's prediction that the chickens would be sorely challenged to produce sufficient eggs was only too true. But the happy hound would eat anything set before him.

Rupert also observed that Raja seemed to spend a lot of time sniffing at his person. He guessed he might not have the most pleasant odor, and begged for a bath. Liam chuckled, and agreed that Rupert might be sufficiently recovered. Water was heated in the fireplace, and poured into a metal tub. Though yet weak and requiring Liam's aid, Rupert felt ever so much better afterwards. But the experience did drain his strength, and it proved necessary to sleep for several hours to recover.

When he awoke, he learned that Lira was out exercising Majesty. Rupert missed seeing the great horse. So upon their return, Liam bore Rupert out to the barn in his arms, so the two could be reunited.

Majesty seemed to realize the danger Rupert had endured, and rubbed his massive head against the lad again and again. Rupert could feel the magnificent horse's energy enter his being, and indeed felt stronger as a result. He insisted on being permitted to walk back to the house, and was able to manage it. Rupert was as pleased as if he'd climbed a great mountain.

After that, his recovery advanced rapidly. He was able to sit up and read for hours at a time, feeling well enough to become restless, and greatly desired to resume his chores and go outdoors. However, the weather had turned chilly and damp, and he was ordered to keep by the fire. His caretakers were delighted that their patient would likely be back to his old self within a few short days. All three realized that they'd escaped what seemed certain tragedy, and felt a rich love and appreciation for one another even greater than before.

One peaceful morning when Lira was out in the garden and Rupert reading by the fire, Liam came to sit down before him.

"There is something you ought to know," he began. "I'd better admit that I know your secret!"

Rupert, blood rushing to his face, could only stare. Might Liam be referring to his golden eyes? Or the ruby ring?

He was fearful to respond, afraid to give too much away. Liam's expression, however, was amused, a sparkle lighting his crystal-blue eyes. Would he truly appear so lighthearted about such a serious matter?

"What? What secret? I don't understand," stuttered Rupert finally.

"Why, the secret you attempted to conceal from Lira and myself; something I hadn't meant to discover, I assure you."

That told Rupert less than nothing...unless he meant the ring? He continued to regard a smiling Liam, who seemed to invite confidence. But Rupert felt most unprepared to speak of this so suddenly. After they had saved his life, he knew he might trust Lira and Liam with anything, but whether it was wise to do so remained yet in doubt. His face reddened in confusion and he looked down.

"Don't look so abashed, my dear boy. I know you meant them for our birthday surprise. But I feared you'd been poisoned at the village, and so I searched the pocket of your cloak. I came upon the necklace and the magnifying glass. I'm very sorry to spoil your plans. I didn't tell Lira, of course. But I believe in complete honesty, my lad, and so felt obligated to reveal my discovery."

Rupert felt flooded with relief and consternation. He'd more or less forgotten the necklace and glass with all that had happened since. He laughed in relief, for he'd feared his true secrets were about to be revealed. But perhaps this was the time to share them at last. The urge to open his heart won out. He opened his mouth to speak, when there came a timid knocking at the cottage door.

Both looked up in surprise. There had never been a single visitor since Rupert's arrival. Liam cautiously opened the door to find a village woman, looking most uncertain.

She was pale and thin, and seemed to apologize even as she spoke. The hesitant woman explained that many citizens had gathered the previous Sunday to see the boy Rupert. Word had spread near and far of his letter writing skills, and more especially of how he'd stood up to the guards in such a miraculous manner. All clamored to see him. There had been many more soldiers than usual at the market as well, so the atmosphere had been extremely tense.

But neither Rupert nor his family had appeared, and rumors aplenty flew about that he'd been arrested, fled, or taken ill. She had wished to see if all was well and thank Rupert again for aiding her correspondence the week before.

Liam invited her in, but she stood hesitant at the threshold. However, when she heard Rupert's voice also insist, she obeyed. She saw immediately that Rupert had indeed been ill, but was quickly informed he was now on the mend.

Alarmed that one of the rumors, at least, had proven true; for it was feared that the king's men had poisoned the boy! Refusing to reveal her name, she wished Rupert well, and left him a small cake she had baked. Knowing of her poverty, it was a valuable tribute indeed. Rupert thanked her and sought to reassure as to his condition. She then gave the young hero a timid smile and made a hasty retreat.

When the lady had gone, Liam and Rupert exchanged looks of consternation. They had been so focused on Rupert's brush with death that the outside world had been almost forgotten. Now it appeared that Rupert's appearance at the village had been continually talked of and speculated upon. Not for the first time, they were reminded that they had come under the king's scrutiny...or at least of that of his men.

By the following day, a steady stream of well-wishers appeared at the cottage door. Word had quickly spread that Rupert had been gravely ill, but had managed a miraculous recovery. Details of his illness began to take on a life of their own, and many whispered that King Ryker himself was responsible, that he had put a curse upon the lad for daring to defy his guards.

Liam grew most uneasy, and finally was compelled to announce that the boy was not yet fully recovered. After he turned away several more callers, the visits finally ceased.

As they ate dinner that evening, however, Lira, Liam, and Rupert were most disheartened at this turn of events. Rupert believed he was not worthy of being regarded as a hero. And he dreaded the thought of causing complications for those he loved. Perhaps he must leave, and return to his forest home; a most unwelcome thought. But Rupert was at last learning the value of caution.

"I believe I should go," he ventured. "My presence here may prove to do you harm."

"No, you mustn't!" cried Lira at once.

Liam counseled against such hasty thoughts. "Your place is with us now. I hope you recognize that. But it would be wise to avoid the village for the present. This talk may die down if we do."

Rupert realized, with a twinge in his heart, that the citizens would count on him to appear again soon. But perhaps he should heed Liam's call for discretion. He had acted recklessly before, and must not do so again.

But it seemed this fine wisdom was coming too late. Because at that very moment was heard the sound of horses galloping towards the cottage, and a terrifying instant later, came a mighty pounding, and a cold and dark voice bellowing words they all dreaded to hear:

"Open up in the name of the king!"

Chapter Ten

Rupert had heard nothing as terrifying as the brutal battering on the cottage door. He stood motionless, as it seemed an eternity passed. He knew, without doubt, his life was to change forever in that instant.

Liam, however, took action. Though the hammering continued, he swiftly ordered a bewildered Lira into the back room, sternly commanding her not to emerge under any circumstances. He then knelt to embrace an agonized Rupert. Regarding him directly, Liam commanded the boy against displaying fear no matter what might occur.

Rupert had only the briefest moment to return the embrace. Liam moved to the door before it was demolished. In seconds, the small room was overwhelmed by guardsmen...at least a dozen, and there were clearly more outside.

Rupert prayed with a guilty heart that this show of force did not mean that they knew of his possible connection with the Golden-Eyed Kings. He feared for the safety of his friends. After all, they were completely innocent of any wrongdoing, and he desired to protect them at all costs.

Liam's tall form stepped forward, attempting to keep his voice calm. "What is your business here? This is a peaceful household."

The leader of the intruders threw up his visor. Rupert's heart sank. It was someone Rupert had seen before, the guard with the icy blue eyes, the one called Ned. He roughly shoved Liam aside.

"It's the boy we have business with, fool. He's under arrest!"

Rupert felt his throat go dry, his heart race. But he could neither move nor speak.

"On what charge do you arrest a mere child?" pleaded Liam.

"Why, the charge of being a bloody little thief," came the sneering reply. "Your precious little lad is a robber of the poor and honest!"

Rupert felt a measure of relief at these words. He knew he had stolen nothing, and the charge was not connected with the lost royal family. Feeling more confident, he stepped in front of Liam, who was yet attempting to shield him from the guardsmen's view.

"Why, I have never taken anything that did not belong to me, I assure you. Please believe me, sir. This must be some mistake!"

"Yes, and the mistake was yours, you little snake!"

The words and the way the pale-eyed Ned pronounced them at Rupert made his heart go cold once more. The sadistic fellow was clearly enjoying himself.

"But what do you think I stole? Who accuses me?"

"Why, he does," replied Ned, as one of his men dragged a gaunt and elderly fellow through the door.

Rupert recognized him. He was the villager who had given him the magnifying glass; insisting it be his gift when Rupert could not pay. The old man looked to Rupert, as if begging forgiveness.

Rupert realized at once that all was lost. The poor vendor knew he'd presented the glass as a gift, but certainly had been forced into a lie. Rupert saw the picture all too clearly, now that it was far too late. King Ryker and his guards would never forgive any disruption amongst the villagers. And how he now regretted his bravado, defying Liam's warnings!

"Well," said Ned in a voice suddenly soft, but no less frightening for that, "what do you say for yourself? Are you calling this man a liar? He claims you stole his glass when you didn't have the coin to pay!"

"I didn't steal it! I thought he gave it me," Rupert pleaded, trying to not get the terrified citizen in trouble. "I'll be most happy to return it."

"Oh, so you admit you have it. You see, all of you, he's confessed!"

Liam stepped forward, placing one protecting arm about a shaking Rupert. "He did no such thing. It was merely a misunderstanding. Allow the boy to return the glass, no harm done."

But Ned only laughed at that. "Hand it over this instant, or we'll tear the place apart piece by piece!"

Rupert almost gasped aloud in fear. What if they *did* ransack the cottage? They might find the ruby ring. And what if they searched the barn and found Majesty? They'd take him away. And they'd accuse Liam of hiding what was obviously a royal ring. The danger had just multiplied a thousand-fold in Rupert's eyes. There was only one thing to do.

"There's no need to search," he cried desperately. "I'll fetch the glass for you!" He raced to the corner of the room where his cloak hung. As he reached into his pocket, he also found the little necklace with red and blue stones he'd so joyfully bought for Lira's birthday. He was struck with the terrible realization that he'd never give it to her now. And further, indeed, he may never ever see Lira or her grandfather again.

Silently, he handed the glass to the fearsome Ned, who snatched it away and then held it up. "You can all witness the brat is a liar and a thief. Prison is too good for the likes of you. If I had my way, your head would be on a pike before morning! But I've got my orders." He grabbed Rupert roughly by his neck and began dragging him from the room.

Rupert gave one urgent look up at Liam, apologizing for all the pain he'd caused. Raja had begun barking wildly at the guards, but Liam scooped him up to keep him safe from the soldiers' heavily booted kicks. The puppy seemed desperate to protect his master, but this was one time when he could not keep him from harm.

Then, just as Rupert was being dragged out the door, another voice was heard. It was Lira who, ignoring her grandfather's order, ran desperately into the room.

"Stop, please," she begged, her voice choked with tears. Before Liam could prevent it, she was at Rupert's side, throwing her arms about him, her sapphire eyes streaming with weeping. "He would never steal anything! Please let him go!"

For an instant, attention from the guards shifted from Rupert to Lira...something that terrified the boy. All the soldiers were gawking at her.

"Well, what have we here?" inquired the icy-eyed Ned as he pried Lira from her beloved friend. "How now, Missy, if you aren't just the prettiest little thing I've ever seen! Where have you been hiding yourself? You'll be making some lucky lackey of the king a likely bride one day; or perhaps His Majesty himself would covet such a pretty lass when you've grown a bit!"

It took all of Liam's effort of will not to punch Ned's smirking face. Rupert was being dragged off to rot in prison, and now this threat to Lira.

Neither of the children had the knowledge of what Liam suffered with for years...that it was the habit of the usurper kings to force any girl they fancied into marriage when they became of age. No one was permitted to refuse. The punishment for the girl, for her entire family, could be prison...or worse. It was one of the most pressing reasons why he'd always insisted the girl conceal her face when leaving the farm.

But it had been to no avail. Now the king's guards knew of Lira's existence. And they would not forget her. No one seeing her face would forget it. So now, sooner or later, they'd return to take her away.

Liam swore to himself, by the memory of her dead mother and her missing, perhaps dead, father that he would never allow that to occur. How he could prevent it, he did not know. But at least he had time, and he would think of something. Meanwhile, he struggled to keep the rage and fear from his voice and reached out to retrieve his trembling granddaughter to his side.

"I believe you've gotten what you came for." He held the tearful girl firmly as his eyes gazed deeply into Rupert's.

Rupert stared back at them. He tried to tell them with a look and a thought how much he loved them, how sorry he was to have caused them harm, begged that they take care of Raja and Majesty too.

But the moment of farewell ended before it began, and the boy was dragged out the door, accompanied by Raja's howling protests.

The night was chilly, and Rupert was allowed no cloak, nor anything else for that matter. Another guard took him from the fearsome Ned, roughly lifting him onto one of the horses, and mounted after him. He swiftly secured Rupert's wrists, so tightly that the pain was immediate.

"Make your farewells, boy, because it's not likely you'll see these kind folks again," he said with a wicked laugh. But before Rupert could speak, the horses charged off and the cottage, Liam, Lira, Majesty, and Raja were left behind in the flying dust.

They rode for what seemed hours through the cold night. Rupert couldn't help but shiver. He wondered if he was still suffering with fever, this just one more horrible nightmare. How he longed to wake up! But it was all too real. He was to be locked up in one of the usurper king's prisons.

Had anyone ever escaped, he wondered wildly? The thought cheered him for a moment. But what if he did? He realized with a searing pain that no matter what, he'd never be able to return to the cottage where he'd lived so happily. Even if he could get away, that would be the first place the soldiers would look. So he could never go back, never see them again. And what of his precious Kara and the treasure? Rupert could not prevent tears from coursing down his face, and hung his head to conceal them from the guard riding in such cold silence behind him.

Then, though it was the middle of the night, Rupert noticed something strange. Along the roadside he saw villagers, standing in silent groups here and there. Word had obviously spread that a large party of soldiers had ridden towards the farm where Rupert lived. The people didn't seem merely curious; they seemed to be silently lending sympathy and support.

No one spoke, but he could sense their feelings of despair that the boy they'd found so intriguing was now being taken away. They could do nothing against a formidable group of heavily armed guards; nothing but make a show of support, even if a timid and silent one. And Rupert was grateful. Because once locked in a dark prison, he'd be fast forgotten, forever.

Rupert estimated they'd traveled about ten miles beyond the village when they arrived at what appeared to be an old castle, one that had been allowed to fall into decay and disrepair.

"Well, take a good look, sonny. This is High Tower Prison, your new home...for what's left of your miserable little life!"

Rupert did look. It was almost dawn and the sky had lightened. He was able to make out the outlines of the once formidable structure, its huge walls at least twenty feet high. The entire building appeared to be made of granite and stone. It must have been beautiful years ago, and Rupert felt instinctively that it had been a former home of the Golden-Eyed Kings.

Of course, the evil King Ryker would take pleasure in turning a Golden-Eyed King's castle into a dark prison; a constant reminder that the days of magnificent justice were truly over. It was like crushing people's hopes for the future and dreams of past glory into the mud.

Rupert was dragged rudely from the horse and forced-marched into the prison. The high walls seemed to close in upon him, and he felt as if entering his own tomb. He couldn't help but shudder, and the sense that this couldn't be real, that it must be a nightmare, returned. But deep in his heart he knew full well there was no waking up.

His mind ran desperately back to all his mistakes that brought about this wretched turn of events. But then, unbidden, returned the voice he'd heard; that voice from his dream, saying again: "*There are no mistakes...only opportunities to learn.*" Could this be an opportunity too? If so, Rupert failed to see it. But he was willing to snatch up any sign of hope, and knew he must persevere to avoid falling into darkest despair.

The heavy gate of the fortress slammed behind them, and Rupert was pushed and shoved down many a dark stairway and passage. The hair on the back of his neck rose when he heard muffled pleas for mercy from behind the thick doors they passed.

They finally halted near the very end of a corridor. The steely-eyed Ned twisted the rusted key that had been left in the lock, and the heavy wooden door was dragged open. The man grinned down into his face as he untied his prisoner. Rupert experienced an exquisite pain as the blood was finally able to rush back into his hands.

"There you go, boy! Good King Ryker hopes you enjoy your new home. And may you soon rot in it."

Giving Rupert a final shove that sent him sprawling, the fellow pushed the door shut behind him with a dark laugh. The cell was not large, and had only one small window, high up on the wall, well protected by bars. The pale dawn made a feeble attempt to shed its light.

Rupert lay on the cold stone floor where the guard's push had landed him. He didn't see the point of getting up. He had never felt so hopeless or alone or terrified. What did it matter if he ever got up again?

But suddenly he did jump to his feet, upon hearing an eerie, almost disembodied sound. And Rupert knew he wasn't alone in the dark.

Chapter Eleven

Rupert stood terrified, motionless, hardly daring to breathe. He strained with every fiber of his being to discern from where the strange sound had emanated. The dim dawn barely lit the cell, which seemed filled with menacing shadows. Slowly he began to back towards the door, though knowing there was no chance of flight. Upon reaching it, he stood stock still again; the only sound was his own heart racing, his own blood pounding in his ears.

Then, it came again; a gruesome, low moan. In Rupert's state of fright, he imagined the guard had placed some vicious animal in the cell to devour him. Perhaps this was some demonic creature with which he'd have no ability to communicate.

But after the third groan, Rupert began to calm himself. It sounded not truly like an animal, but after all a fellow human. His eyes strained to see in the pale light. And finally, in a corner, he discovered a dark shape on the stone floor. Slowly, almost on tiptoe, Rupert approached. The figure did not move, but he could hear the sound of labored breathing; a person after all.

Emboldened, Rupert knelt by the curled up figure. He could now make out that the stranger was covered by his cloak in a vain effort to keep warm.

"Hello," the boy whispered. "My name is Rupert, a fellow prisoner. Who are you? Please speak if you can."

But the only response was of troubled breathing and painful sigh. Gingerly, Rupert pushed back the hood of the tattered garment. The face of a young man was revealed, the face of someone in deepest suffering.

Of a sudden, Rupert felt overwhelmed by compassion for this being, whoever he might be. Having so recently recovered from a harrowing illness, and remembering vividly his own trials, he resolved to do whatever possible to help another in distress.

Sympathy drove Rupert to action. He carefully rolled the man over on his back. He opened his cloak to better assess the situation, and immediately discovered the source of the pain; a wound, likely from an arrow, in his shoulder. There was a large amount of blood staining his tunic and cloak, but at least it appeared to have dried and the wound had stopped bleeding. Gingerly, Rupert felt the man's forehead. It was raging with fever.

How frustrated Rupert felt! He had knowledge of healing herbs, his grandparents having taught him such things as he grew up in the forest. He surely possessed the ability to aid this stranger. But here he was helpless, and that helplessness swiftly turned to anger. How dreadful and unfair to toss people into dark prisons with no thought to treating them with humanity! But Rupert felt determined to do his utmost.

He searched the small cell again, now that the morning light began filtering in. Beside the door was a bucket, and to his huge relief, it contained water; hardly sufficient to nurse a sick man, but better than nothing and better than feeling completely powerless.

Carefully, he carried the bucket over to his patient, who continued to moan and shiver. Rupert covered him again with his cloak. Underneath, he wore a dark grey tunic and leggings, along with knee-length boots. Rupert had seen such clothing before, on some of the king's soldiers.

So this was one of King Ryker's men? Why was he here, locked up, then? Rupert supposed he must have done something against the king or his officers. Perhaps he'd tried to desert the army, since so many recruits had been forced against their will into service.

"Well," thought Rupert with a grim smile, "any enemy of that bloody king is surely a friend of mine!" And he knew any friend at all in this wretched place was a most precious thing.

Rupert offered water to his cellmate, and was relieved when he was able to drink greedily for a moment before falling back to the cold and damp floor. Rupert again attempted to speak to him, but to no avail. He remembered from his own illness that he'd had been too feeble to talk for several days. Rupert resisted the urge to have him drink again, as he had no idea when and if more water would be provided. There was no food at all that he could see.

As it grew less dim, Rupert was able to examine his companion's face. Despite the fever and pain that distorted his features, he reckoned that the soldier was quite young, no more than his middle twenties at most. He had long, unkempt and matted dark blond hair; his face and body were very lean. There was something familiar about his well-hewn features; perhaps he'd glimpsed him at the village market. But no, it seemed another kind of familiarity; as if he was already someone he could trust.

Rupert took a corner of his own tunic and tore off a large square. He dunked it into the bucket, and used the wet cloth to cool the man's burning forehead. He spoke words of comfort, reassuring his patient that he'd soon be well. Rupert even sang some songs...songs that Lira had taught him. At that, the man attempted to respond, but he had no strength.

Hours passed without change, yet Rupert felt grateful to have a companion, and most determined that he not die. That thought was far too dreadful to allow in his head for long. He also forbade himself to think of his circumstances. It was simply too horrible to contemplate, and he could not afford to indulge in hopelessness or despair.

Meanwhile, the day was passing, and there was no sound from outside the prison door. Rupert felt that he and his companion were the two last people on earth. He began to give up hope of more water or food, but as the sun began to set, the key turned in the lock.

Jumping up from his patient's side, Rupert was most uncertain what to expect. Was he about to be dragged out? Beaten? But it was only a faceless guard that pushed open the door a small space, shoved in a tin plate and a small bucket, and dragged the heavy door shut again. Not a word had been spoken.

Grateful that he hadn't been completely forgotten, Rupert raced to examine what had been left. The 'gift' from the guard was most disappointing; two small pieces of stale bread and water, half of which had spilled out. Still, he was grateful, and Rupert now realized he was very hungry.

But his patient's needs came first. He gently lifted the man's head and attempted to get him to open his eyes. However, he was passed out and deep with fever, though the boy was at length able to rouse him sufficiently to partake of water, and Rupert continued to be encouraged at that. He again washed him down as best he could, and thought that the fever had perhaps lessened. Or was that merely wishful thinking?

Finally, exhausted, both from the harrowing events of the last day and from his non-stop nursing, he slumped into a corner and took up a piece of bread. Rupert nibbled at it very slowly. Although his companion was in no condition to partake, he would not eat both pieces. It didn't seem fair. So he had to be satisfied with his portion, and scant though it was, he did feel better after taking nourishment for the first time in more than twenty-four hours.

After that he slept, and much later awoke with a guilty start. It took a moment to recall where he was, and that he had a companion to look after. The young man was still alive, and happy to consume more water. And before long the dawn came, and Rupert was jubilant to realize they'd endured through the night.

The next day passed very much like the previous one, his patient suffering through a painful sleep, but able to drink copious amounts of water. Rupert gave him most of the precious liquid, controlling his own thirst, contenting himself with small sips now and then. Hunger overcame him, and with some guilt, he finally consumed the second piece of bread. Again, Rupert felt grateful for having someone to look after, to help distract his thoughts. How hard it was not to constantly think of Liam, Lira, Raja, and Majesty. And what of his beloved Kara, patiently guarding the treasure in the forest? Or had she long since returned home?

Again, near sunset, the guard returned, leaving more meager supplies. Rupert began to grow dizzy with hunger. He reminded himself that he was young and strong and well able to endure a little hardship. And he felt encouraged that his companion appeared to be made of strong will as well, as he continued to hold on with determination to his life. But how Rupert longed for more than water to help him!

Much to his amazement, his wish was granted. Very late that night, the key turned in the lock and the heavy door swung open. Someone entered, bearing a torch. He wasn't dressed in armor as the king's guards were, but rather in tunic and cloak. This sudden entry made Rupert's mouth go dry as he sought to determine who this man might be.

"Don't be alarmed," whispered the intruder. "I'm here to help you, young Rupert!"

Rupert gave a gasp. Was it possible that such a thing as 'help' existed in this dismal place? Not daring to trust, his eyes strained to uncover the identity of his benefactor.

"Do you remember me? My name is Morley, one of the king's guards. I spoke with you on market day."

Rupert indeed recalled Morley, the fellow with the warm green eyes that had been caring and curious. Suddenly, the words tumbled out.

"Morley, this man is sick, wounded. He has a fever. I've been trying to help him, but all I have is water. Is there a doctor?"

Morley gave a bitter laugh and explained that there were no doctors for any prisoner here. Rupert's heart fell, but the next words sent his spirits soaring.

"I bring greetings from your Grandfather Liam and Lira. They've sent gifts as well!"

Tears immediately sprang to his eyes. He wondered if he'd ever hear those names spoken again! "Tell me, sir, are they well? Did the guards hurt them?"

Morley was able to assure Rupert that they were indeed safe at the farm. Rupert wondered if Morley had anything to do with that.

Morley wore a pack upon his back, and he took it off and began removing what seemed like treasures to Rupert. There were flasks of water, one containing healing herbs, as well as several loaves of bread, a container of honey, cheese, and apples. Rupert felt he'd never seen such riches. At the moment, they seemed more valuable than the treasure that he hoped was still concealed in the forest.

"Your grandfather sent these for you. You see, I went to your family after you'd been taken. The whole village is outraged, and many beyond. Word of your actions has inspired many; that you, a child, could stand up to the king's men. Unfortunately, that's why you were taken prisoner. But we aren't prepared to give up so easily!"

"But aren't you a soldier too?" asked Rupert in some confusion.

"Indeed," was the reply, "but most unwillingly. Many were forced into service, under threat to our lives or the lives of our families. But this is one time I, at least, must act.

"I told your family I would come to you in secret. I must wait until the men are sleeping or drunk in order to sneak in, and can't risk that every day. Your grandfather and I decided on a spot off the main road where he can leave provisions. So, at least you won't be left to starve."

"I am grateful beyond words," cried Rupert, feeling a huge surge of hope and happiness. "But I fear for your safety. Please do not put yourself or your family in peril."

"Don't trouble yourself, lad. For some reason I can't explain, I feel certain you're worth the risk."

Rupert didn't argue further, because Morley handed him a folded piece of parchment. By torchlight, Rupert carefully opened it. It was a note from Liam and Lira.

He had written: "My dearest boy, be brave and strong. We will find you a way out. Believe in us and our love for you." Lira had written, with her newly acquired writing skill, in very large and shaky letters: "Dearest big brother. We love you. I know you'll come home soon. Love, Lira."

Rupert's heart sprang back to life as he read those brief words. They meant everything to him. And he had to smile when he saw that Raja had left his paw print on the paper. Dearest Raja! But a brief moan from the sick man brought Rupert back to the here and now.

"Please, do give me those herbs. This man has suffered enough. How wonderful that Grandfather Liam sent them."

"Yes, he was most concerned you'd fall sick again in this stink-hole. Quick, let's get this into the poor fellow."

"Do you know him?" asked Rupert as he had his patient drink some of the healing tea. "Is he one of your guards?"

"No, I don't recognize him. Perhaps he's a deserter. Hope he'll pull through...even if it means being locked up in this dark pit."

"Neither of us will be here forever. That I can promise you!" proclaimed a determined Rupert.

He was happy to see the wounded man swallow the tea eagerly, and in a moment, sighing softly, he opened his eyes for the very first time. Both Rupert and Morley knelt by his side.

"Hey," Morley observed, "he's looking less pale already."

The young man looked up at Morley and Rupert. His deep blue eyes still shone with fever, yet appeared to focus clearly. Almost instantly, he fastened his gaze upon Rupert, his blazing eyes widening in shock. And for the first time, he spoke.

"Why, Your Majesty! What are you doing here? Am I yet dreaming? I awaken in the presence of a Golden-Eyed King! A Golden-Eyed King! The day has come at last! *A Golden-Eyed King returns!*"

Chapter Twelve

S tunned and amazed, Rupert was unable to move or speak. This young soldier was regarding him directly, proclaiming him a Golden-Eyed King! How was this possible? Rupert struggled to deal with his harrowing inner turmoil, in order to face this most unexpected turn of events.

"Please calm yourself, good sir," pleaded Rupert in a soothing tone. "You've been very ill and still are! Your fever makes you speak strangely. You must lie down and rest."

But the young soldier would not be so easily convinced. "No, this is not a fever nor a dream! I can see your golden eyes clear as the brightest sun!" He turned to Morley, with a determined if frenzied look. "You, sir, do you not see for yourself that this is indeed our prince or our king?"

Morley did turn to stare at Rupert, as the fellow seemed so utterly convinced of his words. But he failed to perceive what the soldier saw.

"Do not speak wildly," begged Rupert. "You must rest. These herbs will help you heal, and you will see more clearly. Now, drink again, and sleep!"

Exhausted, he drank thirstily of the tea. Even that required a major effort and he fell back again. The young man reached out to clasp Rupert's hand, attempting to fight off exhaustion, peering without cease into the boy's eyes. "I will not fail you, I swear!" But in another moment sleep had overtaken him.

Rupert and Morley continued to kneel silently beside him for a long moment. Finally, Rupert rose to his feet. "How strange it is when one is so ill," he remarked with a seemingly casual tone. "I recall dreaming of monsters and butterflies when sick with fever. Poor fellow."

Morley regarded the boy, more than a little perplexed. Since witnessing him act with such cool bravery at the village market, he'd known that this was clearly a most remarkable lad. It was difficult to imagine grown men who could have done the same. And he could not forget his instincts calling him to bow down before the boy. Now this stranger was calling Rupert king! Could this be merely bizarre coincidence?

But to Morley's gaze, the boy with such striking looks possessed eyes of darkest brown. Was the vision of the wounded soldier distorted with fever? Or did it somehow see true? See what no other could perceive? And were Morley's own eyes blinded to the truth?

"I wonder if it is merely the fever that causes him to speak thus? There appears to be more here than meets the eye, young sir."

Rupert hardly knew how to respond. Could he admit he had eyes of golden hue? He'd certainly doubted it at times, but now this stranger claimed to see them! Why should *he* be able to, and yet no one else?

And was this not the most dangerous moment possible to declare his alleged kinship to the lost royal family? After all, he was locked in King Ryker's prison. If word spread of his identity, his life would be forfeit. Plainly, Morley was risking all to come to Rupert's aid; therefore he was certainly worthy of trust. But not with this secret, not at this moment.

"Do my eyes appear golden to you? Do your own eyes deceive you? This poor fellow is very ill, perhaps dreaming the true kings were restored, that he might return home in peace. That is what we all wish. But I am no king, sir."

Morley observed him for a long moment. He could not know whether Rupert was simply a most extraordinary youth with great qualities of courage and leadership...or if he might be something even more glorious.

In either event, Morley was committed to aid him in any way possible. That certainly meant that no rumor of a golden-eyed lad must pass beyond the walls of this cell, for such a rumor would be a death sentence.

"I understand you very well," he said. "But meanwhile, I do have one more thing of importance to show you, for we cannot allow the guards to discover the supplies I've brought."

Morley stepped to a corner and motioned Rupert to follow. He observed that one of the large stones protruded ever so slightly. With some effort, Morley was able to pull it out, and an empty space was revealed. It was perfect for concealing the food and water from any search. Rupert was delighted.

"How did you know of this?" Rupert looked up at Morley in admiration. He must have helped others who had been imprisoned as well.

"My father was locked in High Tower for stealing a loaf of bread to feed his family. When finally released, he told me of it; too late to have helped him, of course. But now that I'm a guard, I can do for you what I could not do for my own father." He spoke those last words with a voice filled with bitterness.

Impulsively, Rupert threw his arms around Morley and embraced him fiercely. After a long moment, Morley pulled away. "Here, see if you are strong enough to move the stone back."

Rupert pushed his weight against it, returning it to its original position, though with a measure of difficulty. Then he pulled it out again. Morley regarded him with pride.

"Still small, but strong indeed!" he said with a laugh. Rupert laughed back.

"Here's one more thing I've brought you." Morley reached into his pack and produced pen, ink, and paper. Rupert's eyes grew huge with joy at the sight.

"I must write to Grandfather Liam and Lira! Will you dare deliver it?"

"I'll try. But I must avoid being seen at their cottage. I'll leave your message at the drop-off point along the roadside. However, that cannot be for a several days, so be patient," Morley cautioned.

"Of course I understand, and I'm forever grateful. Allow me to write a few words. I know you must not linger."

Hastily, he took the writing materials and sat down while Morley held the torch above his head. Rupert scratched out a very brief message, telling them he was well and that the healing herbs they'd sent were helping a fellow prisoner. And that he loved and missed them as well as Raja and Majesty. He blew the ink dry and handed the folded note to his new comrade.

"I'll come again as soon as possible, but be prepared for a delay. Do ration your food wisely."

Rupert assured him he would. Morley removed his own cloak and handed it to Rupert, knowing the nights in the dark stone cell would become only colder still with the passage of time.

But before Rupert could thank him, Morley was gone, the heavy door dragging shut behind him. How Rupert missed him already, and the light from his torch as well! But the dawn would soon come. And though Morley was gone, his mysterious companion remained.

Rupert, his spirits considerably lifted, made a hearty meal of bread and cheese. He had been so very thirsty, having given almost all the water to the sick soldier, and was finally able to drink his fill. After he'd finished, he placed the smuggled supplies into the stone hiding place and carefully and quietly pushed it shut, feeling well satisfied that no one would guess that life-saving food and medicine was concealed there.

Rupert was simultaneously exhausted and exhilarated. He knew he should sleep, or at least make the attempt. First, he again checked on his patient, who seemed to be resting comfortably, and decided not to make him drink again of the tea. That could wait till morning.

The boy curled up beside him and struggled for calm. His heart still pounded at the astonishing thought that someone could testify to his golden eyes. It was both satisfying and overwhelming. And it was no less amazing that he should have found such a resourceful comrade in Morley, and that he could now communicate with Liam and Lira though locked in this dank fortress. He felt his courage renewed and a vivid determination to persevere.

Finally he slept, and woke again well after dawn. He sat up quickly and leaned over to check on the young soldier. He did appear much improved. His breathing was more even and the fever seemed to have greatly abated. Rupert, with a deep sigh of relief, reached for the herbal tea and gently shook his companion's shoulder. He opened his eyes after a moment, and smiled up at Rupert, obeying the request that he drink.

"Do you feel up to eating anything? I have bread and honey and cheese."

The young man grinned. "And who but a king would have such luxuries while locked in a prison cell?"

Rupert forced a laugh. "Do you remember the guard Morley from last night? He brought them for me...for us. Can you eat? It would do you a world of good. Do please try."

"Yes, I do believe I am rather hungry."

Rupert was delighted. He moved to the rock and pulled it out, removed bread and cheese and gave some to his cellmate, who accepted it eagerly. He even had the strength to sit up. Rupert watched him take a small bite, then close his eyes and chew, a blissful look upon his gaunt yet handsome face.

"I did not expect to taste food again in this life," he sighed.

"We must preserve what we have. Our next supply may not come for some time. By the way, please tell me your name. Who are you?"

"Why, thank you for asking, Your Majesty. For I do yet see your golden eyes, though my fever has broken!"

"Please do not say such things!" begged Rupert. "It would be death to us both if someone overheard!"

"I understand. But let it be known my eyes can see, and your eyes are pure gold, no mistake. How this miracle has come about, I do not pretend to know. And how others cannot perceive what is plain to me, I also do not comprehend. But *you* know it's true, do you not?"

"I suppose...I'm not certain. But please, let us not speak of this now. Tell me who you are. You've been my companion for days, yet I know nothing of you. Have you deserted the army?"

"Yes, 'tis true. I was forced into the King Ryker's service these five years. I've witnessed battles and famine and more suffering than I hope you can imagine. Though the penalty for desertion is death, I could endure it no longer. Most of the men feel the same, but they fear for their safety and that of their kin, and so remain. But finally, I felt death was preferable. And I longed for my family. I do not even know if they are alive or dead or have fled the area. I traveled so long and I was nearing home when I was discovered, wounded, and thrown into this cursed place."

"But who is your family? Perhaps I've seen them in the village?"

"My beloved wife died just before I was taken away. My little girl was only a year old then. She'd be six now, and may be living with my dear father. I do hope he's well and still caring for her. As for my name, I'm a bit tardy with introductions. I am called Daniel."

For a moment, Rupert could only mutely stare. He had heard that name before. Could this be? No, it must be impossible! But he at last made himself speak.

"Sir, is your daughter named Lira?"

"By God, yes!" came the astonished reply. "How could you know?"

"And is your father's name by chance Liam?"

Daniel could only regard Rupert in wonder. "So you know them? Have you seen them? Are they well?"

Rupert could hardly speak. But the man's urgency made him finally reply. "Yes, they are very well indeed. They took me in and gave me love and shelter. They are now my family too."

"Tell me, you must tell me *everything*!" came Daniel's plea. But before either could speak again, tears flowed freely down their faces and man and boy embraced. "A miracle," proclaimed Daniel, and Rupert could only agree.

His utter despair at being thrown into prison turned to utter joy! For in no other way could this precious young man have been saved had not Rupert been here to come to his aid. Now he could finally repay Liam and Lira's kindness in the most amazing way possible; by returning her father and his son to them. The very thing they longed for above all else! And Daniel was, it seemed, the only being who could see his golden eyes!

Who could begin to fathom the wonder of it all? Rupert learned a most valuable and stunning lesson - never to despair, however dark the moment might be. Because events might be unfolding and forces might be guiding his course that were beyond his powers to comprehend, and yet were there with him nonetheless.

And the beauty and mystery of life held him enthralled.

Chapter Thirteen

The prison cell was dark and dank, but its inhabitants found the following days to be almost happy. They could not help but feel a sense of awe at the other's identity. To Daniel, Rupert had saved his live, revealed himself to be an adopted member of his own family, and beyond even that, to be his true king! To Rupert, Daniel was the beloved father to Lira and son to Liam as well as the only other witness, besides himself, to have seen his golden eyes!

Their hours together were filled with continual converse. Each had endless curiosity about the other and they greatly desired to hear every detail of one another's life. And here, at last, for Rupert came a vast sense of relief. Now, for the very first time, he would withhold nothing; things he had so yearned to share with Daniel's father, Liam, yet dared not. But since, by some miracle, Daniel could see his golden eyes, Rupert was compelled to open his heart filled with secrets.

Daniel sat for hours on end, listening with amazement to the tale Rupert unfolded. Beginning with his first memories of life with his enigmatic grandparents, learning to live in harmony with the forest and its creatures, teaching himself to read, his grandfather's mysterious disappearances, until that life-changing day he discovered the treasure and thereafter found himself alone in the world.

Of course, Daniel listened with equal fascination to every detail of Rupert's life with his father and Lira. He began with his first moment of seeing Lira riding upon Majesty; that never to be forgotten moment of beauty and grace and freedom. Daniel could not keep the emotion from his eyes when he learned what a beautiful, bold, and intelligent child his daughter had become. And he delighted to hear that his father had remained unchanged through hardship - still courageous, compassionate, and open-hearted.

Rupert demanded to know everything of Daniel's adventures; of growing up on the farm with his father, who had told him tale after tale of the fabulous days of the Golden-Eyed Kings. But in reality, he had been faced with unrelenting darkness under the crushing rule of King Ryker.

Upon turning fifteen, the age when young men were forced into military service, Daniel decided to flee, and knowing no alternative, his father had given his blessing. It took six weeks of difficult and dangerous travel to reach the border of a land which lay far to the north. Here, Daniel found safety; though his heart bled to think he may never see his father again.

His story took a more cheerful turn when Daniel described apprenticing with a kindly lady blacksmith who taught him many valuable things, including the local language and customs. His new neighbors realized he was a refugee from the land of the Golden-Eyed Kings, where brutal usurpers now held sway. And so, he was treated with kindness and sympathy, and gradually, his spirit began to heal.

It was towards the end of a lovely summer day that Daniel took a solitary walk to a silent meadow. His reflections were interrupted by the sound of horse's hooves and girlish laughter. He looked up to see a girl upon a magnificent black steed - an amazing and beauteous girl with her long curling hair, the color of silver moonlight, flying wildly behind her.

Daniel beheld her and fell in love at that instant. He startled the dazzling rider by stepping out from behind the trees. She drew her horse to a halt. He introduced himself, and before the moment had passed, she realized that love had found her as well.

Rupert could not help but feel a chill of recognition. This was, after all, almost exactly how he had encountered Lira, Daniel's daughter. What a strange coincidence! But he returned his attention to the unfolding tale.

Within days, Daniel had met her parents, and begged permission to marry the remarkable Vyka. She had many a hopeful suitor, but never expressed interest in any young man until now. She knew she would love him all her days, and no other. Her family blessed the match, and they were married soon after, and within a year they were expecting their first child.

It was then Vyka's dearest wish to meet Daniel's family. Only his father was left alive, and she, being caring and compassionate, could not endure the thought that he would never see his son again, or meet his wife and child. She made Daniel promise that after the baby was safely born, they would make the journey to his home country, danger or no. And so, when little Lira was a mere six months old, they set out on their journey.

Travel was slow and tedious, but they reached the farm within two months, and the reunion was very happy indeed. Vyka loved her father-in-law and Liam felt great joy to have a daughter at last. And all delighted in the lively Lira, a little beauty who resembled so much her mother, but who had her father's eyes of startling sapphire.

But this happy time was not to last. Within months of their arrival, a deadly fever swept through the kingdom. Many took sick and died swiftly. They all feared for the health of the baby, and contemplated fleeing the area. But living in relative isolation, they hoped the deadly pestilence might pass them by. Moreover, they dared do nothing to bring attention to their presence, lest the soldiers realize Daniel's return, and force him into vicious King Ryker's service.

After a time, the fever began to abate, bringing great relief. But it was then that the terrible sickness fell upon the exquisite Vyka. Despite Liam's skill with herbs and healing, it was clear the battle to save the girl would be futile. It seemed unthinkable that such a lovely, vivid girl of barely seventeen could be torn from this life, her beloved husband and child. But struggle as she did, all was in vain.

Within seven days of falling ill, she was gone forever, and Daniel's heart and soul went with her.

And his terrible sorrows only multiplied when Daniel's presence at the farm was finally detected, and within days of his wife's death, was dragged away by a dozen soldiers before having opportunity to flee. Dragged away to serve a ruler he despised, dragged away to face brutality, battle, starvation, and daily sorrow. And the knowledge that he may never see his father or daughter again, or even to have a quiet moment to sit by Vyka's burial place and mourn.

After each had told their story, they felt even more as brothers than before. And each had a thousand questions for the other. Of course, they spoke of Rupert's golden eyes in the smallest of whispers and only deep into the night. They had also formulated a plan whereby upon hearing the cell door open they would endeavor to appear weak and sick, as they were expected to be on mere starvation rations.

Rupert and Daniel were often hungry, but not starving. The food that Morley had brought was sufficient for Rupert alone, but now had to serve two, and they could not be certain when more might appear. They each had a slice of bread with honey for breakfast, shared an apple and a piece of cheese for lunch, and consumed more bread and cheese for supper. They also reluctantly partook of the moldy bread that the guard grudgingly provided, for no food could be wasted, no matter how unpalatable.

Though their hidden supply was meager, they were grateful beyond measure for it, though not without guilt that other prisoners subsisted on next to nothing, and would likely perish swiftly as a result.

On the fourth night since Daniel had awoken from his fever, they eluded sleep late into the night, voices lowered, attempting to make sense of all that had occurred. Daniel was struck again and again by the strangeness of Rupert's tale.

"I cannot comprehend how and why your grandparents disappeared the moment you discovered the royal treasure," he exclaimed not for the first time. "No grandparents would act that way. And from what you relate, they appeared somewhat cold and distant; rather your keepers than your kindred."

Rupert sighed. "I've often wondered myself at their peculiar behavior. And it seems they did not take any belongings with them. I sometimes imagine they disappeared into the air! I now know such things are possible, since the strange lady at the village market, the one with the basket, did the very same. Do you suppose my grandparents and that lady could somehow be related?" Rupert was intrigued at the thought.

"I hardly can pretend to know," responded a fascinated Daniel, "but it would seem a likely supposition. You have been both hidden and protected all your life, and it is plain that mysterious forces and people are involved. Well, I for one would not object if they appeared in our prison cell. Perhaps they could teach us the art of vanishing. A neat trick that would be!"

Both laughed at that, but suddenly held their breath as the cell door slowly creaked open. As planned, they lay swiftly upon the cold stone floor, feigning sleep, and doing their best to appear pale and weak. But their fears were soon allayed by the very welcome sound of Morley's voice.

"I know full well you're awake, since I could hear your muffled laughter through the door. You must be more cautious! Laughter can only draw the gravest suspicions. No one laughs in High Tower Prison...except for the twisted men who run it!"

Morley's words were serious, yet teasing. Rupert and Daniel leapt to their feet to embrace their welcome guest. He carried a torch and a backpack as before.

"'Tis marvelous to see you again, Morley," cried Rupert with heartfelt joy. I hope you bring good word of Grandfather Liam and Lira, because we have the most wonderful news for them!"

Morley reported that he had not seen them personally, but they had left food and another note for Rupert at the roadside drop-off point. They had evidently found the note Rupert had written, because it was gone. Morley could have reason to assume that all was well.

"But what is this wondrous news you claim? Have you found magic that might cause this dungeon to disappear?"

"Perhaps even more amazing than that," came the joyfully whispered reply. "Morley, may I present to you Daniel, son of Grandfather Liam and father to Lira!"

Morley could only stare, first at Rupert, then to Daniel. He saw confirmation of this pronouncement in Daniel's eyes.

"By God, can this be true? 'Tis indeed strange and wondrous if it be so!"

"Yes, indeed, it is. 'Tis something we've spoken of without cease since discovering the truth. And we beg you to carry the news to my...our family as swiftly as may be. If you dare, please deliver it in person, as we wish no delay in such a fabulous announcement!"

Morley regarded them with awe. "Yes, their joy will be beyond measure! After such longing and suspense, not a moment should be wasted; and to know that you are together, keeping each other well. Why, the lifesaving herbs sent for Rupert were actually used to save Liam's own son; quite unbeknownst to him! Upon my soul, 'tis more fabulous than the tales told by storytellers in the marketplace!"

"Indeed," agreed Daniel. "We cannot fathom the wonder of it ourselves, though we speak of nothing else. We live for the moment when we can all be reunited, for it *must* happen now. All that has occurred cannot be for naught!"

Of course, Daniel greatly desired to confide in Morley the even more wondrous truth that Rupert did indeed possess golden eyes and was their true king! But this was not the moment to reveal all, not while they were prisoners of their greatest foe.

Morley delivered the brief note from Liam and Lira for Rupert. Both Rupert and Daniel read the words of love and encouragement with joy. They also received with pleasure the food and water Morley bore. This time there was more than before since it was known that sustenance was required for two instead of one. But Rupert's adopted family could not know the extra rations would feed their own longed-for son and father.

"Have you heard any news of our intended fate? How long are we to be locked up? What are the charges?" Rupert demanded.

"Charges?" Morley gave a soft, bitter laugh. "There need be no charges, I assure you. You're here at the king's pleasure, and will remain as long as he desires. Most poor souls don't last long. At least you will have sustenance. As to your fate, I'll pass on any knowledge I obtain, you may be certain. But I must be cautious. Please be patient."

Daniel and Rupert could only thank him again and again for risking all to aid them. He smiled, disclaiming any particular valor. And knowing the identity of Daniel made efforts on their behalf the more fulfilling and worthwhile. Morley now believed something most strange and mysterious was occurring, and he was only a small part of the greater design.

After giving his comrades a hasty salute, Morley departed, and darkness filled the cell. They rejoiced that Liam and Lira would soon learn of Daniel's presence in High Tower, together with Rupert, and that both were alive and well. They celebrated by partaking of bread and honey before carefully hiding it away.

Not long after, their thoughts finally turned to rest as dawn approached. They would have slept on, but were abruptly awakened by the ominous creaking of the cell door. They had never had a visitor at this early hour. Rupert and Daniel exchanged a startled look as the heavy door was pushed open, and Rupert experienced a chill of dread.

When the identity of the intruders was revealed, Rupert knew the fear had true cause; for it was the last person he'd hoped to see: the king's guard Ned, with eyes and words of ice.

He was accompanied by a half-dozen men. What could this mean? The captives recalled their plan to look sickly, and Rupert truly paled at Ned's sinister appearance. And he indeed was sick with trepidation.

"Well, sleeping lazily at this dawn hour," drawled Ned. "I suppose that means you find the accommodations to your liking!" He laughed the cold laugh that always sent a chill up Rupert's spine. He longed to turn to Daniel, but it was wiser not to appear overly friendly towards him.

"I bring good news to one of you," declared Ned, his voice soft yet sinister.

Rupert felt a surge of hope. Perhaps one of them might be released? But selfishly, he dreaded to think of remaining without Daniel; yet the thought of freedom for him alone was equally unthinkable. But the boy's heart could only believe that this cold, cruel being would bring the darkest of tidings.

"This Sunday morning, in three days' time, one of you will be set free! Free from all the cares of this sorry world." He turned to Daniel. "You are a soldier of King Ryker. You know the penalty for desertion is death. On Sunday next, your head will be separated from your body at the village square, as a message to all who might follow your foolish example. I hope you and the lad enjoy your last hours together."

He turned to smirk into Rupert's terrified face. "And you, my little snake, be warned that our goodly liege does not take kindly to troublemakers of *any* sort. Your fate will be dealt with without delay. And I presume it will also prove most enlightening for the good citizens!"

With that, Ned turned to leave his horrified audience. He fixed his pale eyes upon Daniel. "On Sunday morning, early, I'll come for you. What a sorry waste that you recovered from your wound. You could have saved us much time and trouble. But ah well, those unhappy villagers deserve their entertainment, don't you agree?"

And in a moment he was gone, and the dark cell seemed blacker than ever before.

Chapter Fourteen

A small and terrible eternity seemed to pass between the two comrades. It dawned on Rupert that he had been living in a false paradise; so confident that all would be well, without considering how such a happy outcome might indeed come to pass. A voice within whispered against despair, but it would require more than vague feelings and wishful thinking to alter their destiny.

"Daniel, this is not to be. We cannot allow it. I swear that neither you nor I should ever be defeated. Not by these vicious and petty men!"

Daniel walked the few steps that separated him from his prince. But he took Rupert by surprise by bending one knee and bowing before him. "My Lord, I believe your words, though logic declares them mere flights of fancy. I vow that my fate is attached to yours, and that we have only begun our journey to restore you to your throne! I do not fear death, but only failing my duty to you."

Rupert could not be but profoundly moved at such an exhibition of faith and loyalty, though feeling most unworthy to receive it. He was a mere boy and quite helpless. How could he have power to save his precious companion?

"Please rise. You are my dear brother. And you speak the truth. Our journey lies along the same path until things are set right for our suffering people. But now, we must be practical. Come, sit by me and let us ponder how we may avoid this disaster."

The tall and slender Daniel rose swiftly and came to sit by Rupert's side. Admittedly, they seemed trapped like rats in a hole.

"I was jesting when I wished for your magician friends to make an appearance," observed Daniel wryly. "But do you suppose it possible to summon them?"

"I wish I knew," replied a troubled Rupert. "I've never done such a thing, nor have any inkling how to go about it. Besides, if they are truly watching over me, they must know of our plight. Yet they have taken no action to come to our aid."

"Perhaps some magic words might summon them forth? I've read of such things in tales of old. But no, it seems you had no need of spells for the lady with the basket to appear. Ah, 'tis a great mystery, and I hope we may come to comprehend it in time. But I fear time is something we sorely lack."

Rupert jumped to his feet. "Why, let us not forget our dear Morley! Surely he will hear of this, as news of your coming execution must be announced to the villagers! There is no way he could remain in ignorance. Morley will find a way to come to our rescue." Rupert began to pace back and forth in the small cell, feeling a great rush of excitement. "Morley will not fail to do his utmost! And he will tell Grandfather Liam as well."

"You are right, of course," replied Daniel with caution in his tone. "But I foresee great danger should they come to our aid. Yet escape would be our only hope. Clemency from the likes of King Ryker is beyond imagining."

"But perhaps the citizens will rise to help us. They found courage to speak against the guards in the marketplace. Perhaps Morley could speak to them and..."

Daniel interrupted such talk. "We should not allow ourselves such a false hope; they are terrified of the guards. The people have no weapons, no training, and no leaders. Undoubtedly, the threat of my public execution would only intimidate them further."

Daniel spoke true. The citizens were not ready for such a giant step. Well, they'd have to pray that Morley would find means to smuggle them out of prison. But Rupert remembered all too well the towering castle walls and the mighty gates of High Tower. And with an execution approaching, the security would certainly increase.

The boy and the young man spent all the day in whispered discussion, each attempting to raise the other's spirits. Rupert even thought of concealment in the small hiding place where they kept their food. But it was far too tiny for even Rupert alone to fit. And they had no tools to increase its size, nothing except their bare hands, and their hands could do nothing against solid rock.

It was disheartening for the two, both of whom had warrior blood flowing through their veins, to feel so helpless. Rupert vowed that once free from these prison walls, nothing would deter him from becoming master of his destiny. Though now but a lowly and powerless prisoner, the boy had never felt more in touch with his Golden-Eyed Kingship. And in his heart was born a determination to free his people from the terrible burden they bore.

Dreadful as their circumstances were, they indeed did not give up hope. They thought over and over again of escape! Where would they go? And they must take Liam and Lira with them, for they would not be safe from the king's wrath. And the treasure! Was Kara still there guarding it? Only Rupert and Daniel knew of its existence, but it could be by no means left behind whatever the risk. And the ruby ring! Rupert wondered with longing if Liam had discovered it at the bottom of the woodpile.

He imagined the stunned surprise at recovering such an object, and realizing it belonged in some way to Rupert. If Liam had found it, he'd have a thousand questions, Rupert was certain. But what if it still lay in its hiding place? It was impossible to leave it behind, but almost impossibly dangerous to return for. The boy could only pray that Morley would warn Liam to take Lira and flee. That is, if the young soldier had devised an escape.

The next day passed in a suspense that seemed to grow with each breath they drew. The execution was to be the day after tomorrow. Surely, if Morley could conceive a plan, it must be implemented very soon! But perhaps the prison was so closely guarded now that Morley could not convey a message...even if the message was that there was no hope.

It was very late that night when the bulky cell door finally was pushed open again. Since the announcement of the coming execution, even their meager rations had no longer been provided. Of course they had their own concealed food and drink, but little appetite to make use of them. They had been left entirely isolated; and now this intruder.

The late hour made them hope it might be Morley. But when the fellow entered, bearing a flickering torch, he did not wear the uniform of a soldier. Instead, he was clad in a dark and heavy cloak, his face completely concealed. He remained motionless, staring at Rupert and Daniel as they held their breath. But then the hood was pulled back to reveal what Rupert believed must be an apparition or a dream. It was Liam!

After a heart-stopping pause, Rupert rushed into his outstretched arms. He was real! Rupert could not speak as great tears flooded his cheeks. But then the boy recalled an even more momentous reunion, one that had been delayed for over five agonizing years.

Rupert stepped back to allow Liam and his son to gaze into each other's eyes. Then Daniel, with a cry, rushed to his father's side and the two exchanged a fierce and marvelous embrace.

"How I've prayed and longed for this day," cried Liam. "And now that it has come, there are no words to express what is truly in my heart. No words at all!" But the power of his profound emotion said all he might have wished to convey.

"Dearest Father, I too have dreamed of nothing else. But how has this miracle come to pass? How have you appeared as if by magic in this hellish place?"

"We've little time to speak. But suffice to say that as a child, when the Golden-Eyed Kings still ruled, this was their home. I often came to pay homage with my family, and was given leave to play with the royal children. I memorized every secret passage and tunnel, and though I was then no older than Rupert, my memory still serves.

"But now, we must make haste. Soon the guards will patrol the passage again. Gather what food you have. We depart at once!"

Daniel pushed back the stone, grabbed the supplies and hastily put them into the knapsacks his father had provided. It took only a moment, and then, donning clean cloaks, they silently as possible pulled opened the heavy door and fled down the passageway.

Much to Rupert and Daniel's surprise, Liam led them into another cell at the end of the corridor. Luckily, no one was imprisoned within, and Liam lost no time pulling up one of the enormous stones that made up the floor. When he pushed it aside, the two others were astonished to behold a stairway leading deep into the ground. Taking his torch and leading the way, Rupert and Daniel followed, but not before Daniel swung the huge rock back into place. No one examining the spot might guess that a secret passage lay concealed beneath.

Down, down they went, then back up again. The way seemed long and meandering. They moved in swift silence; any sound might alert the guards to their presence. Rupert was hoping, praying, and holding his breath. Would the soldiers continue to ignore their cell until the execution? That would give the fugitives a fine head start as they fled to who knows where.

After following the winding stair for what seemed like an hour, but was probably less, they came upon another large stone overhead. Liam pushed against it with all his strength and it finally gave way. Through the opening appeared the night sky and shining stars above. Rupert was ecstatic at the sight! He'd been shut away from the sky and its beauties for an eternity, or so it seemed.

One by one they emerged from underground. They were not within the castle walls at all, but at least a hundred yards into the forest. Daniel and his father silently dragged the stone back into place, and then concealed it with sticks and dirt, hopefully covering their tracks.

With a gesture, Liam signaled to follow, and they did, rapidly and wordlessly. The trio must have gone half a dozen miles through the forest, because Rupert could see the stars moving slowly in their heavenly path as the moments passed. The young fugitive breathed the wood-scented night air with pleasure. This was his home, the forest. And the boy felt confident to meet any challenge that lay before him.

Finally, their leader slowed to a halt by a very small clearing. His eyes searched the darkness, and seemed satisfied they had not been followed. Softly, he gave a low whistle, and almost immediately there came one in return. And a moment after that, several figures emerged from the shadows. It was Morley, Lira, Raja, and Majesty. Rupert's joy knew no bounds!

Lira ran to greet her friend, but before she could complete the embrace, Raja had bounced upon him, knocking the boy to the ground. The hound appeared to have doubled in size yet again. He licked Rupert's face and Rupert embraced his pup with delight. When he finally was able to look up, he observed Lira staring shyly at her father, the father she'd never known except as a baby.

But he knew her, and with a cry Daniel swept his daughter up into his arms. Shedding joyous tears, Lira wrapped her small legs around his waist, kissing his cheek again and again. When they finally drew apart, it was only to peer deeply into each other's eyes; such similar eyes of blazing sapphire blue. Rupert had never witnessed a more beautiful sight.

But he could not forget Morley. "How has this miracle been achieved?" whispered Rupert while stroking the towering Majesty, who rubbed his head continually on Rupert's arm, as if to assure himself that his master was truly with him once more.

Morley, after a hearty clap upon young Rupert's shoulder, recounted that he had brought news to Liam of his son's miraculous survival, that he was locked in the same cell with Rupert, but was now scheduled for execution. Morley had been prepared to risk all to free the prisoners. But to his amazement, Liam had knowledge of the secret passageways, and insisted on carrying out the rescue himself.

"Of course, we are all fugitives now, as the king and his men will never cease hunting us down. But there could be no other choice."

"Morley, I'm so sorry," cried Rupert "This must put your family at risk as well."

"Never fear, young sir. Both my elder brother and younger are now dead in King Ryker's service. Only my mother and her sister survive. I arranged for them to flee. But I could not fail in being of service to you and your friends."

Rupert embraced his comrade. "You've lost your brothers, but we are your brothers now."

Dawn would come in a few hours' time, and Daniel declared they urgently required a plan of concealment. Liam explained that escape had been so pressing; there had been no time to consider their future. But Rupert interrupted.

"There is one place we need go before anywhere else." Only Daniel knew he was thinking of the treasure. "There is something I cannot leave behind, no matter what the risk in retrieving it."

Liam motioned Rupert to his side. "Rest assured that the precious item left in the cottage has been found, and I bear it with me, my boy. You have a great deal of explaining to do when we obtain leisure to talk!"

Rupert was vastly relieved the ring had been discovered, and to see that dire events had left Liam's sense of humor intact.

"There is something of even greater importance that lies not far from your cottage," he whispered with a glance at Lira, conveying that he did not wish the girl, yet in her father's arms, to know.

"Do you mean to return in the direction of the cottage?" cried Liam in dismay. "Why, that is the most dangerous place we could go!"

"Nonetheless, it must be attempted at all costs. Perhaps I can go alone, or with Daniel or Morley, and we could reunite later."

Liam looked deeply into Rupert's eyes. "Though what you say appears folly, my heart requires that I trust you, with everything. But the time for secrets must be truly at an end."

"There is nothing I wish more," agreed Rupert from his soul. But first things first. The treasure's safety came above all. And so it was decided that the whole party would head back in the direction they never expected to go; back to the deep woods behind the cottage. And they relied upon the boy Rupert to lead the way.

Chapter Fifteen

The small party sped through the thick forest, proceeding as quickly as they deemed safe. Still several hours until dawn, their way was shrouded in darkness, though the sliver of a moon and pale stars did their best to light their path. Rupert guessed they might reach the treasure by nightfall, but had no way of judging the exact distance. Though confident of finding the way, several fears did plague his mind.

He was most concerned regarding Majesty. The magnificent horse, burdened with blankets, food, and other supplies hastily gathered for their journey to who knew where, was not accustomed to traveling through dark woods. Every move carried potential danger, as one false step could lead to a rabbit hole or other hidden obstacle.

But as the hours passed, Majesty continued to astonish. The powerful stallion seemed as sure-footed as a mountain goat. How this was possible, Rupert could not guess, but only hoped this amazing phenomenon would continue throughout their hasty journey.

Of course, he had trepidation concerning Lira. Despite the early death of her mother and the long-time absence of her father, she'd always lived a relatively safe and comfortable existence, and was not accustomed to hardships. Perhaps she had not realized the permanent loss of her home, that she was now a fugitive.

The final fear, felt with every beat of his heart, was that the king's guards had already discovered their escape. Daniel's death had been scheduled for the morning of the following day. Perhaps the hateful Ned had found them gone and was even now charging in pursuit.

For all Rupert knew, the area round Liam's farm could be swarming with soldiers; for they would certainly suspect that Rupert might flee in that direction. With luck, they wouldn't reach the spot where the treasure lay concealed. That was a full three miles from the farm, but Rupert couldn't be certain of that, or of anything else for that matter.

"Make haste, make haste!" was Rupert's only thought, and he urged the others constantly forward. Liam had brought food, and parceled out bread every few hours, and they wolfed it down as they went. So Rupert had every reason to be satisfied with their speedy pace, but the closer to the treasure, the more anxious he was that it had been discovered.

It amazed him to realize that he'd never been to check on the treasure even once; always meaning to go, but something had always interfered. He wondered against hope if his precious Kara was yet guarding it. By now, she must surely have returned to her forest home.

Rupert's thoughts wandered to Raja; the pup must have found the forest absolutely intoxicating and filled with marvelous smells. His heart must yearn to wander, explore, and perhaps to hunt as well. But he remained fast by Rupert's side, and would do nothing without the boy's approval.

The fugitives traversed the forest all through the day, and finally, just after dark, arrived at a spot Rupert estimated to be a half a mile from the treasure's place of concealment. Rupert signaled a halt, and gestured for his comrades to remain where they were, plainly intending to go the final steps alone.

But Liam took Rupert by the arm and shook his head. Daniel stepped forward, and after a pause, the boy nodded. After all, Daniel knew of the treasure's existence, and it might prove wiser after all. As the two set off, it also became obvious Raja had no intention of allowing his young master to proceed without him, so in the end, all three hastened ahead, while Liam, Lira, Morley, and Majesty remained behind.

The distance was covered swiftly. Rupert knew exactly where to go, as if he had an inner map guiding him. The pale moon had risen, which provided minimal illumination. His heart began to pound as he finally caught sight of the log that he prayed still held his treasure.

But as he and Daniel tiptoed toward it, a dark form sped from out of the woods moving as fast as lightning. Before Daniel could draw the sword his father had provided, the shadow became visible, and leapt into Rupert's arms. It was his fox friend, his dearest companion, Kara!

When Rupert realized who had raced from the shadows, his heart almost exploded with joy! He embraced the beautiful russet-furred creature, and Kara replied by rubbing her face against Rupert's again and again. Raja responded by running in circles about Rupert and the fox, but somehow knew not to bark or growl. Of course, Raja had never seen a fox before, but this creature was obviously beloved by Rupert, and the pup knew instinctively to treat her as a friend.

When he finally released Kara, Rupert was able to communicate with her by his thoughts, but for the sake of Daniel, also whispered aloud. He begged to know if the treasure was still safe, and Kara was able to inform him that it yet lay undisturbed.

Rupert was joyful at such tidings. Informing Daniel that all appeared well, he dashed to the log to see for himself. Cautiously feeling inside, his hand discovered his cloak, the treasures wrapped within. Drawing out the contents, he could not resist unwrapping it, though knowing they dare not tarry. With Raja, Daniel, and Kara at his side, he revealed the sword, the necklace, and the mirror.

Even by the feeble light of the pale moon, Daniel could only gasp at what he beheld. Rupert had in no way exaggerated when describing this treasure in their dank prison cell. And he knew without doubt that it was now in the possession of its rightful owner: a golden-eyed boy named Rupert! After exchanging looks of wonder, they swiftly wrapped the items again and raced back towards their party. Kara joined them as they sped off.

They were soon reunited with their comrades. The mysterious objects remained wrapped in Rupert's old cloak, and placed silently onto Majesty's back. The others stared in greatest curiosity, but inquiries would have to wait. Kara was hastily introduced. Then there remained only one matter of greatest urgency - their next destination. Where could they find safety in this dark and treacherous world?

Fearful of being overheard, knowing soldiers might be searching nearby, there was also danger from every passing woodcutter, farmer, fugitive, or hunter. Anyone could prove a potential informer to the king's men once word of their flight became known.

Daniel whispered to consider the North Country, the land where Lira's mother had lived. But Liam shook his head; the way would soon be covered with snows. More suggestions were made, but there were always objections. Obviously, this puzzle was not a topic to be decided in a confused and hasty moment in the dark and dangerous wood.

Finally, Rupert had an inspiration. It seemed so obvious he was chagrined that it had not already occurred.

"Why, we must go to the place where I was brought up," he exclaimed. "No one ever disturbed us there. Now it might well be discovered, if the soldiers pursue us without cease. Yet it will serve for a brief time, which would give us opportunity to plan with cooler heads, don't you agree?"

Daniel, Liam, and Morley exchanged looks and smiled down at the eager Rupert. "Leave it to the youngest fellow among us to come up with the best idea," remarked Liam, and even his soft whisper could not conceal the laughter in his voice. "Do you think you could lead us? For we must regroup and determine in which direction our future lies."

"Of course, I could find it blindfolded. And even if I mistook the way, my Kara could show us our path, for it's her home as well. But we must travel without cease. The soldiers could be almost upon us."

"Oh, wonderful!" whispered a radiant Lira. "I've always dreamed of seeing where Rupert grew up. It sounds as mysterious as something from a fairy tale!"

"I fear you may be disappointed. But in any case, let us depart without delay."

And so it happened that the party set out upon what might prove the first of many journeys together, leading to an ultimate destination as yet unknown. And again his comrades appeared willing to leave their fate in Rupert's young hands.

Chapter Sixteen

That night brought no respite for the small band of fugitives. They raced more swiftly than was imagined possible through the black forest, carrying the knowledge that the king's men might be close at their heels. Yet it brought great relief that at last they were heading away from danger, away from Liam's farm, heading deeper into the sheltering forest with every step. Though exhausted, exhilaration at outwitting a fearful foe provided a renewed burst of energy. Even the onset of a penetrating rain did not serve to truly dampen their spirits. On through the night they trudged, never pausing till the pale dawn broke. They finally allowed themselves a brief pause, silently devouring the bread and cheese that Liam divided among them.

For the most part, the comrades were silent, wary of being overheard by anyone or anything, while also conserving energy for their desperate flight. At one point, Daniel caught Rupert's eye. His expression carried a look of wonder.

"Do you realize," he whispered, "that this was to be the day of my beheading? Why, at this very hour I would have been led to the village square to face my death. Yet here I am, alive, free, and with my family and friends. Who could have predicted such an outcome?"

"It is indeed miraculous," agreed Liam. He reached out to embrace his son, and Lira jumped into his arms as well.

Rupert observed the reunited family with deep emotion. Yes, their escape was something almost too amazing to be true. He also enjoyed a grim satisfaction as he contemplated the fury of Ned and his men upon realizing they'd been outsmarted.

And what of the villagers? Would they also learn of the daring escape? Even if the guards remained silent, there would be rumors aplenty concerning the cancellation of the dark event. Rupert recalled how wild stories had run rampant when he had not reappeared at the village market.

In all events, this would be one day of victory against the usurper king. Rupert suddenly yearned for many such victories, and his heart could settle for nothing less than the total defeat and ruin of vicious King Ryker and his followers.

The party remained at rest for no more than half an hour, and then continued on their march. Rupert had much time to think during their mostly silent progress. How strange a turn events had taken! Rupert had longed with all his being to see the wide world. But though he'd left the forest at last, in truth he'd merely experienced Liam's farm, one tattered village, and a gruesome prison. But what changes his very small journey had wrought! And now the boy was returning to the place where he'd begun, but this time with his dear friends, his new family. Whatever journeys he was to undertake in future, Rupert would not take them alone.

They again traveled all day without cease. Finally, even Lira admitted fatigue, and though not wishing to burden her father, permitted herself the luxury of riding atop Majesty. Her tiny body did not pose a burden upon the huge stallion, and he could have easily carried Rupert as well. However the boy refused to consider it. It was a matter of pride that he led the way on foot.

On the second night, rest was permitted for a mere hour at the beginning of the evening, and then again at dawn. Their pace was inhuman, but none felt safe taking a longer repose. As far as could be determined, they were not being followed, but they could never be certain. The companions trudged forward in single file, by now in a daze of exhaustion. Only the animals never seemed to weary.

At last, on their third night, they decided to sleep from dusk until midnight. They did not risk the lighting of fires, though feeling chilly and damp. But their spirits rose at the mere thought of sleep.

Their bread was gone, but they still had apples and cheese, nuts and dried fruit. The comrades, however, were almost too weary to know what they ate. Daniel offered to keep watch while the others slept but Morley objected, insisting they were all in desperate need of rest. It was finally decided they should trust their animal friends to give warning if danger approached, and as they were too tired to argue the matter, soon were deep asleep.

Rupert awoke only with the greatest difficulty, feeling he'd barely closed his eyes. But Kara and Raja licked at his face again and again, not permitting him to resume his slumber.

It was still darkest night, and examining the stars, he realized it was not long after midnight. Rupert knew time had come to resume their journey, but oh, how he wished for more rest! It took all his will power to finally sit up. It was only then that he became aware of the reason his animal friends had disturbed him; something was stirring in the trees not far off.

Rupert looked to the others. They were sleeping as if dead. Though his own heart was racing, Rupert sensed that Raja and Kara were excited and curious rather than fearful. That set his own heart somewhat at ease, and he quietly rose to his feet. Daniel was sleeping close by, and the boy took up his friend's sword.

Giving a nod to his four-legged companions, they cautiously approached the place from where the rustling seemed to be emanating. Raja was almost wild with excitement, and quickly Rupert understood why. He smelled a familiar odor that was quite unmistakable; something that filled him with trepidation and curiosity. Parting the bushes he saw what he hoped and feared to see: a bear cub!

The cub was no more than a few months old; so appealing in Rupert's eyes, but it signaled the greatest danger. Because where a cub was found, his mother could not be far behind. Most likely she was roaming the forest nearby hunting. If she returned to find the comrades near her offspring, she would certainly attack. And there could be no happy outcome. Either some of their party would be killed or injured, or the bear herself would be. And if she died, what would happen to her cub? Of all his forest friends, the bears were the ones that he'd been taught to avoid. He respected their need for distance from humans, and admired their power and beauty from afar. But this was not the time to form an acquaintance.

Rupert slowly backed away pulling the playful Raja with him; Kara however was as wise and cautious as the boy could have desired. He proceeded to shake awake all the members of his party. They were as drugged with sleep as he had been a few moments before, and it was at first difficult to make his frantic whispers understood. Once they realized a bear cub was near, the danger became most obvious. More quickly than anyone could have imagined, they made ready to depart.

Rupert directed his thoughts to Kara, asking if she knew in what direction the mother bear might be. She delicately sniffed the night air and indicated her findings to Rupert, and he swiftly led the party in a wide detour, that they might avoid a violent encounter. Luckily, they succeeded, but the episode served as a reminder that obstacles might not only come in the form of the king's men. And how right to rely upon the animals to keep watch!

Two more days and nights passed when the bone-weary travelers were at last informed that the cottage was but a day distant. There were sighs of jubilation, as much as their depleted condition allowed, and it was decided to permit the unheard-of luxury of actually sleeping through the night.

Spirits seemed to rise with each passing moment. Lira was positively gleeful at the thought of seeing Rupert's former home. And she begged him to at last reveal what he'd retrieved from the forest, for which he'd been willing to risk all their lives.

Rupert exchanged a swift glace with Daniel, silently seeking permission for his daughter to witness the treasure. Smiling, Daniel responded with a brief nod. Yet Rupert knew she must not be told of his golden eyes. That was too large a burden for her fragile shoulders. But his greatest secret must be revealed to the others come what may.

It was nearing sundown the following day when the party at long last arrived at the clearing where the cabin stood. To Rupert's vast relief, it appeared silent and undisturbed. Slowly they approached, and Rupert did the honors of pushing open the door.

The companions stepped inside. All surfaces were covered with dust and cobwebs, but otherwise it looked exactly as Rupert had left it. Only Kara and Majesty remained outside. As the others looked about with curiosity, Rupert quickly lit a fire from the wood still resting by the fireplace. It was the first light and warmth the fugitives had experienced since the prison escape. For Rupert and Daniel, it had been even longer than that.

For a happy moment, they sprawled upon the dusty floor beside the crackling flames. Now that they could at last speak freely, no one seemed to have the strength for words. But what a luxury to feel warm, dry, and safe!

Lira jumped up after a long moment, embracing each member of the party, including, of course, Raja. Her high spirits enabled them to truly relish the moment. The elder companions soon broke into raucous laugher and congratulated one other on surviving such a perilous journey, and moreover giving the king's men a merry chase!

Rupert leapt to his feet, recalling his duties as host. He went to the cooking area to find everything intact, and began to prepare a huge pot of porridge, adding handfuls of nuts, dried fruit, and honey. Before long, each had a huge tempting bowlful before them, along with fragrant cups of steaming tea, their first hot sustenance in many a day, and their spirits revived even further.

Lira thanked Rupert for the repast, and inquired with an eager smile if she might see the object of their curiosity, which still rested upon Majesty's back.

Her request reminded Rupert that poor Majesty yet carried his burden, and along with Daniel hastened outdoors to unload the blankets, food, and other supplies. Rupert kissed Majesty's face and thanked him again and again for his amazing sure-footed stamina. Majesty returned the affection by rubbing his head against the top of Rupert's wildly tangled black locks. After feeding the stallion several apples, he allowed Majesty to walk about freely. Kara was nowhere to be seen, and Rupert surmised she'd gone to find her family, whom she hadn't seen for so very long.

"Do you truly think it's safe that Lira sees the treasure?" wondered an anxious Rupert. "I suppose it would be impossible to keep it from her, since we must carry it with us wherever we go."

Lira's father agreed. "We must hope she will understand the need for complete secrecy. However, she's shown incredible bravery and maturity already; and I say it though she is my own daughter. I could hardly be more proud of her. But trust her or not, she must be told, though not of your golden eyes."

Rupert heartily concurred. And so they together carried the treasure into the cottage. Laying the cloak and its contents before the fire, the others gathered round. And slowly, very slowly, his heart racing...for he'd dreamed of this moment for so long...Rupert unfolded the cloak and revealed to his new family the sword, the necklace, and the mirror.

There was a gasp of disbelief from Liam, Lira, and Morley. For a prolonged, stunned, terrible moment, no one said a word. And finally Liam spoke, though with choked utterance.

"Rupert, what is this? How did it come to pass that you possess such treasures? Do you realize..." But he was overcome and could speak no further.

"Please don't...I'll tell you everything," cried Rupert. And he proceeded to recount, in a rather frenzied and disjointed fashion, what only Daniel had heard till now. Of the strange storm that had swept the forest, of how Rupert discovered the eerie oak revealing the rotted wooden box, how he'd dug, covered with mud until he was able to dislodge the treasure from its hiding place. And of how, from that moment, his grandparents had disappeared from his life.

The again awe-struck boy took up the sword, the first thing drawn from the box, and held it for a wonder-filled moment before passing it to Liam. He took it in his grasp.

"This is the sword of King Marco. I have beheld it in his hands or strapped to his side, on so many occasions. It belonged to generations of Golden-Eyed Kings before him. I had come to believe all signs of kingship to be lost, or in the hands of usurpers."

He softly kissed the sword, and then handed it to his son, who after a long moment examining it with shining eyes, passed it to Morley.

He took it up, trembling. "I do not feel worthy to hold such an object," Morley declared. "I feel as if I'm touching history, our lost golden-eyed past, our kingdom's former glory. And I confess to a great reawakening of hope in my heart. Hope that we might yet find another worthy of these symbols of true kingship."

Morley turned his gaze upon Rupert. For now, how could he doubt that the boy was deeply involved with returning the land to its true destiny? He could not believe these treasures could have been uncovered by someone unworthy of finding them.

Lira had been staring wide-eyed at the sword as well, and reached out to touch it reverently while still in Morley's hands. But she was equally fascinated by the necklace, and the mirror. She asked a timid permission to put the necklace about her own neck, and Rupert embraced the idea. For in his own thoughts, she was already a princess and a hero. Rupert took the stunning ruby necklace and placed it over her head. It hung down to her waist, and the others could admire its glorious beauty and the beauty of its wearer.

And then, Rupert cautiously took up the object that caused him the most curiosity of all - the mirror. Before daring to look into it once more, he held it up for Lira to behold her own reflection, probably for the first time. She gasped in surprise and delight. "See how beautiful the necklace is!" she breathed. The others laughed, amused that she did not appear to find her own astonishing beauty to be of interest. But she was truly as dazzling as the necklace she wore.

Rupert handed the mirror around, and all were curious at its carved silver beauty.

"This must have belonged to Queen Karoleena or another royal lady," observed Daniel. "Did you ever see it when you visited the castle, Father?"

"I don't recall," whispered a still dazed and dazzled Liam. "But that is not remarkable, since I was never in her private quarters. But we may assume that it was hers."

The three men could not help but examine their own reflections. Morley had never been privileged to see into a mirror before, and it had been many years since Daniel or Liam had had the opportunity.

Rupert, observing them, thought all should be pleased by what they beheld. And he could see now how strongly father and son resembled each other. Both had the same tall and lean figure, blond hair - the color of ripening wheat on the son and a lighter hue for Liam, and similar fine features of aristocratic aspect. Only their eyes greatly differed, the father's being narrow and of pale azure, while Daniel's were wide and of darkest sapphire.

Finally, taking a breath, Rupert took back the mirror and dared gaze into it. And there, unchanged, were his golden orbs blazing back at him! Rupert had half-feared the magic mirror might reveal eyes of gold to any face reflected there. But clearly this was not the case.

He was vastly relieved, and, looking up, found Daniel smiling a knowing smile. For he concluded that Rupert had witnessed his kingly reflection, and that, as soon as Lira slept, would come the moment to reveal the truth. And both realized it would be an announcement which, if believed, could change all their destinies forever.

Chapter Seventeen

They remained by the fire for some minutes, an awkward silence prevailing. All seemed to sense there was more to be said, yet were aware certain subjects must not be spoken of before Lira. Rupert finally rose to prepare more tea, feeling a dreadful trepidation that his astonishing secret was now to be revealed. He blessed the fact that Daniel could give his words a measure of credence.

Finally, as if in answer to Rupert's prayer, Lira fell asleep curled up by the fire next to her father, the necklace still about her neck. Rupert fetched a blanket, and covered her. The time was now.

The boy flushed and his heart began to race as if he were about to hurl himself off a high cliff. For once he had spoken, there was no turning back. Either they would believe him, or else think him mad. However, to Rupert's relief, it was Liam who chose to speak. He had reached deep within the pocket of his tunic and pulled out the ruby ring, holding it up for inspection by the others.

"I believe this is not the first time you've beheld this ring," he observed, peering in Rupert's direction. "I'd be most curious as to why you did not conceal it in the forest with the other royal treasures. Because make no mistake, this ring belonged to King Marco, and generations of Golden-Eyed Kings before him."

Daniel, who had heard of the ring's existence from Rupert; and Morley, who had known nothing of it, stared with fascination at the glowing gold and ruby jewel. Rupert's blush deepened as he returned Liam's gaze, and finally drew breath to speak.

"The reason it was not hidden with the rest was because the ring was not part of the forest treasure. It was given me by that lady in the marketplace, the one with the basket."

Morley spoke up. "But I inspected that very basket, along with Ned. We saw nothing but the pup." Suddenly the truth of the matter seemed to penetrate his thoughts. "Why, had we discovered the ring, you would have been arrested on the spot along with your family. And King Ryker would have certainly interested himself in the matter. Possession of a royal ring could only have had the most hideous consequence!"

"Very true," agreed Rupert. "That lady made me promise not to open the basket until I returned home. When you opened it, I greatly feared what you might discover. But it seemed the basket contained only the pup. It was only after I'd later lifted Raja out that I spotted the ring."

"But why did you say nothing even then?" Liam demanded.

"Because...well, I *wished* to speak. Please believe me for that! But it seemed so complicated. I'd have to explain everything; about finding the other treasure...and something else as well. I was so very confused as to what was to be concealed and what to be revealed.

"I had decided to hide the ring in the forest with the other treasures, but could not resist first trying it on. I know it was wrong; I am no king. And when I did put it on my finger, well that's when I fell sick. I feared I might die on the spot, so with my last bit of strength, I placed the ring under the firewood, hoping it would be safe."

Liam and the others continued to stare at him. "And so you believe that putting on the ring led to your brush with death?"

"Yes, of that I am certain." He explained about seeing the mysterious lady, whether dream or real he could not know, who revealed that he was not yet ready to wear it.

The others were attempting to comprehend the mystery, including even Daniel, who had heard the tale before.

"But, if it was not meant for you, why did the lady entrust you with it? Do you believe you should be keeping it safe for another? Then why give it to a mere boy to protect?" Morley wondered.

"Before you attempt to draw any conclusions, there is one more thing I must divulge, though I fear to even breathe the words. But you are my family, and I must now trust you with everything."

Rupert paused and took a very deep breath. Wondering how to proceed, he quietly took up the mirror and handed it to Liam. "Tell me, when you look into this glass, what do you see?"

He held it, regarding Rupert with quizzical eyes. Finally, he did as requested. "Well, I see a man of two-and-forty who feels that his life is beginning anew. And in a manner I do not yet comprehend."

Rupert nodded, and indicated he should hand the glass to his son. Daniel took it up. "I see the face of a man who never thought to find his loved ones or his freedom again. And now I have both."

Daniel handed the glass to Morley. "Well, no solemn observations for me, for I see the face of a very fine-looking fellow! I'm certain you all must envy me!"

Morley's three listeners burst into laughter. His amusing remarks were just the thing needed to break the tension and Rupert smiled at Morley with gratitude. Besides, Morley truly *was* a fine-looking fellow, with agreeably rugged features, long, thick auburn hair, a ruddy complexion, and warm green eyes. Morley gave Rupert an encouraging smile, urging him to unburden whatever lay upon his heart.

Finally, Rupert took up the glass. He did peer into it again for an instant, as if to verify if those golden eyes were still there. He half-hoped they'd be gone, and thus his burden lifted from him.

"Well, when I look into this glass..." He swallowed and could hardly speak for the hammering in his chest. He turned to Daniel, the only one who knew the truth. Daniel nodded back, urging him to proceed. "When I look into this glass, I see *golden eyes* reflecting back at me!"

Liam and Morley gasped, staring aghast at the anxious boy. Liam jumped to his feet. His emotions seemed to fly from rage, to wild hope, to greatest confusion.

"Do you comprehend what you are saying? Your eyes are brown. This cannot be! Or can it? Is it possible? No, they are all dead!"

"I could not believe it myself, I assure you. Please do not think I speak of this lightly," begged Rupert. "Just listen to what I say, then draw your own conclusions. Because when I first saw these golden eyes when I uncovered the treasure in the forest, I knew nothing of the Golden-Eyed Kings! The first I heard of them was the very night I met you and Lira. But before that, I'd examined my reflection many times, and I had come to suspect these eyes might be special; perhaps even portend danger. I wished to conceal them, though I could not fathom how that might be possible. But consider my astonishment when you and Lira were apparently blind to them!

"As you can imagine, it made me question everything. Was I connected to this lost royal family, or was I not? I was merely a boy who had lived life isolated in the forest. I knew nothing of the world or its happenings."

Rupert took a breath and looked to see how his heartfelt explanation was being received. But it appeared no one had anything to say, and so he continued.

"I tried to convince myself that I'd somehow imagined it all. Or that perhaps the mirror was magic and that anyone peering into it would see golden eyes reflected there. But then, there were other things. Lira told me about Majesty and his mysterious appearance, that he was the exact twin of King Marco's horse. And when I rode atop Majesty, I saw...a "vision"...I suppose you'd call it, of a Golden-Eyed King riding into battle. A vision of the past or future I could not tell. And then the lady gave me the basket with a puppy that had been the chosen guard dog of the royal family, and the ruby ring as well. And when she touched my hair, I found myself seeing yet another vision, this time of a Golden-Eyed King riding in triumph!"

Rupert paused, energy coursing through him as his words tumbled out. It was a vast relief to reveal all, especially to Liam, whom he had always trusted, yet never found the right moment to confide in.

"After I was imprisoned, it was Daniel who gave me courage again. For though he was delirious with fever, the first words he ever spoke to me were declaring that he could see my golden eyes!"

Liam looked to his son, his dazed eyes wide with surprise.

"Yes, it is true, Father, I did see golden eyes the instant I gazed upon him. And when the fever passed, I saw them still. As I do now." Daniel spoke gravely as if he were taking the most solemn of oaths.

Morley spoke up. "By God, it's true! I was there when Daniel awoke. He was raving on about Rupert's golden eyes, calling him king! Of course, I thought it was the fever speaking. And Rupert was smooth as silk, saying the poor man was off his head. Actually, I wasn't certain what to believe. For I knew Rupert was a most extraordinary fellow. But his eyes certainly appeared almost black to me!"

After a pause, Rupert spoke again. "I know this must seem a great shock. But I swear all I've spoken is true. At least the truth as I believe it to be. Now, you may conclude what you will. But at last, I have no more secrets concealed. This I swear!"

There was a prolonged silence. Each looked down, deeply withdrawn into his own thoughts. Finally, it was Daniel who spoke.

"I for one believe, with all my heart, that Rupert is our king. Or at the very least, our prince, since, if he survives, perhaps his father might as well? But I believe Rupert deserves our utmost loyalty and protection. He has given meaning back to our lives, and hope to our land. I have already knelt before him, pledging my fealty forever."

Without further hesitation, Morley moved to Rupert's side and knelt on one knee. "I also believe you are my prince, my king, it matters not! From the instant I beheld you in the marketplace, my heart bid me kneel before you, and at last I know why. It is a pleasure and privilege to follow my heart at last. You have my sword and my strength and all I have to offer. I swear it!"

Rupert felt moved beyond measure, yet troubled and unworthy. "Please arise, Morley, and refrain from bowing before me. This is not the time, if ever. I have not earned the right to such an oath."

"You are mistaken, my dearest boy," whispered Liam, barely able to speak. "I know not why your golden eyes are revealed only to my son. Perhaps it is to protect you from grave danger. Or perhaps it is a curse to keep you from your rightful heritage. But either way I accept you from this moment as my liege, and you have my oath to serve you." He stood before Rupert and then bowed low.

This was too much for Rupert to endure. To have Grandfather Liam kneel before him, he felt like the greatest of frauds! *He* should be the one to do the kneeling. Instead, the boy flung himself into Liam's arms.

"Please, never kneel before me! I owe you everything, and you... all of you are my friends, family, equals! I know full well I am most unworthy and have everything to learn. I would not ask for better teachers. But you do me far too much honor." For now Daniel had come to kneel once again before the boy as well.

"We only pay you just homage. And as our king, you must learn to accept it. But it is true that from this moment, we must treat you as our equal, if only to prevent Lira from sensing the truth. For this burden would be too great for her. But if you are to be a true monarch, you must accept the gift of love and loyalty from your devoted subjects." Daniel spoke these words looking deep into Rupert's eyes, and Rupert embraced him, and then Morley.

"Please do remember, we cannot be certain I am a Golden-Eyed King until *all* can testify to it, and we can know we are not deluded. I prefer to consider kingship a possibility only, and I pray that you do so as well. Now let us put this aside, for we have much to attend to, especially the puzzle of where our destination lies from here. For escape must be our first concern."

"Ah, yes," agreed Liam. "But let us not forget an even more pressing matter which we must observe on the morrow. For, unless I have lost track of the days, it is Lira's seventh birthday!"

Rupert smiled in gratitude, glad that Liam had lightened the mood, knowing Rupert was most discomforted by the burdens suddenly thrust upon him.

Yet, perhaps the boy was right; until all could see these amazing eyes, they could not know the truth with certainty. Liam remained puzzled as to why none but his son could perceive them, but hoped this, and yet other mysteries, might be revealed in time

"I have something here that is also yours," Liam finally continued. He reached again into his pocket and produced the necklace of blue and red stones that Rupert had bought in the marketplace for Lira. Rupert received it with surprise. It seemed a thousand years since he'd proudly paid those few coins to purchase the gift. Emotion churned within him, remembering being brutally dragged off to prison, believing he'd never see Lira again, on her birthday, or any other day. He turned to hand the necklace to Daniel.

"You should give this to your daughter," he said with a generous heart. "She should rightly receive it from you." But Daniel refused, knowing full well how Rupert had dreamed of giving it to his friend.

"In that case, I have many things that would make suitable gifts." He pointed towards the rows of shelves lining the wall. "Here are many of my books that I know she would love. Morley, pick some out as your gift to her. And I have wonderful scarves that my grandmother made as well."

Liam interrupted. "I have my own gift for her. He reached into his knapsack and produced a wooden figure about eight inches in height. It was a skillfully painted carving of Majesty, with Lira riding atop him. It amazingly captured the beauty and grace of horse and rider.

"Lira will adore that!" exclaimed Rupert. And suddenly the four of them were busily planning Lira's special day.

Rupert was grateful that the focus had shifted from him at last. He could not shake the feeling of being most unready and unworthy. He was cheered and encouraged, however, at having such staunch and fearless counselors to rely upon.

It was time at last for much-needed sleep, and before long there was no sound to be heard but the night wind in the trees. However, it seemed that the evening's events were not yet over for Rupert. For once again, the vision of a mysterious lady invaded his slumber, in dreams that seemed more than real. And when he awoke deep in the night, breathless, Rupert knew he had been given a gift of knowledge: knowledge of where they should flee. A place that never would have entered his thoughts. A place he barely knew existed. And Rupert could hardly wait for the dawn, so he might reveal it to the others!

Chapter Eighteen

Rupert was awoken the next morning by Raja's insistent licking of his nose. Once his master had opened his eyes, the pup raced to the door. The message was clear; Raja needed to be released. Rupert stretched and got to his feet. Liam was already awake, but the others slept soundly on. Rupert would have been content to sleep longer as well, for it had been many days since experiencing the comfort of a roof and a cozy fire. But Raja's needs came first.

He tiptoed to the door, and then, seeing Liam hard at work baking bread, Rupert went to his side and gave him a radiant smile. The boy had never felt closer to him than the previous night, when the truth had been finally revealed. He received a warm look in return, and then Rupert hurried to the door.

Raja lost no time in racing out. Rupert watched him frolic, and then went to bid a good morrow to Majesty, grazing on the thick grass just a few yards away. As always, the sight of this powerful beast filled him with awe. Majesty, as customary, lowered his head so that Rupert might stoke his face. It almost appeared as if Majesty was bowing to him. He laughed and instructed the steed that he was not prepared for salutes from him either.

Realizing he hadn't ridden Majesty in many a day, the boy quietly led the towering stallion further from the cottage, so the sound of racing hooves might not awaken the others. In a moment, finding a fallen tree trunk that he could stand upon, Rupert swung up upon Majesty's back. Holding on to his flowing white mane, the boy signaled the horse to canter about the clearing. The wind blew through Rupert's waving black locks, and the boy experienced a magnificent sense of joy and freedom.

Leaning forward, embracing his horse's muscled neck, the sensation of bringing himself even closer to the mighty beast as he flew across the earth was wondrous! Of course, Raja was soon racing alongside and Rupert experienced a profound sense of unity with the earth, sky, and the world of living creatures.

He continued to ride for some time, watching the stars fade and the sun rise. His heart felt enveloped by a powerful feeling of peace and perfection. Rupert, knowing such moments were rare, vowed to treasure them, especially since darkness and danger must surely lie ahead.

Finally, he slid down from Majesty's back, whispering words of gratitude. He headed back to his friends, Raja beside him. The seductive perfume of baking bread filled the air. The others were in the process of waking.

Rupert was eager for Lira to realize this was her birthday. He went to assist Liam. With a wink, he whispered that although they did not have proper ingredients for a cake, he did bake a special loaf of birthday bread; a loaf filled with dried fruits and apples, which Lira might find an acceptable substitute. Almost immediately Morley, Daniel, and Lira were up, inhaling the fragrant air.

"Why, what a delicious scent," cried Lira. "It's been so long since we've had fresh bread. And I'm starving too. I hope you baked lots and lots!"

"You may eat as much as you like," beamed her grandfather, "for today is special - your seventh birthday!"

Lira gasped in surprise. Her father swept her up, holding her high over head while the girl giggled wildly in delight. Finally, he lowered her and kissed her blushing cheek.

"Happy Birthday, my darling girl! How I've dreamed of this! I was only with you for your very first birthday, and I fear you don't remember that!"

She kissed her father back and soon Morley, Liam, and Rupert claimed their share of hugs as well. And Raja was not to be forgotten.

"Oh, this is truly the happiest birthday I've ever had!" she proclaimed. "All my dreams have already come true! Because ever since I was little, I only had two wishes. One was that Father would come back. And the other was, though I love the farm, I always wished to see the world someday. Although I do hope we'll see something besides forests eventually," she ended wistfully.

All laughed at that. "Yes, darling," replied Daniel. "For the moment, we must abstain from traveling by road, but if we reach any degree of safety, we should certainly see all the towns and cities and castles you crave!"

"I always dreamed of seeing the world as well," remarked Rupert ruefully. "Though life as a fugitive was not exactly what I'd envisioned. There was an old saying my grandmother used: 'Beware of what you desire!'"

The others chuckled. "Sounds very wise," observed Morley. "But come, let us chatter as we eat. For I'm wasting away to a skeleton at this rate!"

The comrades sat down around the small wooden table. It struck Rupert as most peculiar that they had five bowls, plates, and spoons. There had only been three people living there, he and his grandparents. But his grandmother had always kept enough utensils for five. He'd questioned her about that more than once. She'd only remarked that you never knew when extra would come in handy. It gave him a strange feeling now. Almost as if she'd known that this day might come.

The freshly baked loaves were carried to the table. "This will have to do as your birthday cake," apologized Liam. But Lira was most delighted. They gave her the first piece of the fruit-filled bread, and there was hot porridge as well. It was not long before the repast was devoured, but there were more in store.

"Happy Birthday!" they exclaimed in unison, and Lira jumped up in joyful surprise. Her gifts had been wrapped in a blanket, and she slowly unfolded it to find the books from Morley, the knitted blue scarf and cap from her father, the necklace from Rupert, and the beautiful carved horse from her grandfather. Her face blushed with pleasure while thanking each of the givers in turn.

"I hardly needed any presents, as I already have everything I could wish for. But there is one more thing I hope to request: to put off my dress and wear boys' clothing. Because dresses are not very suitable for our journey, don't you agree?"

The others regarded her, bemused. They'd never seen a girl anywhere dressed like a boy. But she spoke true; her blue frock had been reduced to a very ragged state, constantly caught in bushes and brambles along the way. And her bare legs were covered with scratches.

"I do believe my grandmother kept some of my old clothes," said Rupert. "But you must ask your father's permission," he amended hastily.

Daniel willingly agreed to the idea. "It is a fine thing to have such a practical daughter. I'm glad you pointed out the deficiencies of your garb. By all means, Rupert, see if she finds something more suitable."

She dashed to her father with a radiant smile. Then Rupert led Lira to a small chest in the corner of the room, used for storing his meager wardrobe. Opening it, there were several tunics and pairs of leggings that he'd left behind. He dug to the bottom, and found garments that were now too small for him.

Inviting her to take her pick, she carefully considered an excited instant before selecting a dark blue tunic and gray leggings. Lira grabbed them up and dashed into the next room, appearing a moment later to display her new attire.

They all clapped in approval. She did not look like a boy, no matter what the disguise, but she did appear charming indeed. And she was right, male attire was certainly more practical for the time being.

"And I want to wear my hair out of the way as well. It seems to get caught on every passing bramble." She ran to her backpack and pulled out a hairbrush and a dark blue ribbon. Rupert recognized it as one bought for her at the village fair. "Father, will you please brush my hair and put it into a braid for me? You can tie it with this ribbon."

Daniel slowly took up the brush, recognizing it instantly as one owned by her mother. It brought up a wave of deep emotion, but Lira did not see, as she had turned her back so he might arrange her hair...the wildly curling tangle the color of silver moonlight...the very hair that had graced her mother Vyka's beautiful head.

Daniel kissed the brush, and then his daughter's locks as he began his task. She tried not to complain, because it was indeed in something of a tangled snarl after their hard journey. But finally he had it crackling smooth as silk, and made one enormous braid that hung to her waist and secured it with the ribbon.

"There, you look the proper lad," teased her father, which produced more mirth, because even in this strange attire, she looked more beautiful than ever. Having her hair drawn back served to set off her features to even greater perfection. Lira, as always however, seemed unaware of the effect of her beauty upon anyone who beheld it. She was flushed with excitement at the adventure of wearing boys' clothes.

Liam returned to practical matters, and wondered if there might be fresh clothing for them among Rupert's grandfather's belongings. For the coming journey would be most challenging, and there would be no possibility of approaching any village for a very long while. They feared they must be among the most wanted fugitives in the kingdom.

Rupert showed Liam his grandfather's trunk. Much to his surprise, for his grandfather seemed to wear the same garments day in and day out, they discovered a large number of tunics and leggings, along with knitted scarves, gloves, and warm caps! There seemed to be enough to provide the men with several changes of clothing.

"I am astonished. But now I do recall that my grandmother seemed to sew and knit constantly, far more than necessary. When I questioned her, she always made the same reply: 'You never know what the day might bring.'"

Rupert was intrigued. *Had* his grandparents known this day would come? But that was impossible, wasn't it?

"Well, we may not know if this was mere coincidence," ventured Liam. "But we can be grateful that we will be better prepared for our journey."

These words gave Rupert his opportunity. "Speaking of our journey, have you any notion as to where we might go?" he began.

"I believe that will take much discussion," observed Daniel. "I had hoped that we could head to the North Country, but 'tis probably true the snows will make the journey most hazardous."

"The south would be far too perilous," cautioned Morley. "The fighting along the southern border tends to be fierce. King Ryker is intent upon invading those lands if given half a chance."

"I do believe...rather, I *know* where we should go!" The others turned to regard Rupert, appearing certain and confident. "A lady appeared to me last night in my dream. The same one, perhaps, that came when I was sick. But whoever it was spoke very plain: 'You must go to the land of Queen Karoleena'...though, in truth, I know not where that may be."

Morley shook his head, but Liam and Daniel exchanged astonished looks.

"Queen Karoleena!" exclaimed Lira. "Why she was the wife of King Marco, the last of the Golden-Eyed Kings! But I know not where she came from. You must know, Grandfather Liam, for you knew her when you were a boy! Where? Where did she come from? Do tell us!" Lira clapped her hands and jumped up and down in excitement. Raja caught her mood and raced about the room howling.

"Yes, I know where she came from. But Rupert, you don't understand. That would be an impossible journey. Perhaps several thousand miles, perhaps far more! Filled with hardships beyond reckoning. I do not know the way, nor do we have even a map to guide us."

"But *where* is this land? What is it called?" demanded Rupert.

"It is called 'Raja-Sharan' and it lies far, far to the east. It might as well be on the moon, my boy. Put the idea out of your head!"

But Rupert, entranced by the exotic sound of the words, was not to be dissuaded. "But why would that lady tell me something impossible? It only *appears* to be impossible because you believe it so! We cannot know until we have attempted the journey. Who knows what we may be capable of? Besides, if it is the land of Queen Karoleena, wouldn't the people there be allied to... to the Golden-Eyed Kings?" Rupert refrained from mentioning that he might be one himself, mindful of Lira eagerly listening to every word. "Perhaps they would help us; and anyway, it would be so far away that King Ryker could not pursue us."

Morley spoke up. "The boy may be right. After all, if north and south are too dangerous, where else can we go, as there is a great sea to the west, and few who attempt to cross it return. But, of course, I for one am open to other suggestions."

An idea suddenly dawned on Rupert. "Raja-Sharan! And I named my dog 'Raja', which I had read meant 'king' in a land far away. Is this that very country?"

Liam had to confirm the fact. "Yes, 'Raja-Sharan' means 'The Land of Kings'. The rulers there are called 'rajas' and the queens are called 'ranis'."

Rupert felt awed; naming his dog after this land was no coincidence. The lady in his dream must be right!

"Please do believe me! I feel certain we *must* attempt the journey. We can't remain here, certainly; it grows more dangerous by the moment. And it is possible we might find refuge before reaching Raja-Sharan. Are there not friendly lands between here and there?"

"Who can say?" replied Daniel. "There has been little word of outside events for many years. We have no way of knowing friend from foe across our own borders. But none has any inspiration of where we should flee; except you, Rupert. So perhaps we should heed your plea."

The others were silent. They knew, with the exception of Lira, of his golden eyes. They could well believe he might be receiving special guidance.

"I, for one, think we should go!" declared little Lira. "It sounds like a wonderful adventure. But whatever is decided, please do tell us all you know of Queen Karoleena and Raja-Sharan!"

"I agree," said Morley. "For the history of the Golden-Eyed Kings has not been a subject for discussion, except in whispers, since their deaths. I myself know nothing of Queen Karoleena or her homeland."

"Then I will tell you what I know," sighed Liam. "Most of these events happened before I was born. I did hear of them from my father, and passed these stories down to Daniel. And yes, I met Queen Karoleena and King Marco frequently as a child."

"Was she very beautiful?" Lira wanted to know.

"Yes indeed, but not in the way of ladies in our kingdom. Most here are very fair of skin and eyes and hair. But she came from far to the east. Her hair was black as night, as were her eyes. Her skin was a dark honey hue. As a boy, I remember being fascinated the first time I beheld her; she looked amazingly beautiful to me. And obviously King Marco agreed, for it is said he fell in love with her even before they met."

"But how would that be possible?" Rupert demanded.

"Have patience and I will tell you. First of all, her name was not Karoleena. She was truly called 'Khar-shar-leen'. But when she married King Marco...he was still Prince Marco then, she wished to appear less foreign. So she chose a name not uncommon here. But I remember King Marco used only her true name."

Liam began the tale with a far-off look in his clear blue eyes. It was when Prince Marco was in his sixteenth year that his loving parents, King Willem and Queen Shara, determined it was time to search for a bride. Marco was their only son and heir, and thus his duty was to marry and produce a golden-eyed son of his own.

The prince had no objections. Though young, he had proven himself in battle, and achieved note as a skillful horseman and hunter. Moreover, he was most intelligent and curious about the world, a great lover of books, and spoke a number of languages. It was his destiny to marry, but Marco wished to do so for love as well as political considerations.

And so the search began. Marco had already met the daughters of many noble families. Many were rich as well as lovely, but none moved his heart. But as ambassadors arrived from lands near and far, presenting their eligible ladies, he never felt his soul stir. Of course, the young ladies did not make the journey themselves. But representatives from their royal houses arrived bearing lavish gifts, and often brought portraits of their princesses; or at least vivid descriptions of their charm and beauty. But Prince Marco rejected every candidate.

His doting parents began to feel growing annoyance. Just what was the lad looking for? He could not provide an answer. Only that it had not yet appeared.

But one day, when Prince Marco was nearing his eighteenth year, he returned from a gallop upon his favorite horse, the magnificent golden Rico with flowing white mane and tail, to be greeted by an amazing sight. Riding into the courtyard of High Tower Castle, he found a dozen black horses, riders beside them.

The steeds were covered with red silk; their saddles trimmed with silver. The men were dressed in black and silver, and unlike any the young prince had ever seen. They had dark complexions, long black hair shining with fragrant oils, and long beards. Their garb was also foreign to his eyes; long red silk blouses worn over billowing black silk trousers. They wore heavy belts of silver and silver necklaces as well.

Prince Marco dismounted and demanded to know who they might be. But no one, it seemed, spoke his language. He attempted to communicate in several other tongues, but none could respond. But they all recognized his golden eyes, and bowed before him.

Hurrying within, Marco found his parents deep in discussion with another of the foreign party. He was dressed in similar fashion, but with a turquoise blouse and a silver and ruby necklace about his neck.

To Marco's relief, the man was able to communicate, at least, after a fashion. He was an emissary from the eastern land of Raja-Sharan, come to offer their princess Khar-shar-leen as a bride. For even in such a distant kingdom, the fame of the Golden-Eyed Kings had not gone unnoticed. The soothsayers of their Raja and Rani had spoken, announcing this marriage was fated to occur. The man spoke with greatest confidence, as if the match would be approved without doubt.

King Willem and Queen Shara exchanged bewildered yet amused glances. It did not occur to them that any objections were already too late. For Marco, upon hearing for the first time the name 'Khar-shar-leen' felt his heart speak as never before.

Breaking protocol, he spoke up without his parents' consent, with endless inquiries about his future wife. She was almost fifteen years of age, had been well-educated, and spoke the language of this country. She was brilliant and beautiful and would make a most worthy wife. He then produced a small painting, no bigger than the palm of his hand, of the face of his princess...or the 'Ranila' as she was known. Marco beheld the image of the most exquisite girl he'd ever seen.

After that, there was no turning back. Marco insisted the marriage be arranged without delay. His parents hesitated, fearing an alliance with such a distant land would prove of no strategic advantage. But the ambassador declared that one never knew when a distant ally might prove useful indeed. The king and queen were startled to learn that in Raja-Sharan the coming marriage was taken as an accepted fact, and the bride was already on her way. Marco was overjoyed, and determined that the wedding should take place the very day of her arrival.

Her Highness and an enormous escort appeared a month later, laden with bride-gifts of silver, gold, jewels, spices, and silks. But though his parents were well pleased, Marco cared for nothing but his princess, and they met at last face-to-face. She was even lovelier in person, but more importantly, the Golden-Eyed Prince instantly felt his heart and hers were one; that they would always share the greatest love and loyalty.

Princess Khar-shar-leen also loved Marco at first sight. He was like no man she had ever beheld in her own world; so tall and strapping, with flowing golden locks and dazzling golden eyes. He looked like a being from another world! But more than that, she knew he was brave and loving and loyal; they would always find happiness together.

And so they did. The only misgiving for Marco was that his bride brought with her several very strange attendants. They claimed to foretell the future and even be casters of spells. But Karoleena, as she was now known, believed in them implicitly. Marco's parents had warned their son against such people, for they were not to be trusted.

But Marco would refuse his bride nothing, and since she had left her whole world behind to marry him, he would not turn back her retinue. And so the soothsayers remained and seemed, for the most part, to stay out of his way. And the prince and princess lived many a happy day, eventually becoming king and queen with children of their own, ruling with love and harmony until the hideous day that Zorin destroyed everything that was good and beautiful in the land.

All listened with rapt fascination to Liam's narrative. But, in truth, they had learned little of Raja-Sharan, for little was known about it. Even the vivid tales Liam had heard as a child seemed more like something from a fairy tale with amazing creatures and mysterious wizards. He had no idea whether they were true or mere fancy.

But Lira was convinced, thrilled at the thought of such a distant and exotic place. So was Rupert. The others greatly feared such a long and desperate journey, with the king's men likely at their heels. And who knew what other obstacles might present themselves? Finally, Liam spoke again.

"I do not see how this odyssey could be possible; yet I also do not readily see an alternative. We have been guided by young Rupert in recent days, and have not done badly by following his instincts. So let us do so again. And see where the road east may lead us!"

He looked to Daniel and Morley who nodded in agreement, for they could think of no wiser alternative. And so, much to Rupert's joy, it was finally decided that toward Raja-Sharan they would go!

Chapter Nineteen

The remainder of the day was spent in preparation for their most arduous journey. Rupert hoped to leave on the morrow, though the others wished for a further day of respite under a sheltering roof. It was decided to be ready to depart with the dawn, but the possibility of instead staying longer lingered.

Liam had discovered the stores of healing herbs that Rupert's grandparents had grown and determined to leave none behind. Lira was occupied inspecting Rupert's many books; for though she had received several as a birthday gift, she hoped to bring even more along.

Morley and Daniel were examining the small pile of arms that had been kept in the cabin. Rupert had known only of his grandfather's rusted and unused sword which hung above the fireplace. But at the bottom of the trunk of clothing, he uncovered several knives, bows, arrows and other swords as well. Now those weapons were being cleaned and prepared for whatever dangers might lay ahead.

Rupert had a nagging feeling that he was forgetting something, and found himself drawn again to the trunk of clothing. Now all that remained were his grandmother's few dresses, tunics, and long skirts. Of course, they were far too large for Lira, but he had a peculiar idea they should be taken along; though for what purpose Rupert could hardly imagine. He rolled them into a bundle and sheepishly added it to the growing pile to be placed upon Majesty's back.

Perhaps the most vital necessity was food. The supply that Liam had taken when fleeing the farm was most inadequate, as events had occurred at a lightning pace. The cottage, to everyone's relief, did provide a substantial supply of oats for porridge, dried fruits and nuts, apples, honey, and potatoes. There was also a large sack of flour, needed for baking bread, but no way to make use of it on the journey, as they hardly expected to be able to light a fire, let alone do baking.

Morley did not appear to worry overmuch. "Whatever happens, we should not go hungry, since the woods are always full of game," he observed cheerfully.

But the casual remark caused a dark change in Rupert.

"Kill game!" gasped Rupert, turning a pale face to Morley. He loved his animal friends with all his being. He could not eat a deer or rabbit any more than he could imagine eating Kara, Raja, or Majesty! Of course, the custom of the land was to partake of meat on the rare occasions it could be obtained. But the boy could not, in fact, endure the thought.

Without another word, the others instantly comprehended. Morley shook his head.

"Forgive me, Rupert. Do not alarm yourself. I swear no animal will be harmed by me. We shall do very well with our stores or what grows in the forest. Besides, we'll not always be confined to the wood. We shall be able to purchase food eventually."

Liam smiled. "Do you know, I'd quite forgotten that in the land of Raja-Sharan, they do not partake of meat. At least their royal family does not, and so the people follow their lead. To my knowledge, Queen Khar-shar-leen never ate meat in her life. And King Marco rarely did after their marriage."

Rupert was most intrigued. "Truly? Well, now I find myself more eager than ever to reach Raja-Sharan. I, for one, should feel quite at home!"

"By the way," said Daniel, "speaking of purchasing food, do we actually have any money? As for me, I have but one small coin that would hardly buy a cup of tea in a marketplace."

"Do not worry for that," his father assured him. "I possess sufficient means for our journey, I believe; gold and silver hidden from the bloody usurpers. We can obtain what we need when we dare approach a town. We might even hope to buy horses eventually."

Rupert welcomed the thought of horses, for the way was far indeed, and he was certain that his companions would rather ride than walk. His mind still being on animals, he had a sudden thought.

"Grandfather Liam, what happened to the goat, the cow, and the chickens that were at the farm? I realize you couldn't take them along, but...are they all right?"

"Ah, I should have remembered to tell you sooner," he replied soothingly. "I had no time to make arrangements, but I did let them roam free, with a large quantity of food in the open barn. Be certain they will find their way to nearby farms, and be welcomed."

Rupert knew that could by no means be certain, but acknowledged that Liam had done the best he could under dire circumstances.

In a few hours, the preparations were more or less complete. The house was again filled with the smell of baking bread, for they would take as much of it as they could carry.

Rupert most urgently desired to meet with his animal friends. He had not had the opportunity since his return, and realized full well he would probably not see them again - or at least not for a very long time. Eager as he was for the coming journey, his heart ached at the thought. And how could he bear to part with his dearest Kara? Would she agree to come? He determined to bid his painful farewells alone. The boy asked Daniel and Morley to watch the pup, and then set out.

Arriving at a clearing not far from the cabin, he began whistling for his friends. But strangely, there was no response. Rupert had expected to be greeted by a large retinue of his childhood playmates, his only companions until he had left the forest. Where could they be?

The boy continued his summons for several minutes. After all, he had been gone a long while, and perhaps they no longer listened for his call. Yet somehow he did not believe that. Why would they not come? A chill ran through Rupert as he feared something must have happened - something bad.

Cautiously, he moved further into the forest. He was now about a mile from the cabin. Something seemed not right to Rupert. He was on alert, suddenly as cautious as an animal sensing danger. He stood stock still and the hair on the back of his neck stood up.

Rupert smelled something awful yet unmistakable. Something that smelled like death. He turned to his left. Several small trees blocked his view. He walked mechanically towards them. The boy circled round to see what lay concealed from his view. He saw and fell to his knees. He whimpered for a brief moment. And then he began to scream. And then wail. And time stood still.

It was only a moment later that the sound of twigs being broken underfoot reached Rupert's ear. Men were coming. It could have been King Ryker's entire army, but he could not care. He was incapable of thought, only of hideous pain.

The footsteps stopped, and he became aware of people standing about him. He did not bother to look up, but out of the corner of his eye, recognized Lira's gray leggings and Raja's legs and paws. The boy sensed the others were there too. But he could do nothing but let them see.

Rupert could not master his emotions, nor did he wish to. For lying dead in his arms, while he still knelt upon the earth, was his beloved fox friend Kara, a black arrow piercing her side. So beautiful; but now still forever, covered in blood. He felt as if an arrow had pierced his own heart. And something was born in him besides hideous grief. It was rage!

Liam was at his side, whispering soothing words. "My darling boy, I'm so very sorry. But we must leave this place. We must depart at once!"

Rupert could only continue his howls of pain; a sound that seemed alien to his own ears. He had not realized he was capable of creating such a cry; as if he'd turned into a howling wolf.

Daniel knelt by him as well. "Rupert, I beg you listen. I know this black arrow. Black is the color of the king's special troop, the elite guards. You were right, we must depart at once. I know you suffer greatly. But you must not cry out. They could be anywhere within earshot. If they catch us now, we'll *all* be dead."

But Rupert did not care. He could only feel the tearing of his soul at Kara's loss. He had never lost anyone. His grandparents' disappearance did not count, since they willingly abandoned him, or so he felt. But precious Kara had been murdered. And it was all his fault, for the king's men would never come to this part of the forest but for him.

And from deep in his heart, another feeling was born. Something he'd never known he was capable of feeling. He felt *hatred* for these soulless beings. He wanted to kill them. Kill them himself! Rupert yearned for revenge. Some deep instinct told him this desire was wrong, but the boy was incapable of opposing it. Nor did he wish to.

His wailing finally ceased as he held up Kara's bloody corpse, kissing it again and again. "These men killed her for nothing," he hissed. "They do not eat the meat of a fox, nor did they even take her fur. They killed her for sport! For amusement! Out of cruelty! They have no souls! I hope they all die! I hope they all rot!"

Lira beheld Rupert in great distress. This was not the boy she knew or loved. Yet her elders regarded him with understanding and compassion. They had all suffered terrible losses. And the desire for revenge was in their hearts as well.

But they feared for Rupert. He was so young, and perhaps their future king. Rupert could not be allowed down such a dark path. However, this was not the moment for fine lessons. This was the moment to flee.

"Come, Rupert," begged Morley. "We must go. Remember, to Raja-Sharan, as you wished. The king's men are very near. Kara has not been long dead. It's a miracle they haven't already discovered the cottage. We must get Majesty. You wouldn't want them to catch Majesty would you? Or Raja?"

Rupert still felt an icy cold anger envelop his heart. But he finally rose to his feet, embracing Kara in his arms.

"Very well, but we must bury her first."

"I'm so sorry, dearest boy, but there is no time. The soldiers might circle back, and if they discover her grave, they'll know we are near. Leave her as you found her. Kara loved you and tried to protect you and your treasure. She would not wish you to risk yourself on her account."

Liam had knelt down to be face-to-face with Rupert. His heart broke to see the rage and pain reflected there. The gallant sense of adventure, courage, confidence, and compassion that had always sparkled had been replaced by something so very dark and bitter.

Rupert stood frozen. Finally Raja moved to his side, jumped up, and licked his face. Then he licked Kara's torn body as well. He seemed to be saying good-bye to his fox friend. The boy's heart expanded in grief to see it.

Rupert gently lay down his beloved companion, treasured virtually all his life, and placed her upon the very spot he'd discovered her, lest the murderous guards return. He quietly embraced Raja, and turning his back on the others, headed swiftly in the direction of home. Lira moved to catch up, but her father restrained her. And they moved in a silent single file through the darkening forest.

The party had not gone far when Raja halted. He turned and looked to their right. They froze, peering in that direction as well. They could see nothing, but one by one, the companions smelled something. It was smoke.

Liam said prayerful thanks that it was not coming from the direction of the cabin. And it seemed to be a small fire. He was grateful for that as well, because, though he dared not name the thought aloud to Rupert, Liam feared the soldiers would not hesitate to set the forest ablaze in an effort to capture them. Rupert would surely go mad at the vision of his animal friends dying in a terrible inferno. But it was seemingly just a campfire. It was growing dark, and their pursuers were likely settling in for the night.

The others silently acknowledged awareness of the fire. It was half a mile off at most. They were in terrible danger. But Rupert, eyes blazing, longed with all his heart to seek out those very men and fling his body at them. Bite them, scratch them, grab Daniel's or Morley's sword and kill them all! How he wished he had taken his grandfather's weapon. Then nothing would have prevented him seeking justice for Kara!

The three men seemed to sense his thoughts. Even Raja was uneasy. Morley took Rupert roughly by the arm and pulled him back towards the cottage. Rupert attempted to break free, but Morley's arm seemed suddenly made of iron. Rupert felt hatred for his friends as well as his foes. He gritted his teeth, in an effort to prevent shouting out words of anger. And finally, almost miraculously, they reached the cabin.

It became darker by the moment. There was no moon, and gloomy clouds hid the pale stars. No one was permitted to speak. They were ready to depart, for preparations had been made all through the day, but they yet had to place the load upon Majesty's back. Daniel and Morley swiftly saw to the task, and then drew on their knapsacks. Liam moved to assist Rupert, but the boy pulled away with a resentful stare. And in a moment, the party was out the door and on its way.

There was greatest danger all around, but perhaps most dire was that Rupert's heart might harden forever. Too much was at stake to allow such a tragedy to come to pass. How it could be prevented, they could not foresee. But now escape could be their only focus. For now the odds were against them even surviving the night.

Chapter Twenty

Once again the companions found themselves fleeing through the forest. But this time they knew for certain that King Ryker's men were hard upon their heels. They fled due east, in the direction of Raja-Sharan, which, at the moment, seemed as distant as a far-away star.

Rupert still insisted on taking the lead, Raja at his side. The others had always been confident with him showing the way, but now, Rupert was not himself, and unable to think with calm or clarity. But he knew this forest and they did not, so no one argued the matter.

They trudged without pause through the night and were soon experiencing the effects of hunger and exhaustion. But their desperate situation gave them a desperate energy. The comrades could only hope their pursuers had halted to rest and traveled on foot, since it was treacherous terrain for horses. So there was a ghost of a chance the comrades might outrace them.

As dawn approached, Lira finally surrendered to fatigue, and, by gesture, asked if she could ride atop Majesty. But her father shook his head. Daniel knew that she'd make a horribly vulnerable target if marksmen were to discover them. And he knew well enough that many among the recruits would not hesitate to kill a child.

Having been forced into King Ryker's service for five agonizing years, Daniel realized that many hated the orders foisted upon them.

But carry them out they would, if it meant their own survival. Moreover, a number of the men were in their element, glorying in the suffering they inflicted. Daniel, for one, could never comprehend such cruelty.

Rupert was barely aware of his companions' struggle to keep pace behind him. His only goal was to move as quickly as he ever had in his life. With all his soul he desired to separate himself from where Kara lay dead, away from this formerly sheltering forest which had always been his home. It had been taken over by evil forces, or so he felt. Now Rupert had become an intruder in his own land. He never wanted to see it again.

His dark thoughts were interrupted by Liam, suddenly at his side, handing him a piece of bread. He shook his head in refusal, but Liam gave him a sharp look, indicating that he must maintain his strength. Rupert nodded, snatching the bread, rushing ahead again, with Raja racing to keep pace. Liam let him go, knowing there was, for now, no way to reach the boy's rage-laden heart.

Rupert, bread in his hand, could not bring himself to partake. He attempted to pass it to Raja, but was refused. It was certainly the first time Raja had rejected food! The mournful pup stared into his young master's eyes, and the boy could read his thoughts clearly. The dog was telling him to eat. Rupert felt indignant that even Raja was trying to order him about; but that indignation fought with an ironic smile. He finally broke off a small piece and devoured it. Raja would consume the bread if Rupert shared it with him. And so Rupert took a little more, and his faithful pup followed suit.

Rupert disliked admitting it, but the sustenance renewed his energy. He took out his flagon of water and drank a few swallows, sharing that too with his friend. He trudged on ahead, leaving the others even further behind, wishing he was all alone on this journey; just he and Raja. Then he needn't speak to anyone, or see the look of concern and pity in their eyes. There seemed to be nothing Rupert desired to say, nothing he wished to hear.

The dark night at last faded into a bleak rainy dawn. Rupert breathed deeply to clear his thoughts and gather strength for an endless day. His head ached acutely, and the boy wished to curl up in a ball and sleep. But who knew when the next opportunity to rest might present itself?

Without warning, a crushing force crashed into him, knocking him off his feet entirely. In a confused flash, Rupert realized two things: that what had knocked him down was Raja, and that an arrow had whizzed by his head and was now vibrating in a tree trunk directly above him! Rupert, the breath knocked out of him, attempted to rise. However, Raja strove to prevent it.

Rupert looked up upon hearing the ominous sound of footsteps crunching twigs underfoot. One of King Ryker's soldiers, clad in black boots, black leggings, and a black and silver tunic approached cautiously. He held a bow and arrow, a black arrow exactly like the one that had killed Kara. This might be the very man who had done her to death. Filled with fury, Rupert attempted to stand, while Raja continued to shield his young master.

"Don't you move, boy!" ordered the cold-eyed guard. "I'd be pleased to put an arrow through your heart, but I might spare you if you'll tell me where your friends are."

His foe appeared surprisingly young to Rupert, younger than Daniel or Morley. But he was no less deadly for that. Hatred for this killer strangled any utterance.

"Looks like that pup is mighty fond of you. I'll willingly oblige his desire to sacrifice his life for yours. That is, if you don't talk!"

"No!" Rupert screamed. Somehow, in a burst of fury, Rupert was able to leap to his feet. "I'll kill you if you touch him!" he shouted.

The young fellow laughed darkly. "Well, looks like you're more concerned about your mutt's life than your own. No matter to me."

As he raised his bow Rupert, without thinking, charged, with Raja glued to his side. But Rupert knew their cause was hopeless; an arrow would be swifter than they.

The sound of an arrow flying through the air did reach Rupert's ears, followed by a small gasp of pain and surprise. Boy and hound froze as they realized that the soldier had been shot through the heart! For a moment, Rupert could not comprehend what had occurred. He or Raja should have been the one falling slowly to the ground.

There was sound of swift footfalls; Morley and Daniel were racing towards him. Daniel had bow and arrow in hand, and Morley his sword. Breathing heavily, they paused to examine their victim. The youthful soldier was dead; his eyes open as if in astonishment.

They turned to Rupert. Daniel gave the still-frozen boy a one-armed embrace, then moved to his victim. He took up the fallen guard's bow and arrow, sword and dagger, dividing them between himself and Morley.

Rupert, almost in a trance, came to their side, looking down at the slain soldier. He had never seen a dead human being. The boy could feel no glory, no sense of revenge for Kara. In the back of his mind, he heard the sound of a woman's wailing: the voice of the dead youth's mother, weeping at her son's fate. Or perhaps she would never learn of what had occurred, and would wait forever for a child that would not return.

At that moment, Rupert truly comprehended that they were at war. If he and his friends survived, they would forever be fugitives, unless miraculously able to return in triumph. It was all too painful to think of. The boy had seen so much blood in just one day. Yet joining the fight was their only path. Silently, he held out his hand to Daniel. He was too small to use a sword, but demanded the dagger. Daniel and Morley exchanged a look. Morley nodded, and Daniel handed the golden-eyed boy the dead man's weapon. He tucked it into his belt.

Leaving the body where it lay, the three and Raja circled back a few dozen yards. There they found a most anxious Liam, Lira, and Majesty. Morley held up the foe's sword, and the others immediately understood that they'd encountered an enemy and had slain him. Liam observed the dagger in Rupert's belt but said nothing. He held up one figure with a questioning look.

"A scout," whispered Morley, "but there may be others about."

Liam nodded. Lira stared at Rupert, eyes wide with concern. But he did not return the look. He simply set out again. They were approaching a part of the forest where Rupert had never been. Therefore, it didn't necessarily follow that he took the lead. However, none bothered to object.

The comrades strode on swiftly, all through the day. Rupert, almost sleepwalking, attempted to comprehend the recent hideous turn of events. It was unimaginable that just a few short months ago he was living a completely different existence in a completely different world. It was all too bewildering, all too rapid a change. But there was never any leisure to adjust to the new facts of his life.

To his dark amusement, Rupert found himself longing for the quiet safety of those lost days with his grandparents. He laughed inwardly, thinking how eager he had been to explore the world and find what might await him there. Well, that had certainly come to pass. He would have done well to heed his grandmother's warning to beware of what you wished for.

It was indeed most strange, but somehow the horror of the soldier's death had calmed his spirit. The flood of hatred and revenge had been washed clean by the sight of so much blood. Killing was dark and dreadful, no matter who was doing it. Above all, the boy longed for peace…not only for himself and his friends, but for everyone in this suffering kingdom, in the world. But peace was not something willingly granted, it seemed. It had to be fought for, sacrificed for. And that meant more killing. What a strange puzzle it was and he was not wise enough to comprehend it. But age did not always bring wisdom, Rupert realized now. For sometimes even kings could be the most unwise of all.

Finally, as the sun was setting, the boy came to an abrupt halt, allowing the others to catch up. All were most wearied, and Rupert gestured they might pause, however briefly. Their backpacks were opened, and more bread was produced, along with dried fruit and nuts. The comrades ate and drank in silence, seated upon the damp ground, needing desperately to get off their suffering feet.

Lira sat upon her father's lap, and after eating, fell asleep in his embrace. Daniel kissed her forehead and stroked her wildly curling flaxen hair, and that simple gesture brought brief tears to Rupert's eyes.

There are still beautiful things in this world, he realized in awed surprise. Beautiful, wondrous things, making everything worthwhile. Love of family and friends, loyalty and bravery. Sacrifice and courageous hearts. He suddenly felt honored to be among such people.

He stood, not wanting the others to witness his emotion, and went to Majesty's side. As always, the horse lowered his towering head so Rupert might stroke it. Instead, Rupert laid his face on the stallion's, sharing a moment of deep communion. He placed his arms around the horse's massive neck and allowed himself to weep silently; but these were healing tears. And the others, looking away, could sense it with relief.

But they could not dare to remain. With Morley's help, Lira was placed upon her father's back. He would carry her through the night.

Liam went to Rupert's side, smiling down at him, and finally, Rupert was able to smile wanly back. He felt drained as never before, yet somehow realizing that with each coming day, his strength would return.

As they started out again, the boy was struck by an amazing realization. Kara had saved his life! Saved all their lives. Her senses would have warned of the approaching enemy. She could have run towards the cabin to warn Rupert…or fled in the opposite direction leading them away from her friend. If the troops had followed to the cabin, all would have been trapped and surely slaughtered. So her death had prevented that or the discovery of the cabin at all.

He also believed that they had been saved by his decision to leave Raja behind. Raja had sensed Rupert's peril, and managed to alert the others. Had Raja not led them to his master, the boy almost certainly would have been captured; being so out of control with grief he hadn't been able to consider his own safety or that of his friends.

As Rupert trudged on, he marveled again that, just when things appeared darkest, unseen events might be unfolding that were safeguarding his path. He had realized that possibility when his despair at being imprisoned had led to saving Daniel, reuniting him with his family, and revealing him as the one to recognize his golden eyes. Rupert had believed he'd learned not to despair when horrible events crashed down upon him. He now concluded it was likely a lesson he must learn many times over.

Now reawakened in his heart was the feeling of being guided, instructed, and protected by some force beyond his comprehension. His confidence and courage began to return, sensing that he and his friends were not alone on this perilous and mystifying journey. And Rupert hoped with all his heart that someday the many mysteries yet concealed would come to be revealed. How eagerly he now looked forward to that day! And perhaps those answers lay along the treacherous path to Raja-Sharan.

Chapter Twenty-One

The next days passed in a blur of tension and fatigue. The comrades had to summon every last bit of stamina to keep one foot moving in front of the other. It required overcoming their human limitations, going without rest or food as much as they dared. Daniel and Morley knew that scouts operated miles from the main group of soldiers. Therefore, their deadly encounter with the black and silver clad archer could indicate their pursuers were as yet some distance behind. But they could not be certain; and that fact drove them ever forward.

The weather did not cooperate with their flight. It began to rain most heavily, turning the earth beneath their feet to slimy mud. A cold, stiff wind accompanied the rain, and they were chilled to their very bones. Rupert shivered with each step, knowing the others suffered equally. He was concerned for Lira, but she maintained her stoic attitude. It was only very late at night when her strength would finally give out, and she would then be carried on her father's back for a few brief hours.

Rupert hoped the dreadful conditions would cause the soldiers to seek shelter. It must be impossible for them to follow their tracks. Perhaps they were even now wandering in circles. Or so he hoped.

Rupert felt as if falling asleep even while trudging forward. Groggily, his thoughts turned back towards his grandparents' cottage and the brief time he and his friends had spent there. So much had occurred; he had shown them the treasure, revealed the truth about his possibly royal blood, and even celebrated Lira's birthday. But what Rupert kept reliving over and over was the blazing fire, the hot porridge, freshly baked bread, and the joy, the absolute joy, of sleeping with a roof over his head in a cozy room. Though this had occurred so recently, the memory seemed as from another lifetime. Oh, to feel warm, dry, and safe!

Of course, Rupert knew all suffered equally. But they could not even commiserate with one another. To complain, to even laugh darkly about their plight! Morley was certain to have something amusing to observe concerning their bedraggled state. Or Liam would have wise words of comfort. Lira would be bound to cheer them all, while Daniel would say something to inspire. But they were obliged to maintain silence, knowing the enemy could be anywhere.

Very gradually, the forest was becoming less dense. It was clear they were leaving the woods, and Rupert had no idea what might lay beyond. He felt apprehensive. At least the forest offered a measure of concealment. Once they emerged, they would be even more obvious targets for their pursuers. But everything had an end, including the dark and dense wood that had been his home

As nightfall approached, the rain pelted down more heavily than ever as the wind howled. There were frequent incidents of slipping or falling in the mud. Miraculously, Majesty seemed to be as sure-footed as ever. But even ever-energetic Raja was beginning to plod instead of prance, his head hung down low, in an attempt to hide his face from the elements.

It dawned on Rupert that they were all quite mad! They must have rest. It would be impossible to go on much longer. He could not imagine the soldiers were following in this deluge. The comrades should seize the opportunity for shelter.

He turned about to face his friends, because as usual, he and Raja were leading the way. The party soon caught up and regarded him questioningly. His comrades had the look of walking ghosts, so pale and exhausted were they. Rupert could not help but feel pride at their endurance and gallantry. Finally he dared to speak, though not above a whisper.

"We *must* rest. We'll kill ourselves at this rate." The others could only nod, almost too drained to utter a word.

After a brief pause, Morley spoke up. "I've been thinking that very thing. We need shelter; let us seek some spot where we might keep this blasted rain from drowning us like rats!"

The others nodded wordlessly, and Daniel signaled to split up and search for a haven. Lira went off with her father, Morley and Liam proceeded separately, and Rupert went in yet another direction with Raja and Majesty. Rupert sent his animal friends the message that they were seeking shelter. Raja looked up at Rupert with his tail wagging for the first time that day. He seemed as anxious for a respite as his human companions.

After trudging blindly about for several minutes, Raja stopped stock still to stare at a small cluster of trees. Majesty had also come to a halt and then pawed the mud with his mighty hoof. Rupert understood instantly that they'd made a discovery.

Raja, having his master's full attention, bounded off, with Rupert and Majesty at his heels. They came to a halt before three scraggly trees growing in front of what appeared to be a small mountain of rock. But when Rupert investigated further, he saw something wonderful - the entrance to a cave!

Cautiously, Rupert entered. Raja romped inside before him, assuring the boy that it was safe, though very dark. Rupert did not have a torch ready, yet continued forward. The cave was quite large, with a high, jagged ceiling. It was bare and stark, but to Rupert it was as beautiful as a palace. They could be out of the rain, sleep, perhaps even dare to build a fire. He doubted the searchers would uncover it, for the entrance was well concealed. He joyfully embraced Raja and Majesty, thanking them for discovering this wonderful haven.

Rupert and his friends raced back to the rendezvous point. They had promised not to be long, and Daniel and Lira had already returned, looking bedraggled and forlorn. But they broke into smiles at the sight of Rupert, dashing towards them with clear excitement.

Before he could speak, Liam and Morley also appeared. Morley spoke first.

"I found an overhanging rock. It does not provide much shelter, I admit, but it's better than nothing." He then noticed the huge smile lighting up Rupert's countenance. "I do believe, however, that our young Rupert has had better luck!"

Rupert laughed, and it was good medicine for his comrades to hear it. "Yes, Raja and Majesty found a cave. It's precisely what we need. It's not ten minutes from here, so let us hurry!"

There were no arguments, and all followed his lead, though with many a tumble in the endless mud. There was a huge sigh of relief and glee at the sight of the promised shelter, and in a moment, they were safely inside. The comrades dropped onto the dank cave floor, too depleted to move, the sound of their heavy breathing interrupting the deep silence of their temporary home.

But then Rupert remembered Majesty, who had been carrying a very heavy burden day and night. Forcing himself to his feet, he moved to Majesty's side, and began removing his load. In a flash, Morley and Daniel came to his aid.

Lira looked up at Liam. "Do you suppose we might have a fire? Or would it be too dangerous?"

The others determined that a small fire might indeed be risked. They'd build it well inside the cave, hoping most of the smoke would not escape. That would mean breathing some of it in, but the thought of warmth, including warm food, seemed worth the sacrifice.

Luckily, they'd gathered pieces of wood before the deluge had begun. It had been covered as best they could, and it was still relatively dry. Before long, a fire was burning and porridge and tea in the making. They'd finished all the edible bread, though some had been discarded, being too moldy for consumption. All were very hungry.

The comrades sat silently as the repast was prepared, and then wolfed it down. The hot food did much to restore energy and spirits. The sound of the rain and wind outside the cave made their bare shelter seem even cozy, and they soon became quite drowsy.

But before they were permitted rest, Liam ordered a change into drier clothing. Even these were damp, but at least were more comfortable than the filthy, drenched, and tattered rags they'd worn for days. After that, they curled up together for warmth and slept heavily until well past the dawn.

When they awoke, it was to the continuing sounds of the pounding storm. How grateful they all were to be out of the elements! Rupert stretched luxuriously then slowly sat up, feeling stiff all over. He looked toward the cave entrance to see Raja and Majesty coming inside.

Raja raced to his side, licking his master's face a good morrow, then shaking the rain off his own body while splashing much of it onto Rupert and Morley, who was still asleep. The boy laughed aloud, giving Raja a hug to show there were no hard feelings for the early morning shower. He stood and went to observe the day. The downpour and howling winds showed no sign of abating. Surely the soldiers were not attempting to follow in this deluge.

The others slept on. Rupert took it upon himself to light another fire and prepare breakfast. Soon the lovely aroma of simmering porridge and fruit brought the others awake. Lira raced to Rupert with sparkling eyes.

"I ate so much last night, but here I am so very hungry again! Do make lots, for who knows when we'll eat hot food after we depart this lovely cave!"

Rupert laughed. "I, too, think this cave is marvelous. Who needs a palace if one is dry and warm?"

Morley stretched himself awake. "Ah yes, indeed a palace is superfluous to the likes of us. We have food, warmth, each other, and best of all, our poor tortured feet can be spared for a few moments' time. This is paradise!"

Liam agreed. "Yes, indeed, we may each decide for ourselves what paradise represents. This will do very nicely for the moment."

And Daniel added, "To have my dearest daughter, my father, my new family, as well as my freedom, this is perfection. I hardly dare desire more; though I daresay a bowl of porridge will not be refused."

With light hearts, they sat together to partake of their meal. It was remarkable that one night of shelter and warm food could so speedily restore their spirits.

"I do hope this storm lasts for days," said Lira wistfully. "Then we could truly have time to enjoy this charming home. And perhaps I might have time for my books. I haven't for ever so long. I'm afraid I'll forget all I've learned."

Her father stroked her hair as she spoke. He could never get enough of the mere sight of her. After so many years of wretched yearning, it was difficult to believe they were reunited at last.

"I'll help with your lessons, with pleasure," Daniel reassured her. "And let us also not forget to have me brush your hair. For despite the braid, it is now in a very sorry state."

Lira looked up with a smile, ran to her backpack and removed her mother's hairbrush. She also pulled out a volume she'd chosen at random. Though she'd received several from Morley on her birthday, she'd hastily snatched up a few more as they had to flee.

She carried the brush to her father, and sat upon his lap. He had finished eating and was enjoying his tea. She held up the brush, but before he took it, he began to unbind her thick, matted, and tangled braid.

"This might take a while," observed her father. "So don't fidget, if you please."

"I promise, if you'll promise to be gentle. And while you brush, I'll inspect this book."

"Which one is it?" Rupert wanted to know.

"Let me see...it's called "Tales from Far-Off Lands." Lira read with little difficulty. She held it up for Rupert. "Did you like this book? Is it interesting?"

Rupert was perplexed. "I don't recall ever seeing it before. Strange." He frowned. "I've read all the books in my grandparents' home time and again. How could it be that I cannot recollect this one?"

"Oh, perhaps you read it when very little," observed Lira. "Anyway, I'll read a bit out loud and see if you remember." She opened the slender tome, holding it up before the firelight. A piece of folded parchment, which had been concealed between the pages, fell to the ground.

"What's this?" wondered Lira, picking it up for all to see. "You'd better look, Rupert, since it must belong your grandparents. It might be private." The others smiled, assuming it to be something trivial. All that is, except Rupert.

He took it from Lira's outstretched hand and slowly, carefully began to unfold it. Suddenly came the sound of crashing thunder; then a huge bolt of lightning temporarily illuminated even the grey darkness of the cave.

Rupert's heart began to race and his hands to shake. He stared at the faded parchment and blinked to make certain he was not dreaming. For in his trembling hands, there lay a map. A map showing the way from his forest home to the far-off land of Raja-Sharan!

Another deafening roar shook the cave, and again lightning blazed through the air. And in that instant, Rupert realized something else. The cave had been discovered. And intruders stood before the entrance at that very moment!

Chapter Twenty-Two

Rupert had been the first to sense the presence of the intruders, but in a flash, all were on the alert. Raja dashed toward the cave entrance before Rupert summoned him back. The three men armed themselves with lightning speed, and Majesty, his ears pinned back, seemed well aware of the danger. Rupert snatched up his dagger.

Liam gestured Rupert and Lira toward the back of the cave while he moved forward with Morley and Daniel. Rupert realized - they all realized - that they were trapped if the king's men had discovered them. There was no place to run.

Suddenly, a voice called from just outside. To their amazement, it was a gentle, feminine voice. "Hello, do forgive us for alarming you. We seek shelter from the storm; that is all."

The inhabitants of the cave regarded one other in relief. This was not what they had feared or expected. Cautiously, the three men moved to the entrance. There stood three women, covered in dark cloaks, wind and rain howling, thunder and lightning roaring and blazing. Liam waved them forward; the strangers took a few steps inside, seemingly most grateful for the offered hospitality.

Rupert and Lira remained where they were. But Rupert found himself overwhelmed with alarm. For a brief moment relief had poured over him, realizing these women, rather than a band of vicious soldiers, had intruded on their haven. But regarding the cloaked figures, the boy felt a terrible chill down his spine.

The three ladies pulled back their hoods, revealing their faces. There was something very strange about the seemingly innocent gesture, for they appeared to have moved in unison. And what was revealed did not reassure him.

Though they were very beautiful, Rupert disliked them on sight. All had flaming red hair; the eldest a deep, dark shade, the younger two slightly lighter. The trio possessed glowing white complexions, red lips, and very large green eyes, strange eyes that tilted up at the corners in an eerie cat-like fashion.

Rupert stepped back even further, drawing Lira with him. He hastily shoved the map deeper into his tunic. And Lira, the most confident and outgoing of children, also desired to keep her distance. Rupert looked down at her, and she gave him a questioning look in return. It seemed that neither liked the look of these pretty ladies.

"Do let me thank you for your kindness," said the eldest of the trio. "And allow me to introduce ourselves. I am Cora, and these are my daughters, Bella and Alicia."

The three turned to smile at the three gentlemen, peering intently into their faces. It seemed to Rupert that the mother Cora kept her eyes fixed upon Liam, while Bella stared directly at Daniel, and Alicia at Morley. Something very strange was afoot, thought Rupert. But apparently the gentlemen did not find anything amiss.

"Do come and sit by the fire," urged Morley. "We would like to learn why such lovely ladies would be about in such a tempest." It seemed that Morley inquired out of a strong sense of curiosity, rather than of suspicion, as Rupert so clearly felt. How he wished to truly interrogate them!

Again, in unison, the ladies removed their cloaks. They were dressed in similar fashion, with long dark skirts and tunics of blue with yellow sashes. Something else immediately struck Rupert. Their cloaks were hardly damp, let alone drenched as they should have been. Their hair was shining and in perfect array, their skirts and even their shoes appeared dry and without a hint mud. Why, they must not have been in the storm at all!

But how was that possible? And why weren't Liam, Daniel, or Morley growing more suspicious by the moment? They continued to stare at the strangers with fascinated admiration.

The ladies stood by the fire, warming their hands gratefully. But Rupert believed they were not truly cold or uncomfortable at all.

"I can tell that you are honest gentlemen, so I will trust you with the truth. My daughters and I are fleeing from the unwanted attentions of King Ryker's friends. One of my neighbors, Lord Dryden, lost his wife and wished me to marry him. Not only that, he wanted my eldest daughter for his son, and my younger girl for his nephew; all most odious fellows, let me assure you.

"Of course, we had no intention of agreeing to the scheme. But the consequences would have been dire had we dared refuse. We requested time to consider the matter, and as soon as it was granted, we took flight. We have been traveling for many days, and in fact, have nowhere to go. But we wished to escape an unthinkable fate, so it mattered not where our journey took us."

This speech was delivered prettily, with a gentle tear or two to add to the poignant tale. But Rupert *knew* she was lying. And he could not help but notice that, though her eyes were fixed on Liam almost without cease, she had several times darted a glance in Rupert's direction. Her daughters had done so as well. Whether the men had taken note of this, Rupert could not tell.

"Why, you poor ladies!" exclaimed Daniel. "I am well pleased you had the courage to flee from such a circumstance. For it would have been a tragedy indeed to see such beauty fall into most unworthy hands!"

Rupert and Lira exchanged looks of dismay. It was so very transparent that she had spoken false. Why couldn't the others see?

"We've been very rude, I fear, Mother dear," said the elder daughter Bella. "Should we not inquire as to why these fine people were braving the storm? Perhaps they are on an important journey?"

Again, Rupert was greatly disturbed. What business was it of theirs where they were going? Daniel opened his mouth to reply, but

Rupert swiftly stepped forward, Raja by his side. He placed himself between the ladies and the men.

"We are hunters," he stated coldly. He greatly disliked posing as a killer of animals, yet it was the first excuse that came to mind. It would also help to explain the many weapons the ladies could not have failed to notice. "We have not the king's permission to poach his game, so we are of necessity forced to travel deep into the forests to escape detection. We had been abroad many days in the storm until we found this shelter. Alas, I fear there is no room for you."

He concluded his speech looking directly into the eyes of the eldest woman. Her determinedly sweet expression faltered at Rupert's cold countenance.

"Why, we don't desire to trouble you, my dear boy. We shall be on our way if you so wish." She directed those words to Rupert, but looked appealingly into Liam's face instead.

"You'll do no such thing," Liam exclaimed. "Rupert, where are your manners, sending these poor ladies out into the tempest? It is unthinkable!"

"Of course you must stay," urged Morley. He indicated they should be seated by the fire.

Rupert felt a knot of fear in his belly. The last thing he desired was to see them welcomed further.

"We thought we might head out far to the east," said the beauteous Cora in a seemingly casual tone. "We have no knowledge of the way, but prayed for someone to guide us. Perhaps our prayers have been answered?" she concluded, looking up at a dazzled Liam with those green cat-eyes.

Rupert's fear was turning to panic. She wanted to go to the east! The very direction they were headed. And he had just uncovered the concealed map to Raja-Sharan. This could be no coincidence. The women had appeared at the very moment of his discovery.

Were they magicians or witches? They must have the ability to appear and disappear, like that mysterious lady in the village market. How else to explain their appearance in a dreadful storm with no sign of exposure to the weather? They'd seemingly put Liam, Daniel, and Morley under a spell, because his comrades did not seem to be using their usual caution, judgment, or good sense.

Rupert knew he could wait no longer. Standing directly before the intruders, he raised his arm and pointed to the mouth of the cave. "I fear you have worn out your welcome. You must depart away!" His voice took on a deeper resonance and there was great power of command in his speech.

For a moment, his audience stared at him wordlessly. No one moved, until Lira found herself racing to Rupert's side.

"Yes, you should go. Father, tell them to leave. They're not nice!"

The youngest daughter attempted to smile at Lira. "Why, you pretty little thing! How sad that you are so unwelcoming. But come, let us be friends," she urged in a sweet, coaxing tone. Yet Lira was not to be convinced.

"No! I want you to go. Go back to where you came from!"

The men regarded Lira and Rupert in puzzlement. They appeared to be half-asleep. Rupert was now convinced they must have fallen under some sort of enchantment. But, by some luck, neither he nor Lira seemed susceptible. The boy spoke again, and somehow, despite his youth, all the authority of his Golden-Eyed Kingship came to the fore.

"Be gone, I say! I see clearly. We have no use for the likes of you!"

The gorgeous strangers stared back defiantly as Lira stood behind him holding his sleeve. Finally, the women exchanged glances and then silently rose. The lovely creatures regarded Rupert coldly but with a grudging admiration.

"Yes, your eyes *do* seem to perceive what others cannot. We wish you no harm, but rather indeed hoped to assist you. There is much you could learn from us. Please permit us to remain," coaxed the being who called herself Cora.

But Rupert shook his head decisively. "Every word from your mouth is a lie. We have no need of your assistance. Depart at once!"

Outside, lightning flashed again, and as thunder crashed hard upon it, the three women were gone, vanishing as mysteriously as they had appeared. And at that instant, Liam, Daniel, and Morley fell to their knees, hands to their heads. Rupert and Lira rushed to their sides.

"What has happened here?" whispered Liam with difficulty. "I cannot seem to recall."

"Nor can I," added Morley, "except that my head feels like a tree fell upon it!"

"No, I would say an entire mountain fell upon my poor head," Daniel gasped.

Rupert and Lira quickly provided water to drink, and after a moment the men were able to sit by the fire. Their headaches faded soon after, but the three had only the vaguest of memories as to what had occurred. Rupert and Lira quickly recounted the bizarre encounter with the three sinister beauties.

"Well, if they were as beautiful as you report, I wish I could recall them," complained Morley with a grin. But all realized that something most puzzling had occurred.

"I ask myself what they could have wanted. Do you suppose they were thieves, after our weapons or treasure?" wondered Daniel.

"Rupert, do you think they were witches?" asked a shaken but fascinated Lira. "I've heard tales of such people. Who else could disappear like that?"

"I do not know. They somehow vanished like the lady in the village market. But these women seemed far more devious. And the timing of their appearance could not be more suspicious. For I fear they were after this!" Rupert reached into his tunic and produced the map. "This was what lay concealed in Lira's book." He slowly unfolded it before his companions. They were absolutely stunned.

"A map to Raja-Sharan!" exclaimed Liam. "And you say you've never seen that book before? What could this mean?"

"I am now certain that we *are* fated to go there, as Rupert was told in his dream," declared Daniel.

"Moreover," added Morley, "Rupert's grandparents provided us with everything else we needed, including more clothing and weapons than Rupert knew existed in the cabin. So if they provided all that, why not this map?"

"I do not pretend to comprehend this," remarked Rupert slowly. "How could they have known these events would occur, or that Lira would choose this book to take with her? But I do know that those ladies appeared just as I uncovered it. That can be no coincidence. I am certain they either wanted the map, or to come with us."

"To help or to hinder?" Morley wanted to know.

"Who can tell?" commented Liam. "But we must be most grateful that their spells could not affect Rupert or Lira. You children saved the day for us grown-ups."

Morley sighed. "I suppose if more beauteous females cross our path, we must make Rupert and Lira do all the talking."

"Well, it makes the road to Raja-Sharan all the more intriguing," responded Rupert. "For if they wanted to interfere with our plans, I can only believe our plans are good. And we can still be grateful *they* discovered us rather than troops. Still, we should be on our way immediately the storm lets up."

"Of course," agreed Daniel. "But shouldn't we first study the mysterious map?"

All gathered round to examine it in earnest. What they saw thrilled Rupert and Lira, but filled the adults with trepidation. The way was indeed very long; a journey of countless months even if all went well. There were dangerous borders to cross, perilous rivers and mountains to confront, and a vast desert as well. But at least now with a map to guide their path, their prospects brightened.

Everything that was bold and adventurous in Rupert's blood sang, rising joyfully to the challenge of their coming epic journey. But perhaps the most treacherous obstacle was what faced them immediately: eluding King Ryker's merciless men. The companions would not be safe until they crossed the nearest border and entered the Kingdom of Zurland. And from the looks of that map, that could still be weeks away.

Rupert regarded his beloved comrades, believing that as long as they held true to one another, they could surmount any difficulties. And as his eyes fell to the three deep blue cloaks the vanishing ladies had left behind, he was struck by a new idea; a clever idea that made him smother a mischievous grin. But Rupert wondered if his companions might ever agree. And he realized it might take all his powers to convince them.

Chapter Twenty-Three

The tempest raged on, but the occupants of the cave were grateful. It meant more time to rest, more time in a dry shelter. Once their flight resumed, what awaited was a treacherous trail of mud, and their relentless pursuers.

As the companions sat by the comforting fire, reveling in the luxury of continual cups of hot tea, they engaged in lively speculation concerning the intriguing intruders. There was no way to be certain how or why they had appeared, or indeed if they came on their own or at the bidding of another. All those who knew of Rupert's golden eyes pondered if the ladies knew of his true identity. But since that could not be discussed before Lira, much remained unsaid.

They also pored over the map; most grateful to possess it, but perplexed as to how it had fallen into their hands. Believing Rupert's assertion that he'd never seen the book in which it had been concealed, only added to the mystery.

There was also a debate over which of several routes to take towards distant Raja-Sharan, for each offered its own difficulties and attractions. But Rupert wished to focus on the more immediate challenge of eluding King Ryker's men.

"How far do you reckon to the eastern border?" Rupert wanted to know. "For we'll never have a moment's security until we cross into Zurland. Or do you suppose the guards would pursue us even to foreign territory?"

"If commanded to, they'd follow us till the ends of the earth," observed Liam. "But I suppose they'd be subject to arrest if they marched into another king's province."

"Of course, they'd have no authority anywhere but here," responded Morley. "But nothing is beyond them. They might take up disguise and continue to track us."

"Agreed," said Daniel with a nod. "But they'll assume we'd be captured long before crossing any frontier. Would they pursue us indefinitely?"

"Oh, of that you may be certain," said Morley grimly. "For they'd have to face royal wrath if they failed."

"Would King Ryker kill them?" Lira inquired with trepidation.

"I'm afraid so, or at the very least put them in prison for a long time."

Rupert hoped this might be the moment to propose his unusual idea, but aimed to bring it up gradually. "Of course they must search for us without cease. But who exactly are they looking for?"

The others were puzzled. "Why, they're looking for us!"

"Quite correct, Lira. But let us ponder this a moment. Firstly, how many are they looking for?"

"Why, I assume three men and two children, a boy and a girl," responded Daniel.

"But why? They knew we escaped together, though I hope they don't yet know how. As far as they knew, we were strangers. Is there any reason to presume we would stay together upon our escape? Did they know of your identity, Daniel?"

Daniel regarded his prince a long moment and shook his head. "I don't believe so. I was discovered yet some miles from the village. I carried no identification. I was shot by an archer, and cast into prison; clearly a deserter from King Ryker's army."

"So they would have no idea that you are Lira's father or Liam's son. They must have suspected that I would run back to them, but could easily assume you would have fled on your own."

"The boy is right," chimed in Morley.

"And what about you, Morley?" Rupert pressed. "Would they know for certain that you aided our escape?"

"Well, they'd be mighty suspicious. I had access to the prison, after all, besides showing you a bit of sympathy at the village market. That is something Ned would not likely forget. Moreover, I 'just happened' to disappear at the time of your escape."

"Even so, if you did help us willingly, why believe you had joined us? You might have wished to flee in another direction entirely," observed Rupert, attempting to sound calm and logical. He was still steeling his nerve to declare his most unusual proposal.

"So what exactly are you suggesting; that the guards could only be certain that you, Liam, and Lira were together, but that Daniel and I might have fled on our own?"

"Does it sound so strange?" inquired Rupert. He looked to Liam for his opinion.

"Yes, it could be the case. You are right, we don't know for certain if they are looking for two children and me, or three men with two children."

"And even if they assume we're together, they should be looking for three men, a boy and a little girl. So why don't we make the chase more challenging?"

"I'm all for that!" declared Morley. "But what are you suggesting; that we split up?"

"No!" cried Lira in protest. "We must remain together come what may!"

"Yes. We're a family, and must stay united. But I've come upon an interesting stratagem that might make our journey far safer, enable us to purchase supplies, even sleep under the roof of an inn. For you'll agree that traveling non-stop over rugged terrain, exhausting ourselves almost beyond our capacities, is hardly something we could continue indefinitely."

Liam smiled, wondering what the remarkable Rupert would come up with *this* time to startle or amaze them all. "Well, you obviously have a scheme in mind, and I'm certain we're most eager to hear it!"

"Well, I'm not certain how eager you'll be after I propose it. But please don't reject it out of hand. Here is what I think. They're looking for one, two, or three men traveling with a boy and a girl. But what if no men are in the party? What if there are three women?"

The men gaped at Rupert in some astonishment.

"And exactly how do you propose this fantastical turn of events?" inquired Morley. "Will you summon back those three witches to exchange places with us?" He finished with an uneasy chuckle and a penetrating look, for Morley believed there was no end to the strange things his prince might propose.

Rupert laughed nervously. "No indeed! But those ladies did leave us their cloaks, which inspired me. Actually, Lira is entitled to her share of credit or blame, as she chose to wear boys' togs. Think of it: from a distance, anyone might suppose her to be a lad. So, our pursuers would see two boys, rather than a boy and girl they've been searching for. Remember, few know our true appearance, only Ned and a number of his men. All others have only the vaguest of descriptions. It shouldn't take much to throw them off track."

"Let me be certain I understand you," said Morley with a growl. "You expect Liam, Daniel, and me to dress as *women*?"

"Oh, it's ever so enjoyable for me to wear Rupert's garb," Lira chimed in. "You'll have lots of fun dressing as ladies."

But the men did not seem to share her opinion. Daniel and Morley looked sour-faced, though Liam was beginning to smile reluctantly.

"But it would work!" argued Rupert. "I knew there was some reason I was compelled to bring along my grandmother's clothing. I could imagine no use for them, but I followed my intuition, and here we are! Of course, you would have to shave your faces. But otherwise it shouldn't prove too difficult if you wore these cloaks and hoods and kept your heads down, as most citizens are prone to do."

"What about Majesty?" Lira wanted to know. "He'd attract lots of attention, and Raja too."

"Good point, my clever daughter," smiled Daniel. "The king's men probably know about Raja."

"Yes, but not Majesty. No one supposes we're traveling with a horse. We'll load him with our gear, and cover him with mud. He'd look like an ordinary pack animal...well, not ordinary, but perhaps people wouldn't notice. And, of course, we could make Raja as dirty and mangy as possible!" Rupert felt absolutely carried away with the boldness of his plan.

"How is it that *you* are the only one to escape disguise?" inquired Morley coolly. "How very convenient!"

Laughter rang out as Rupert looked abashed. "You do have a very valid point! But at the next village, we can obtain feminine attire for me, and I'll join in the masquerade most willingly. Our party would then appear to be three women and two female children...or one older girl and one small boy. That should certainly confuse our pursuers beyond all imagination."

"Without doubt, since I am thoroughly confused already," groaned Morley.

The three men had enough difficulty imagining themselves dressed as females, let alone their future monarch. But they had to admit the idea, crazy and unorthodox as it appeared, had real merit.

"Well, it would certainly be the tactic of 'hide in plain sight'," observed Liam. "We cannot continue as we have, or we'll soon be worn down and starving. And a most arduous journey to Raja-Sharan lies before us."

"We can certainly put off female costume when we cross into friendly territory," Daniel observed hopefully, "which Zurland may prove to be."

"We agree it's time for a new strategy. Grandfather Liam has funds to purchase all we need. But of what use is that if we cannot approach any town? I wish I knew some magic enchantments to enable us to change form, but since I don't, this plan is the best I can do."

"Yes, it's just like you, Rupert to come up with something crazy like this! That's why it might actually work. But what makes you think your grandmother's garments would fit us? Or these three cloaks the mysterious beauties left? I presume they were not near as tall as we," observed Morley with a grimace. Rupert was his liege and he had pledged undying loyalty, but this was hardly the manner he'd envisioned proving it.

"You're right, Morley," said Rupert with a frown. "I had not considered that. My grandmother was not a large woman. I fear her attire might not do at all. But would you try?"

Rupert ran to the back of the cave where his grandmother's belongings lay in a bundle. He untied it; skirts, long tunics, and sashes were revealed, as well as several long dresses.

For a moment, the men stood staring at the rumpled heap. The *idea* of the disguise, and the act of donning skirts seemed two quite different matters. But finally Morley stepped forward and snatched up a skirt, a drab dark-brown one. Pulling it on over leggings and boots, it fit very well. Rupert wondered how his small grandmother's skirt could possibly cover Morley, who stood nearly six feet in height.

Morley, deciding he might as well complete his humiliation, took up a cloak that the red-headed women had left behind, and flung it over his shoulders. It, too, appeared as if it had been made for him! Morley's pained expression was not helped by Lira's constant giggles.

"Father, Grandfather Liam, you must try too. For look at Morley! From afar, no one could guess that he was a big strong man!" cried Lira with genuine enthusiasm. For she loved dressing as a boy and didn't comprehend why the men should be less willing.

And so Liam and his son found themselves grudgingly donning long skirts and cloaks. They fit very well too. The men regarded each other sourly, but belatedly got into the spirit of the moment, and all the occupants of the cave dissolved in raucous laughter. Even Raja barked in puzzled excitement.

And Rupert, with his wild imagination and resourcefulness, had perhaps found the unlikely means for safe passage towards the nearest border. Although this was one inspiration his friends perhaps wished Rupert had never envisioned!

Chapter Twenty-Four

Most strangely, the rainstorm continued unabated. Although this was to their advantage, providing another day of rest and preparation, Rupert began to feel a growing restlessness. Far-off Raja-Sharan beckoned, and he was eager to begin the journey anew, now armed with his unorthodox strategy and the map which had appeared under such mystifying circumstances.

Rupert and his friends pored over the document incessantly. Lira, too, was alive with anticipation, already beginning to live her dream of seeing the wide world. While their elders saw many obstacles, Rupert and Lira only envisioned potential for adventure and discovery.

Liam, after studying the parchment with a grave expression, estimated they'd traversed some one hundred and fifty miles to date. Morley and Daniel concurred, amazed that they'd come so far under such trying circumstances.

"Imagine how swiftly we shall progress once we make use of the roads," Lira commented very cheerfully.

"Oh yes," agreed Rupert. "We should make much faster time when not trudging through forests and mud. Even if we are to be wearing skirts! By the way, Lira, don't you think you should begin to wear dresses again, since the rest of us will be?"

Lira frowned. "Oh no, where's the fun in that? Please, Father, say that I may remain a boy!"

"Of course, you may. It makes sense, for the soldiers would be looking for a very blond little girl. We can't change your hair, but we can change you into a lad. I only wish I could remain one!"

But Lira did not laugh at that. "But why don't you wish to dress as ladies? I so enjoy disguise. Why don't you?"

"Well," began her father cautiously, "we men like to think we are very brave and ready to fight. If people knew we were pretending to be women, they might think us afraid."

"But don't you think women are brave too?" cried Lira, suddenly upset. "Think of how brave my mother was. Why, she left her home country to come here to meet your father and allow Grandfather Liam to meet her and me, though knowing bad soldiers were everywhere. Isn't that very brave?"

"Of course, my darling girl, it's just that..."

But Lira interrupted. "And what about Queen Khar-shar-leen... leaving home and family forever to journey to a strange land and marry someone she didn't even know! That's very brave too! And some ladies become soldiers and fight; Grandfather Liam told me so."

Her grandfather spoke up, trying to placate the indignant girl, while the men appeared slightly abashed. "Of course, women are very, very brave, Lira. We didn't mean to suggest otherwise. Sometimes they show courage in a way different from men, but 'tis bravery all the same. Actually, some of the grumbling is due to the fact that most men don't like to play 'dress- up'... ladies often enjoy it, but men seldom do. Any change from our usual habits will draw complaints."

Lira regarded her grandfather skeptically.

"It's true, Lira," added Morley. "You remember when I was a guard in the village market; I had to wear that blasted suit of armor. It might have looked scary, but I hated it...like being in a prison. Give me everyday garb any time."

"Very well," said Lira slightly mollified. "As long as you admit that ladies are very brave too!"

"Of course they are!" cried Daniel as he swung his daughter up over his head, further restoring her good humor. "Who could be braver than you? You're the smallest and youngest amongst us, yet faced great danger, and kept up on the march without complaint. Why, you're the bravest of us all!"

"Three cheers for Lira!" proclaimed Rupert, as all joined in with a great shout, while she blushed with pleasure.

"I just had one more question. Will you be able to conceal your weapons under your new garments?" Lira inquired sweetly.

The men regarded each other sheepishly. Apparently, no one had considered that. "It appears you're not only the bravest, but the cleverest as well," said Morley, grinning at the girl. "I do hope our swords will be well hidden. But carrying the bows and arrows would prove impossible."

Morley strapped on his sword, pulling the skirt and cloak over it. He strode about the cave in large, manly steps, amusing his comrades. "Well, what do you think? Is the sword obvious?"

"I think one would hardly notice," said Lira in her most judicious voice.

"It will pass muster, I believe," agreed Daniel. "And we should be able to conceal our daggers as well."

"We could put the bows and arrows on Majesty, at the bottom of his load. They might well escape notice then," said Rupert hopefully.

Liam concurred, and declared that once the endless rain had ceased, they should make for the nearest road east. According to their map, it lay approximately eight miles distant. After finding the way, they planned to follow it to Hanover, which appeared to be fifteen miles further on. If they could leave the cave the following day, they might arrive there by Sunday, just in time for market day. And there they might purchase necessities, and move quickly on their way.

"Do you suppose we might stay at an inn?" inquired Lira wistfully.

"I don't think we should press our luck. Let's count ourselves fortunate if we blend in with the crowds, obtain what we need, and escape undetected. That should be challenge enough for our first adventure as ladies," replied her grandfather.

"Should we purchase horses?" Rupert wondered.

"Only the king's men do not travel by foot," Daniel reminded him. "But when we cross the border we may hope to become riders at last."

"So suffer, our poor feet must, till then," said Morley with his usual humor. "At least we should look to purchase new boots. We'll probably wear out a dozen pairs before we ever reach Raja-Sharan! And while we're at it, should we not choose new names for ourselves? Since we are to be ladies, and Lira is to be a boy."

Lira and Rupert were amused at the thought, though Liam less so.

"The less speaking we do the better. Our voices might give us away. But you're right; we should have names ready, should someone inquire."

"That's easy!" cried Lira. "Because you'll now be 'Grandmother' and Father will be 'Mother'!"

"Let's pick new names, but keep them as close to our own. Less confusion that way," said Rupert, smiling from ear to ear. "Though I don't believe Raja and Majesty need to be included."

Lira wanted to do the honors, and decided that she would be 'Luka', Grandfather Liam would be 'Grandmother Vyka', (after her mother), her father would now be called 'Dalia', Morley would now be 'Mara', and Rupert, 'Rebeka'. There was a dizzy confusion as they struggled to get their new titles into their heads.

"Well, let's again agree to speak as little as possible. But you chose well Lira," approved her grandfather/grandmother.

And at long last, the rain abated as dusk was approaching. They determined to depart at first light, daring to hope they'd now outwit their pursuers. Rupert, for one, believed the further they traveled east, the fewer the soldiers that might know of their escape.

That night, Rupert tossed and turned, restless, ready to move on. Sometimes, against his will, his beloved Kara flashed into his mind's eye. He would toss again, attempting to shake the image of her bloody body from his brain. He so loved her and missed her, but it did no good to dwell upon that pain. He also deeply regretted there had been no opportunity to bid farewell to his other forest friends.

And strangely, the boy even missed his grandparents. There were a thousand questions he wished to ask of them. There might be far more mysteries involved in their disappearance than he'd first assumed. And the feeling of being 'guided' continued. He hoped it was true, because they would be in need of constant assistance as their perilous march continued.

Dawn came at last, and the comrades were eager to face the day. Majesty and Raja were equally glad to leave the cave behind. The ground, however, was thick with mud, and they sank ankle deep into the mire with each step.

Grateful for their high boots, they trudged ahead. Only Lira was in disguise, for it was agreed that skirts would prove an impediment. As soon as they came within a mile of the road, the men would don their new clothing.

Upon departing the cave, all had done their best to 'disguise' Majesty with mud from head to tail. Loaded down as the steed was with their supplies, and looking quite filthy, he managed to appear less imposing. Furthermore, Rupert had communicated their plan, and the stallion responded perfectly, lowering his proudly held head until it positively drooped, giving him an old and tired appearance. Rupert was amazed that Majesty could be such a fine play-actor.

Raja, too, was covered with mud, though Rupert and Lira did not have to apply it. Rupert simply sent the message to become as filthy as possible, and the delighted pup rolled about until finally commanded to stop. His once golden body was now as black as his nose.

Progress was slow, as mud and fallen branches were all about. But the group was in high spirits at the thought of marching right through the king's guards undetected.

It was mid afternoon when Morley believed they were approaching the road. The men pulled on skirts and cloaks, their swords well concealed, and continued on. Rupert now was eager to purchase his own disguise, knowing his description must be known; a boy with black hair and dark eyes. He suddenly felt very exposed.

After another hour on the march, Majesty and Raja came to a halt. They obviously sensed something. Morley held up his hand for the others to pause, then moved ahead cautiously. In a moment he was back.

"The road lies just over this hill. A small party of farmers has passed, but all's clear now. Let us make haste, so no one will witness us emerging from the wood."

Morley led the way, and what appeared to be three women, two small boys, an old tired horse, and a filthy dog took to the road. Their hearts hammered at being boldly out in plain sight after hiding for an eternity. They felt vulnerable, one and all. But this was the path they'd chosen, following Rupert's inspiration. They must proceed and hope for miracles.

The road itself proved disappointing. It was in no way paved, and almost as muddy as the forest. But conditions should improve in a day or two when the sun had time to dry the mud to earth again.

The party proceeded silently with lowered heads. Following Majesty's example, the tall men hunched over, hoping to appear smaller and perhaps older. The adults were wary, eyes roaming left and right alert for possible trouble. But Lira and Rupert's hearts were lighter, acknowledging the danger, but also the anticipation of what might happen next.

Rupert himself had never been to a town the size of Hanover. From the map, it did not appear to be large, but certainly bigger than the one village he had seen. And Lira was eager for any new experience.

Raja halted again, and all looked to see the cause. He was staring straight down the road, but the companions observed nothing. They continued cautiously on, and before long came upon a sad sight.

A frail young woman sat forlornly by the roadside, a baby strapped to her chest, a cart filled with potatoes resting beside her. She looked weary, almost in tears. The others exchanged glances, wondering if they dared pause or whether it was more prudent to simply continue on. But somehow it was not possible to pass her by.

Rupert, the only one not in disguise, moved a step forward after Liam gave an approving nod. "Excuse me, madam, but are you quite well? Are you in need of assistance?"

The young woman looked up. She appeared thin and sickly. "Why, aren't you kind," she said, with a feeble smile. "I am heading to the Hanover market, but I find my load difficult to bear. My baby is but two months old, and it seems I haven't yet regained my strength."

"And your husband?" inquired Rupert, before he realized it might be impolite to ask such a personal question.

Helplessly, she began to sob. "The king's men took him away just last week. We hoped he could avoid service, what with his crooked leg. I suppose they need men very badly now, because they took my poor Micah. I fear he won't be able to keep up with their marching. Perhaps they'll let him go so he can come home."

The men exchanged looks through their heavy hoods. They knew well enough that her hopes were likely in vain.

"Well, we are headed for the market ourselves," whispered Liam. "We will happily provide escort. You look quite worn out, my dear. May we share something to eat? We have enough, I assure you."

The woman looked up in surprise. The voice seemed strange and hoarse, and the kind offer even stranger. Not many bothered to help another in these sad times.

"You are kind beyond measure," she responded. "My name is Sarah, and I thank you very much indeed. But I couldn't think of troubling you."

"No trouble at all," replied Rupert hastily, as he noticed her peering at Liam with a curious look. Whether it was because of his unusual offer or his peculiar voice, Rupert did not know.

"Here, walk with us. Or perhaps you should sit in the cart as we push it for you. You do seem in need of rest, if you'll pardon me saying so." In fact, she appeared hardly to have strength to walk a few steps, let alone the many miles to Hanover.

Sarah was too exhausted to argue the matter, and smiled softly up at them. Rupert handed her into the cart, and she settled herself among the baskets of potatoes. She nestled her infant in her arms, as it continued to sleep soundly. Lira reached into her knapsack and produced two apples and some nuts, and handed them to Sarah.

"Why, thank you young sir," she said, and began to devour the apple, shyly but with hunger.

Daniel took up the handles of the cart, and began to push it along, obviously without undue effort. But after an instant, Morley joined him, eyeing Daniel meaningfully. It would be a heavy load for one lone woman, and Daniel had to recall he was posing as a female! So, the two of them handled the cart while the others trailed behind.

After a few short moments, the sound of thundering hooves met their ears. There could be no mistake. A troop of guardsmen was fast approaching! The comrades attempted to display no undue alarm, and merely continued plodding along, heads down. Rupert felt his heart race, and knew the others felt the same thrill of fear.

The ominous hoof-beats drew ever closer...and then they were at the party's side. A dozen heavily armed soldiers glanced down in merest contempt at the bent old horse and filthy mutt accompanying a party of women, children, an infant, and their pathetic cartload of potatoes. Barely slowing their pace, they rode off with little more than a smirk in companions' direction. And the villains vanished in a cloud of careless flying mud, spattering them all.

It took all Rupert's self-control not to shout aloud in jubilation! He felt Lira's hand suddenly in his, squeezing hard. It was her way of celebrating. They had passed their first hazardous encounter. Morley coughed discreetly; the best he could offer for his part in the rejoicing.

But Rupert knew there were huge smiles concealed beneath the cloaks. And the boy was especially joyful they had stopped to help this suffering citizen. For their good deed had become part of their disguise. For which they might be doubly grateful.

Chapter Twenty-Five

Though they continued their trudge through the thick and slimy mud, their steps were light with joy. The comrades had faced the enemy, yet emerged unscathed and victorious. And the victory was all the sweeter since their foe was quite unaware that a confrontation had even taken place.

Rupert, for one, had never felt such jubilation. Well, perhaps escape from prison might compare, but this moment was none the less blissful. Moreover, he was especially proud the tactic of disguise had been his own, though with due credit to Lira. He fully wished to savor this delicious moment with his friends, but could do nothing to arouse Sarah's suspicions.

The companions continued towards Hanover until the sun began to set. As always, it was most inadvisable to travel after dark. The party found a peaceful cluster of trees not far off the road, and settled there for the evening.

A fire was quickly built and porridge and tea prepared; for the first time not having to fear discovery. Their new disguise was to be in the open, appearing as innocent and innocuous as possible. The party silently blessed the presence of Sarah and her child. The little one's occasional wails only added to their sense of security. Surely, no one supposed the fugitives to be traveling with a woman and her infant.

Sarah continued content to look after little Zela, most grateful for aid from these strangers. She could not help but notice, however, that these strangers were indeed very strange! Yet she felt it prudent not to inquire. She was confident they meant no harm, and would assist her way to Hanover. And that was more than she could hope for.

As they sat by the crackling fire consuming their repast, Morley chose to address their guest. Mindful to disguise his normally low-pitched voice, he was somehow able to convert it into something higher and lighter. The others were almost convinced a female was indeed speaking. Rupert had to suppress laughter, wondering what other hidden talents his companion had heretofore concealed.

"Pardon me for asking, Sarah my dear, but where will you go after Hanover?" he inquired.

"Why, of course, I shall go home. I must await my poor husband's return. We have but the smallest of cottages, though it is most precious to me. It is where we've spent out entire married life together," replied Sarah. Her voice was weak, and she could not prevent a tear from sliding down her wan cheek when recalling her Micah in the hands of King Ryker's infamously cruel army.

"But have you no one to help you?" pressed Morley. "If you'll forgive me, dear, you seem as weak as a kitten."

"It's true that even before little Zela was born, I was not feeling my best. But my dearest husband took such good care of me... of us after the baby arrived."

"Have you no family?" asked Rupert. It was very clear that she could not hope to manage on her own.

"Oh, yes, I do have an elder sister. She lives in Crossly, a village east of Hanover. She has a husband and two children. I love them dearly, but haven't seen them for a year or more."

"Well, could you not stay with her, at least until you recover a bit? We'll be happy to escort you, since we'll be continuing in that direction," offered Rupert without thinking to consult the others. But he could see no cause for objection. They could hardly leave her in Hanover with no way to return home.

"Why yes, dear," said Liam in his not very convincing whisper. "I do believe the lad is right. Please allow us to escort you, if you believe you will be welcomed there."

"Oh yes, they'll be ever so happy to see us, for they've never met the baby. Well, I suppose it would not be amiss to visit for a while. For even if my husband were to return very soon, he would surely search for me at my sister's village if he could not find me."

The others realized that it might be a very long time, if ever, before she saw her husband again. They truly wished to see her safely settled. And they couldn't help but have a selfish thought to their own safety, since traveling with Sarah and Zela only aided their cause.

"Well, it's settled then!" agreed Daniel, wanting to see how convincing his own feminine voice might be. Rupert judged it was better than his father's, but less successful than Morley.

Meanwhile, Lira experienced newfound joy; for this was the first time she was not the only girl in the party. She had hardly spent time in feminine company, and seldom even seen a baby, except for the brief glimpses obtained at the village market.

She was fascinated by little Zela. Shyly, Lira requested to hold the baby, and was readily granted permission. It took all her self-control to remember that she was posing as a boy, because all the little-mother instincts of her heart came to the fore. The baby was sweetly perfect in her eyes.

Rupert, for his part, was equally enchanted, and was allowed his turn to hold the tiny being. It moved him in a way he'd never felt before. As he gazed down upon the child, the boy felt the burden of his tentative kingship in a new way. He had long wished to rid his land of the dark and evil rule of King Ryker. But now he truly comprehended why it was so vital. It was to allow little babies to grow up in peace. Not to face starvation, servitude, or suffering as their only future.

Rupert felt a thrill imagining that before this baby had grown, there might be a *new* ruler in his kingdom: one with golden eyes, who would bring Sarah and her baby a world fit to inhabit. And perhaps even a world where her husband might return to them both.

The travelers finally slept, and it was a heartening experience to allow a roaring fire. Of course, Rupert remembered the many nights of no fire at all; when they'd been at a forced march through the forest. The contrast was heavenly, and he wished the rest of their long journey to Raja-Sharan might be in the open instead of being condemned to hide like rats.

The dawn broke with a glorious pink and orange sky. The promise of clear weather raised spirits. It was six or seven miles further to Hanover and they hoped to reach it by late morning. By the time they'd eaten and taken to the road, the sun was up and the party found they were by no means the only travelers. There were farmers, some pushing carts, a rare few having the luxury of a broken-down horse to pull their loads. Most were families; parents appearing dispirited and burdened, while ragged children dodged to and fro.

Rupert and Lira wished to dash about as well, and permitted themselves to play an endless game of tag. It did the men good to hear their laughter. They were feeling cautiously optimistic themselves, hoping their mission of obtaining supplies might prove without incident.

The road grew more populated with each passing mile, and what a strange sensation it was to be surrounded by crowds after so long in concealment. Rupert felt exhilaration at approaching the biggest town he'd ever seen, and knew that Lira also shared his anticipation. He could see her glowing face even under the cover of her hood. And sooner than expected, the towering walls of Hanover rose up before them.

As they approached, Rupert's expectation increased. He held tight to Lira's hand, Raja beside them, as the party approached the massive gates that lay open at the town's entrance. The boy attempted to ignore the dark-armored and menacing guards that stood sentry.

As the companions entered the city, the children were immediately entranced. There must be several thousand people, and it was an overwhelming sight. There were countless stalls, offering food, clothing, household wares, farming implements, musical instruments, books, spices, jewelry...and much, much more besides. What a feast for the eye. And there was even entertainment; acrobats, musicians, and a man swallowing fire! Or at least he appeared to be.

Rupert and Lira walked together, open-mouthed, determined to drink in every sight and sound, barely aware of the sullen gloom that dominated the atmosphere. How glad the boy was, and how right, to take up disguise that enabled them to walk openly in the world!

Their elders had more practical thoughts, though delighted in Rupert and Lira's wide-eyed wonder, for their business must be attended to with little delay.

First, Liam suggested a meal. As they explored the possibilities, they observed that each vendor offered but one dish; some included cooked meat, but out of respect for Rupert, they immediately bypassed those. However, Raja could not help but sniff the air with appreciation.

Finally, they settled on a stall offering vegetable stew, and sat upon a wooden bench to eat, of course inviting Sarah to be their guest. Soon they were partaking of a watery concoction laced with beans, potatoes, and cabbage, thinly spiced with garlic. They were also served thick slices of dark bread spread with stale butter. The comrades, as well as Raja, considered it a fine feast.

After their repast, they prepared to explore, but the sight of a dozen soldiers marching through their midst gave Rupert pause. Again, they remained unnoticed, but he was reminded that he was not yet in disguise, and thus exposed and vulnerable. As much as he wished to see the sights, it was wiser to be discreet, and suggested he attend Sarah and the baby.

The others understood and approved. So while they went off to purchase necessities and sell Sarah's potatoes, Rupert remained behind and volunteered to hold the baby as well. Not only did he enjoy it, but realized any casual eye would observe a mother and two children. Sarah seemed to instinctively comprehend that she was helping her new friends blend in. However, it was also easy to sense Rupert's excitement.

"Why, I do believe I'm feeling much better," she said, attempting to be convincing. "Why don't we see something of the market?"

Rupert looked doubtful, but observing there were many places to rest should she tire, agreed.

And so, baby in his arms, the three set out to explore. The companions had determined to meet back at the food stall in an hour's time, so he did not worry should they return to find him gone. And Rupert knew where he wanted to go first - the book seller. He remembered to inquire if Sarah needed to purchase anything, but she declined.

As they made their way through the teeming crowd, every sight was intoxicating. But he could not help but finally notice, despite the jugglers and fire eaters, that there was an air of subdued anxiety prevailing. These people were going about the business without spirit or energy.

With an anxious knot in his stomach, Rupert observed darkly-clad soldiers everywhere, keeping the populace cowed by their mere presence. It was like throwing a wet blanket on a fire; smothering the joy out of the townspeople and visitors.

They discovered the book stall. As in the village market, many were awaiting a chance to have letters written, or having read the ones received. This time, Rupert knew to remain silent. But he'd hoped to inquire of his grandfather. He reminded himself, however, that his grandfather could never have traveled this far to buy Rupert's books during his mysterious disappearances. Changing his plan, he merely glanced at the volumes displayed.

"Why, can you read?" inquired Sarah.

"Well, just a very little," responded Rupert, and suggested they move on before arousing her curiosity further.

He headed back towards the food stalls. It was his assignment to purchase nuts and dried fruit for their journey, and he acquired large sacks of walnuts, apricots, and raisins. Returning the baby to Sarah, he loaded the staples into his knapsack.

Rupert, holding Zela again, continued to explore. The sight of so many people energized and amazed him. He could only wish that there were more expressions of happiness; so many appeared strained with sorrow. And it was clear that many lived without hope.

Without warning, a gang of soldiers came crashing through the crowd, angrily pushing people aside. Rupert felt a flash of terror, wondering if he'd been somehow recognized - or perhaps his comrades were in trouble. Before they could step back, Sarah, Rupert, and the baby were shoved rudely to the ground. Rupert twisted his body to avoid crushing the infant. Raja just managed to escape being trampled himself, and ran to Rupert.

The breath had been knocked out of him, and his left shoulder felt sore, but he was more angry than hurt. The boy turned to Sarah. She had been knocked senseless. He sat up next to her, patting her face and calling her name. In a moment, she feebly opened her eyes. He assisted her to her feet, as she reached for her wailing baby. Rupert observed at least a dozen other citizens had been carelessly flung to the ground.

The market was rapidly losing its charm. Any innocent pleasure could be destroyed by those sadistic men. It was so wrong to have one's spirit constantly beaten down. It only made Rupert's heart more determined to break this bondage, to free his people. Though he knew that day was distant, it made him only the more impatient.

Sarah and Rupert silently proceeded to meet the others. And before long, the party was back together, having made their desired purchases. Morley, assuring Sarah that he had obtained a goodly price for her potatoes, handed her a large sum. She realized it was quite impossible to sell mere potatoes for the price of a precious jewel, and without doubt was being given a very generous gift. Sarah refused again and again, but Morley insisted, with a lady-like laugh, that he was merely a very good bargainer. She knew he was lying, but finally accepted with gratitude an amount sufficient to care for her and her child for many days to come.

Most of their purchases were added to Majesty's load, and the rest carried on their backs or Sarah's cart. She and Zela rode, allowing themselves to be pushed by Morley and Daniel. Rupert was relieved that his friends had obviously not had a run-in with the brutal guards.

He was beginning to truly comprehend what daily life was like for the long-suffering citizens of his kingdom. And the burden was his to set things right. Somehow Liam sensed his mood, and placed a warm, comforting hand upon his shoulder.

As they headed toward the gate and the road east, another sight greeted their eyes. Two men were being dragged off by soldiers; hands bound behind their backs, punched and kicked while pulled along by their sadistic captors. The townspeople regarded the sight with pity, but knew to keep their distance, and swiftly turned their heads away.

"Thieves, arrested in the king's name," declared one of the troop.

Of course, Rupert could not know if they were truly thieves or not. They were most likely as innocent as he had been. The sight of their wives and small and ragged children, chasing after their loved ones in tears, only made fury grow in Rupert's chest. But there was nothing at all he could do. Not now. Not yet.

Before long they left by the same great gate as they'd come, and were again heading east. Rupert should have been rejoicing that their day had gone so remarkably well, but instead felt a burden as well as a success. For his responsibility to the kingdom and its suffering people was becoming more real with each passing day.

Chapter Twenty-Six

When they departed Hanover and resumed their way on the eastern road, it was just past noon. The path was filled with travelers, some bound for the market, others towards home. Patrols of soldiers were often to be seen, but their party received only the most casual of perusals.

The village of Crossly was a scant seven miles distant, and the comrades reached it by late afternoon. It was prettily situated at the foot of a hillside, but an air of gloom hung over it like a heavy fog. Crossly was holding its own market day, which was coming to a close as they arrived. Rupert looked about as the village green emptied. There were a few food stalls, sellers of fruits and vegetables - a most modest display. But one unexpected attraction caught his eye.

A woman sat upon a stool, with another seated beside her. Several others stood awaiting their turn. The lady did not appear to be selling any wares, and that fact alone drew his curiosity. But there was something else; a strange air about her that gave the boy pause.

"Sarah, who is that? Do you know her?" Rupert inquired, before recalling that this was not her home.

Sarah, along with the rest, turned in the direction Rupert had indicted. "Oh, I do believe I've seen her before. She's come to my village. I cannot not remember her name, but she is a fortune-teller. She reads palms or tea leaves, I believe."

Rupert was instantly intrigued. Could people truly foretell the future? How he would love to inquire! But what if she could see his golden eyes; or the fate that might await them all? Surely even that slight possibility would make it far too hazardous to test her veracity.

"Such people are frauds," declared Liam flatly, forgetting for a moment to use a more feminine whisper. He hastily cleared his throat, then continued. "At any rate, I do believe 'tis far better not to know what lies ahead. It could take away one's hope."

"Not if the future is good," exclaimed Lira. "It could be ever so exciting to know, don't you agree?" she asked, turning to Rupert.

"I, for one, think the possibility intriguing. However, on second thought, it might be like reading the conclusion of a book first. All the suspense would vanish."

"Besides," added Morley in his somewhat convincing lady-like tones, "I would wish to make my own decisions, come what may. It would not please me if my life was truly fated."

"Perhaps she might know when my darling Micah will return?" said Sarah, her voice quavering. "But I should hesitate to dare put the question to her: for what if the answer was not to my liking?"

"Yes, I do believe it is best to live in hope," Daniel responded firmly. "Besides, who knows if this lady has true vision or no. So let us think of her no more."

Rupert could not help but be fascinated that there might exist someone who might foretell his future. For he could only imagine a destiny of dazzling promise or utter destruction. But his optimistic heart hoped that his path might lead to wonders yet unknown.

The companions continued on until reaching the far-end of the settlement. Skinny dogs and shabby children were everywhere. At last they arrived at the cottage of Sarah's sister, who was working in her tiny garden when the strange-looking party drew near.

"Lillian!" cried Sarah as she called out to her startled sibling. With Daniel's aid, she climbed down from the cart, Zela in her arms.

Her sister, after a moment of stunned immobility, broke into a radiant smile. She was a very kindly-looking woman some years older than Sarah. In a moment, the two were locked in the warmest of embraces, and as happy tears flowed, Lillian greeted her little niece Zela for the first time. In another moment, Lillian's husband and two children, a boy about twelve and a girl of nine, were part of the enthusiastic greeting. Rupert and his friends felt happy relief that Sarah and her baby were obviously to be left in loving hands.

When emotions settled, Sarah made introductions all around, recounting how these wonderful strangers had come to her rescue. They received the most heartfelt thanks from Lillian and her family, and were instantly invited to stay for supper.

But much as the group welcomed the very idea of a home-cooked meal, they could not possibly accept. After all, it was one thing to keep their hoods up while outdoors, but they could hardly maintain their disguise while guests in someone's home. And there was another reason that Liam and the others were anxious to depart; one of which Rupert was not yet aware.

"We thank you most heartily for your kind invitation," said Liam. "But we hope to cover more ground before dark." He turned to Sarah and embraced her swiftly. "It has been a great pleasure. You and baby Zela will be in our thoughts."

She thanked them again with all her heart, embracing each in turn. She and her family stood together before the dilapidated cottage and waved them on their way.

The companions set off, as Rupert and Lira looked back several times. They would miss her company, and especially that of baby Zela. All were aware that traveling with a woman and infant had aided their cause. Yet it was equally true there was now a sense of relief. At last they could openly converse, and the men could resume their natural speech.

"Well, I'm certainly delighted that she found her family," remarked Morley in an exaggerated, roughly masculine tone. The others burst into laughter to hear it.

"But your impression of a lady were most remarkable!" exclaimed Daniel. "I was quite envious of your talents."

"Not as envious as I," declared Liam. "My attempts were most unconvincing! I was fearful of putting us in danger."

"You *were* rather awful," affirmed Lira, still giggling.

"Yes," agreed Rupert. "Perhaps next time you should let Daniel or Morley do the talking."

With the happy banter, Rupert's good humor was restored. In another hour the sun began to set, and again the comrades sought a resting place. They found an apple orchard, and settled down quickly, building a fire. Apples had fallen everywhere, and Majesty was having a well-deserved feast. Rupert was delighted, and stroked the stallion's imposing head and neck, thanking him for portraying a broken-down nag so very well.

As water was boiled for tea, Rupert looked to prepare their usual porridge, but Liam forestalled him.

"I believe a different menu awaits, for it is a very special day!" He ordered Rupert to close his eyes, and he did so, puzzled but intrigued. "Very well, you may open them now," he was told after several moments had passed.

"Happy Birthday!" his friends exclaimed. Lira stood holding a goodly sized cake, obviously purchased in Hanover. The others surrounded her, and at their feet a blanket lay concealing something, most likely his presents.

Rupert was taken completely unawares. He had been oblivious to the fact that this was indeed the third day of the tenth month, and was overjoyed and grateful that his companions had not forgotten. His own grandparents had never marked the occasion. So this was, in fact, his first birthday celebration. And today he was eleven years old!

With a whoop of joy, he ran to embrace his new family, but taking care against knocking the precious cake from Lira's hands.

"Thank you all so much! This is my first birthday remembrance ever! And how happy I am - happy beyond measure, to celebrate with all of you, whom I love so very much!"

Though touched, his companions were dismayed at the coldness of his grandparents. They now hoped Rupert would always celebrate with those who truly cared for him.

"Well, first comes the cake," exclaimed Lira. "For Rupert has always desired to taste chocolate!"

Rupert needed no urging, as they sat cross-legged upon the ground and allowed Rupert the honor of cutting his cake. The delicious smell emanating from the confection set his mouth watering. He served his friends before taking a huge slice and biting in. It was heaven! "Surely nothing else on earth could taste as good!" he exclaimed.

"You may partake of as much as you wish," declared Liam. "But we purchased other things to feast upon; freshly baked bread, butter, cheese, and vegetables. But we did not wish to be so cruel as to postpone your introduction to chocolate."

"Well, I've appetite enough for everything," he responded, cutting a second slice, but making certain there were sufficient helpings for all. And after gobbling that down, Rupert prepared thick and delicious sandwiches from the delights purchased at Hanover. Lira wished to do the serving, but Rupert insisted. He felt forever in their debt, and desired to show it, even in this smallest of ways.

"The contrast between my tenth birthday and this, my eleventh, could not be greater," he declared between bites. "I was living isolated from the world, and now have a new family, a new life. I owe everything to you. I can only thank you again and again, and declare my undying love and loyalty."

The comrades were greatly touched, especially Liam, Morley, and Daniel. If he was indeed their true king, they owed their undying devotion to *him*. And so, they were most honored by Rupert's sentiments.

After the feast, their celebration was not yet complete, as there still remained gifts to bestow. Rupert hardly felt the need for anything other than their display of love and friendship, yet experienced an eager curiosity as to what they had chosen.

Morley stood first. "May I present you, my dearest Rupert, with this true token of my esteem," he said, holding up a small package wrapped in paper.

Rupert accepted it, unwrapping it slowly. It was a medallion to be worn about the neck, round and made of bronze, with a carved lion upon it.

"This belonged to my younger brother Jacob, slain in King Ryker's service. He was very dear to me, and I gave him this before we were both forced into the army. I recovered it after his death, wearing it in his memory ever since. Now I have a new younger brother, and so I pass it on to you."

Rupert was affected beyond words. He clutched the medallion, then looked deep into Morley's eyes, acknowledging the true magnitude of this offering. Rupert raised it to his lips, and placed it round his neck. He went to Morley's side to embrace him. For a moment, Rupert could say nothing.

"I will always wear this...all my days, I swear it. And I will honor Jacob's memory, and hope to prove worthy of truly being your brother."

"No need for that, my dear Rupert, for you've proven that many times over." They embraced briefly again.

"Do let me go next!" cried Lira. She pulled her gift from under the blanket and shyly handed it to her friend. It was a sash of golden-colored silk, beautifully made, and fringed at the ends.

"I have heard that princesses sometimes give their knights a sash to carry into battle. I know I'm not a princess and you're not exactly a knight, but if you carry this, you will remember me forever. So do promise never to forget me, come what may!"

He took the silken garment from her hands and wrapped it around his neck. The color almost exactly matched his eyes; golden eyes that Lira could not see.

"As if I could ever forget you, Lira! That's just impossible. But I do thank you, and you also have my pledge of undying loyalty." Lira smiled with delight as Rupert swung her in the air and kissed her cheek.

Next in line was Daniel. "Here is something you truly deserve to possess." He produced a dagger and handed it to Rupert. It was quite unlike the rude weapon taken from the fallen archer. This appeared quite old, with a silver handle and sheath, beautifully engraved. "This was a gift from my wife's father when we married. All those years I was a slave in the army, my father kept it safe, as he did my precious daughter. Now I pass it to you, my brother."

Marjorie Young

Again, Rupert was touched, comprehending the true meaning of loyalty and trust included with this gift. He held the weapon in his hands, knowing well that he had to accept responsibility for using it, for someday making war on a bloody tyrant. It was a burden as well as a blessing, but those aspects were intertwined, and he had to fully embrace both.

After uttering his heartfelt thanks and warmest of embraces, he turned at last to Liam.

"Well, that just leaves me, I believe. Despite such outstanding gifts, I refuse to be outdone. So please accept this token with all my affection," Liam declared while handing Rupert a sizeable bundle wrapped in paper.

Rupert opened it eagerly, only to find himself blushing red as the roar of laughter filled his ears. For Liam had presented him with his disguise: a girl's wardrobe of several skirts, tunics, and even one dress, along with a feminine cloak of dark blue. After so many solemn thoughts and words, this struck Rupert as a perfect moment of absurdity, and the boy could hardly recall laughing so resoundingly. His response spurned the others on, and soon Raja was dashing in excited circles, howling away himself.

"Put it on," begged Lira, and willing to do anything to please her, Rupert soon found himself clad in a dark-blue skirt and gray tunic tied with a blue sash. Along with his new cloak, he could possibly pass for a girl, at least from a distance.

"Welcome to our ladies' club," declared Morley to more laughter.

But Liam was not finished. He produced a silver ring, and handed it to Rupert. It looked antique and was carved with an old-fashioned design. It was far too large for Rupert, but it gave him a mysterious thrill to hold it.

"This was presented to my Grandfather Harold by King Marco's grandfather, King Jaden, for valor in service. It has been passed down in my family. I wish you to have it."

"Oh no, this must go to Daniel!" exclaimed Rupert.

"But Daniel wishes me give it you," replied Liam looking deeply into Rupert's eyes and heart.

182

Rupert understood. It was a memento from a Golden-Eyed King. They wished to pass on the ring to him...their own true leader. He would accept the honor, resolving that if he ever reclaimed his throne, he would return it to Daniel.

Rupert removed the medallion that Morley had presented him from around his neck. The golden-eyed boy added the ring to the chain that held it, and put it back on. Now both items lay close to his heart.

"I can never thank you enough...all of you!" There was a moment of silence. But then the boy smiled. "I believe there are no more fine words to express how I truly feel. But please know that I would move heaven and earth to serve you in any way. And now, let us finish that delicious cake!

And so they did, spending the rest of the night in joy-filled converse, amazed at their destiny, delighted in their unity, and for the moment, relishing their sense of security. But the party had no way of knowing that the very next day, news would reach their ears that would throw all their plans into deepest turmoil, and set their minds racing with shock and alarm.

Chapter Twenty-Seven

The following day began happily enough. As usual, Rupert was awoken by Raja's rough tongue licking his face. It was just before dawn, Rupert's favorite hour. After greeting his pup, he gazed for a long while at the dazzling starry sky, sighing with contentment, still experiencing a glow of joy from his first true birthday celebration.

A moment later Rupert was upon his feet, taking care not to disturb his companions. He led Raja some distance away, where the two romped among the fragrant apple trees.

Rupert examined his dog in mock alarm. Though not many months old, Raja had grown astonishingly; his 'pup' must weigh well over eighty pounds. And he'd more than double that before reaching maturity. Rupert wondered if he'd himself grown since leaving his forest home. He certainly *felt* older.

Majesty cantered over for his morning greeting. The stallion had been relieved of his burden, and had spent the night racing about to his heart's content. Rupert would not allow the opportunity to pass without a gallop, but before he could mount, Lira was beside him. It had been ever so long since they'd ridden Majesty together and she wished to do so again.

Rupert agreed with all his heart and boosted the girl atop the giant horse before climbing on himself. In an instant they were racing among the trees, watching the stars' last fading light and the sun's pink and purple entrance to the day.

Lira laughed in abandon and Rupert at first felt equally joyful. But soon he experienced a strange intuition: one of warning and trepidation. He'd witnessed several visions while riding Majesty, but this was different; merely a chill of foreboding. Still, Rupert was determined to let nothing spoil this beautiful day.

After a prolonged gambol, they dismounted, allowing Majesty to run freely before taking up his load. Rupert and Lira fed him tasty apples in thanks for the ride.

Lira remarked that Majesty seemed to love apples as much as Rupert loved chocolate. Rupert wondered when they might partake of the delicious treat again, and was reminded that Liam's birthday was approaching on the eighteenth day of the month, and Daniel's three days later. That set them to a whispered discussion concerning gifts...and of course, cake. Lira had learned that Morley's birthday was upon the first day of the New Year, and they must by no means forget to mark that as well.

By the time they returned to the campfire, the morning meal had been prepared, and the party sat to partake of porridge.

"It's sorry I am to offer this humble repast, Rupert," apologized Liam. "For I'm certain you'd prefer chocolate again."

"Yes, chocolate cake, chocolate porridge, or chocolate cheese! Perhaps I wouldn't appreciate it if I had it every day. But I'd be willing to test that theory."

"Might we buy some today?" wondered Lira. "Will we be passing more towns or villages?"

Rupert produced the map from his tunic. "It appears there is a village about ten miles on. A larger town is twenty-five miles beyond that. However, it might be wiser to halt only if necessary. We'd better not press our luck."

"I believe you're right," said Daniel. "It might only take one sharp-eyed soldier to notice our disguises are just that. So let us head east as swiftly as we may." And, with that, they made ready to depart.

The market day was over, but there was still a regular flow of traffic on the road. Farmers, soldiers, tradesmen, and others made their appearance. As always, the comrades kept their hood-covered heads down. Though the party no longer included Sarah and her baby, they continued to attract but little notice.

Rupert reflected on how astonishing their luck seemed to be, for since they'd taken to camouflage they encountered no opposition. The boy felt an optimistic glow, almost as if nothing could go wrong despite the unsettling premonition experienced earlier.

They'd traveled through the morning before arriving at a crossroads. As the party approached, a crowd of a dozen or more were gathered in discussion. This in itself was unusual, since citizens were anxious to avoid drawing attention from the guards, and any gathering was certain to do just that. But no soldiers were visible, so perhaps they felt free to converse. An air of tension emanated from the group, and the comrades stood at the outer rim to uncover whatever might be their topic of debate. But their natural curiosity turned to greatest alarm as they understood what was being said.

"I saw him myself in Blackstone not two days since," declared a gaunt older man, perhaps a farmer. "He was being displayed on the village green. He's just a lad, and scared to death, though he did his best to look brave. The boy spoke right up and declared it was mistaken identity. But of course, the soldiers just battered him about for daring to speak."

"Had you seen him before?" questioned a woman with a cart of produce. "If they did arrest the wrong boy, could not someone identify him?"

"Apparently no one in Blackstone, anyway. I've lived nearby for years, but can't recall the lad. Not that I claim to know everyone hereabouts."

"But it's too awful. What will they do with the child?" the distressed lady inquired again.

"They'll bring him back to High Tower Prison. The soldiers plan to exhibit him in every town and village along the way to show what happens if you dare attempt to escape King Ryker's justice."

The fellow spat in the mud in a rather daring display of contempt for his ruler.

"Well, I doubt the poor lad will make it that far! It's over two hundred miles, and with such cruel treatment he'll not last the week," another citizen commented regretfully, but with resignation. It was obvious to him that nothing could be done to remedy the sorry state of affairs.

"Why, of whom do you speak?" whispered Rupert with dread. He remembered to speak softly, now that he was in disguise. But it was difficult not to cry out his question, though terrified of the answer.

"We speak of a boy called Rupert. He'd been locked up for thievery and somehow escaped High Tower Prison. How he managed that I cannot fathom. Why, the lad's a hero. What a great pity he's been caught!"

Rupert felt he'd received a hideous blow. The air left his lungs in a gasp. How could this have happened? He'd been so exuberant at escaping High Tower, and it had never once occurred that an innocent person might be arrested in his place! The boy clenched his teeth to keep silent.

"Yes, well, if you wish to catch sight of him, he'll be here soon enough. The town of Wolfbridge, not ten miles up the road, is likely their next stop. But it's a sorry sight, let me tell you. Better to avoid it, I say. Alas, he's not the first child to be mistreated at the hands our king. And he won't be the last, that's for certain," concluded the care-worn farmer with a shrug. And he turned and continued on his way.

The gathering broke up after that, leaving Rupert and his party alone by the crossroads. They regarded one other, stunned. Liam gestured to walk on, and silently they did, though Rupert felt he might explode with suppressed rage. He longed to hear his friends' thoughts on the matter, but they must seek a less public place. The comrades traveled onward for another mile, then retreated to a quiet grove not far from the roadside.

"This is the worst possible thing that could have happened!" cried Rupert when he was free to speak at last. "We cannot allow that boy to be taken in my place. We must rescue him! There is no other choice!"

"Please calm yourself, my dear Rupert," begged Liam. "We all feel the greatest distress, but cannot allow emotion to cloud all judgment."

"But how did this happen?" wondered an agonized Lira. "Why did they think that other boy was Rupert?"

"It is not difficult to imagine," remarked Daniel grimly. "Remember, no one knows Rupert's true appearance except for Ned and a few of his men. The others could only have been given a vague description, so any boy about Rupert's age with dark hair, eyes, and complexion could be suspect. And such are a great rarity hereabouts."

"Oh, but wouldn't Ned tell the other soldiers they arrested the wrong person?" suggested Lira hopefully. "After all, Ned will see the boy when they bring him back to High Tower."

There was a pause as Lira's point was considered.

"Firstly, we cannot be certain he'll survive the journey," remarked Liam. "And beyond that, I do not believe Ned would see fit to admit the mistake."

"I have no doubt he'd execute the boy just to save his own face," said a bitter Rupert.

"I must unfortunately agree," said Daniel. "And after executing the lad, he'd simply send word to keep looking for the real Rupert."

Morley cleared his throat, wishing to speak, yet hesitating.

"I beg you in advance to forgive me," Morley began. "I say it only because we must consider *all* aspects of our dilemma. I realize my words will seem quite odious, as they are to myself.

"But consider this. We realize with this news that the king's men are still searching for us without cease. The arrest of this boy, though unfortunate, might indeed be a blessing in disguise!"

Rupert gasped and made to interrupt, but Morley held up his hand.

"Ponder this. If they truly believe Rupert to be caught, they will discontinue their pursuit...at least until the mistake is discovered.

That would give us time; time to swiftly make our way to Zurland in safety. Remember we are at war. And war requires terrible sacrifice."

Morley stared deeply into Rupert's eyes as he spoke those last words. Rupert understood. He was being reminded that, as future king, his first responsibility was to save his kingdom by saving himself. Someday he'd lead an army against the brutal King Ryker and liberate his people. Any suicidal action now could destroy all their future hopes.

These were harsh thoughts, but Rupert realized - though his kingship might lay far into the future - he would even now be required to make the most burdensome of decisions. And he must be prepared for council which might prove relevant yet most painful.

After a moment of silence, he went to Morley's side and embraced him. "Please do not worry. You have not offended me. For you are my friend and brother, and I will always desire your true thoughts."

Rupert sighed and continued. "What you say is most worthy of consideration. Though I, for one, cannot imagine permitting this poor lad to go to his doom. I recognize that people...children...suffer daily under Ryker the usurper, but they are as yet beyond our help. Nevertheless, to have this boy punished in my stead; I cannot endure it." The young prince regarded the others, his resolve boundless.

"Well, perhaps the truth lies somewhere in between," observed Liam. "We must help this boy if at all possible. But we must first gather facts. We should proceed tomorrow to Wolfbridge, where the boy is to be displayed, and glean what information we may. At the very least, we must learn how many guards are in the escort. We'll know what we can realistically hope after that."

It was with great difficulty that Rupert refrained from crying out what was in his heart. He felt that even if a hundred soldiers were guarding the boy, they must still attempt rescue. But he had not the right to demand an act of madness. He would prove unworthy of being their future leader if he did so.

After all, Liam was right - Morley too. They must consider *all* aspects of the situation. And gather more knowledge of what obstacles might lay in their way. But Rupert believed that if he did not do his utmost to rescue this boy, his future kingship would be as nothing. Because he would always feel that he'd sacrificed innocent blood to gain his throne.

And so it was decided to remain where they were for the night and arise before dawn to reach the town of Wolfbridge. Rupert knew the next day would bring him face to face with the boy who had been taken in his place. And he would have to look the lad in the eye and decide if his life must be sacrificed to save his own.

Chapter Twenty-Eight

They spent a very anxious night, each having their own dark and disturbing thoughts on this most unexpected dilemma. Liam, Daniel, and Morley hoped to have further converse with Rupert, words of counsel concerning responsibility as their future liege. But there proved no opportunity, for Lira was experiencing a most restless night and they would not risk her overhearing such matters.

Lira, indeed, was facing the very rare experience of wakefulness through the dark hours. Certainly, she feared for the poor boy that faced such a terrible fate, and agreed with Rupert that rescue must be attempted, no matter the odds. But there was another matter keeping sleep at bay. It was Rupert himself, and what she had observed earlier that day.

The girl fully understood that in the normal course of events, grown-ups made the decisions and children were meant to follow. But something very different was apparent in their group. She observed that her grandfather, father, and Morley all seemed amazingly deferential to Rupert; as if somehow the final resolution was his to enact. It puzzled her greatly.

Without doubt, Rupert was most wonderful and extraordinary - so bright, resourceful, and courageous. And she remembered it was Rupert who had discovered the royal treasure, led them through the forest, envisioned the dream that set them on the path to Raja-

Sharan, and even conceived the design of being in disguise...with a little help from her! So it was far from puzzling that the adults might hearken to him respectfully. However, she sensed something further. Lira could not help but feel the others possessed knowledge of Rupert that she did not. Because from what she'd observed, the decision of whether to help that poor boy appeared to rest on Rupert's young shoulders.

There were moments when the men seemed to treat Rupert as their leader, their liege. Almost as their king! The momentous thought caused Lira to gasp aloud. But it was true, she realized. Yet how could that be? He did not have golden eyes...*or did he*? Could he be under some curse or spell that prevented people from seeing them? Perhaps it wasn't mere coincidence that he'd discovered the royal treasure? Perhaps it truly belonged to him? But how could the others know and she not? Could they see his golden eyes?

Lira turned over again, pulling her blanket about her. She gazed at the glowing night sky and smiled. She could easily believe that Rupert was true royalty. Who could be more wonderful or more worthy? But she would not jump to conclusions.

The girl thought back. When Grandfather Liam told Rupert about the Golden-Eyed Kings, he had appeared confused and taken aback. Had he believed he'd possessed those signs of kingship? Perhaps his grandparents had informed him? Or perhaps he'd seen his reflection in the royal mirror and made the discovery himself? But she was certain that her grandfather had not seen them, and she certainly had not. And when Morley saw Rupert for the first time in the village, it appeared he hadn't either.

That left her father. Perhaps he'd observed golden eyes when he and Rupert were in prison together? Yes, that seemed the only possibility. And he must have told the others, but not her.

She was irked at the thought, knowing they'd feared she was too little to keep a secret. We'll...she'd show them! She would not speak of it. Especially since she couldn't be positive it was true. Not yet. But the more she reflected, the truer it appeared. What a thrilling thought: that there was, by some miracle, a golden-eyed survivor, and that he was her darling beautiful Rupert!

The dawn at last broke. Rupert and Lira romped with Raja and rode Majesty, for their animal friends required attention no matter what the circumstances. After a hasty repast, they set out for Wolfbridge. The comrades had no idea what time the soldiers might display their prisoner, and so, keeping a very swift pace, they arrived by mid-morning.

Already a crowd awaited on the village green. Evidently, word had spread. Villagers and random travelers chose to gather, perhaps out of curiosity, sympathy, or a combination of both. From the sight of people milling about, Rupert and the others surmised they had arrived in good time. Remaining on the edge of the assembly, they attracted no attention.

The party had to wait but a short while before soldiers appeared, pulling their young prisoner behind them. Only one man rode horseback, clad in dark armor, his visor down. Coming behind were a dozen others, dressed in dark leggings and tunics, all on foot. In the midst of this group was the boy, hands bound, a hood covering his head. He stumbled and tripped, and was cruelly dragged along by his captors. The lead foot-soldier led his men to the center of the green as the crowd made way.

"Here you see the renegade boy, Rupert," proclaimed the fellow who held the rope. "He committed vile crimes against the good people of this land and against his noble king. A brazen thief, he dared escape from High Tower Prison. We now return him hence, where his head shall be removed from his body as he deserves. And such will be the case for anyone daring to disobey the just and mighty King Ryker!"

With that, he reached down, drawing back the hood concealing the boy's face, so all might see this villainous creature clearly. There was a gasp of sympathy at the youth of the captive, but it was quickly stifled.

As for Rupert, it was as if a knife had been plunged into his heart. The comrades had approached near enough to observe the boy distinctly. He had been beaten and abused, yet stood tall and displayed no fear, a fire of defiance in his dark eyes.

The stranger was clearly several years Rupert's senior. His waving unkempt hair was very dark, as were his eyes. Both boys had complexions several shades deeper than the norm for citizens of this land. There existed perhaps a vague resemblance, akin to distant cousins.

Rupert felt he *was* regarding a family member, assuming total responsibility for this boy's fate. No doubt remained that a rescue must be attempted. It was now unthinkable to leave this innocent person to be beaten and beheaded in his place.

Clearly, his friends would also be assessing the situation. Well... twelve soldiers on foot and one on horseback; and only three grown men and two children to oppose them. The truth of the matter seemed all too obvious. But Rupert was not prepared to be practical. His only course was to act.

After a brief pause, allowing the crowd a clear look at their victim, the soldiers dragged the prisoner off. They were soon gone from sight and on the road west toward distant High Tower. The crowd remained silent and mournful, but none dared speak aloud of the matter.

How Rupert longed to awaken the townspeople from their apathy! Why, if united, they could overwhelm the guards and free their prisoner, no doubt. But with a sick heart and a practical mind, Rupert was forced to acknowledge that the beleaguered citizens appeared in no way ready for such a step.

The disheartened companions maintained silence as they prepared to move off. Not knowing for certain in which direction to go, they hesitated. Their destination lay to the east, but the soldiers had headed west. For a time the party was frozen in indecision, knowing they were far outnumbered, but desiring with all their hearts to aid the boy. At last, Liam gave a nod toward the eastern way. Rupert began to shake his head violently when Daniel spoke up, in a whisper.

"We will discuss this, but must find a safer place. Let us continue on. We must not appear to be following the soldiers or draw their attention in any way."

Rupert gave a reluctant nod and the party trudged forward. In less than a mile, they came upon a deserted field strewn with boulders. It was noon by then, so they produced bread and cheese and would appear innocent enough to passers-by. But none had an appetite.

"There are only thirteen soldiers!" declared Rupert. "That's not so very bad, is it? For surely we can use bows and arrows to even the odds. We may succeed with his rescue if we attack while they sleep!"

"Just what I'd had in mind," observed Morley with a grim smile of approval. "We can pick them off one by one. Not gentlemanly behavior I admit. But we'd be destroyed in any honest fight."

"Kill them while they're sleeping?" questioned Lira doubtfully.

She looked at her companions with new eyes. This was foreign territory to her. But even the small girl realized that the prisoner would not be freed by asking the soldiers nicely. There was only one way. Or was there?

"Perhaps we could sneak in and free him while the guards slept! And they wouldn't know till morning, which would give us time to get away."

"Not enough time, my darling," said Daniel, regarding his exquisite child with the saddest expression. She was so small. How he wished she were home, safe, with no concerns but which book to read next. But there were few if any children in the land with that luxury. And so she had to face facts, grim as they were.

"Lira, even if we could succeed, the soldiers would be furiously on our trail by dawn. They and hundreds of others before the day was out. We cannot hope to make a miraculous escape as before. To rescue the boy we must depend upon killing those soldiers and concealing their bodies. That would give us a small head start at least."

"Well, perhaps our feminine disguise will aid our cause," said Rupert with a desperate hope. But the idea of slaying so many weighed heavily upon him. Surely the majority had been forced into service, as Morley and Daniel had been.

"I still do not like the odds," declared Liam, attempting to appear calm and detached. His heart bled to reflect upon what that lay before them should they chose to attempt rescue. Yet, should they refrain, though they might survive, their hearts would be forever scarred.

"If we are to act we must do so without delay. Hopefully, this very night!" declared Rupert with conviction.

"Yes, I agree," said Morley. "There can be no purpose trailing the soldiers. That is the direction from which we've come, and I, for one, have no desire to retrace my steps. We must act at the first possible moment and take the boy with us. We'll disguise him and hope to pass undetected."

"But what of his family?" Lira wanted to know. "Surely we must try to reunite them?"

"Yes, of course we'll do our best," agreed Rupert impatiently. "But I feel more strongly than ever that we must make for Raja-Sharan in haste!"

They continued to discuss the matter in all aspects. Rupert felt as if his belly had been filled with burning coals. Tension raced through his body. He believed he'd never be able to eat again. Or rest either. At least until the boy was freed from his terrible destiny. Rupert could not blot out the hideous image of his battered face, a visage that, he had to admit, did in some ways resemble his own. Who could fathom that, in this benighted kingdom, dark hair, eyes, and complexion could lead to a death sentence.

At last, Liam held up his hand. "I do believe it's time for determination. Shall we risk all to rescue the boy, or take the perhaps wiser course of proceeding to Raja-Sharan in comparative safety?"

There was a silence, and then Rupert spoke. "I cannot permit this boy to go to his death. But I recognize the hideous danger. Even should we succeed, the soldiers will be after us with fury. Yet I can conceive of no other course. However, please do speak your own hearts. I truly will not be offended."

One by one they did so, very briefly.

"I welcome this fight," declared Morley. "After scurrying through the forests and hiding in skirts, it will be most invigorating to face the foe openly for once. That boy needs our help, and I believe our plan would allow us to do so. So I say yes!"

Daniel spoke with a far-away look. "I recall all too vividly being locked in prison awaiting my own death. This is but a child, facing the same terrors. I cannot allow him to die in such a manner. Should we perish, at least he would not die believing no one on earth cared for his fate. If he has no family, then we must be his family!"

Liam spoke next. "I am eldest here, though perhaps not wisest. I dread risking all, including the lives of two children, to rescue another child. My head commands that we close our hearts and move forward with our journey. Yet my heart reminds that I risked my life and Lira's to rescue you, Rupert and Daniel. How can I do less for another equally precious being?"

Lira also chose to speak. "Yes, this is so very terrible. And I'm afraid of harm coming to those I love. But there's nothing to be done. Because I know that if Rupert or I were captured, you would all come to our rescue, no matter what the odds, come what may! So how could that be right, yet somehow wrong to rescue a boy we don't know?"

And so, they found themselves in accord, though flooded with trepidation. Now it only remained to use the last of the daylight to design their attack.

Their plan was very simple and very stark. Lira would remain with Majesty and Raja while the others dealt with the sleeping soldiers. The adults preferred Rupert to remain behind as well, but he would in no way allow that to occur.

The three men would slay the soldiers as they slept and then free the boy. Everything in their hearts cried out against it - to murder men in their sleep! But Liam, Daniel, and Morley would be outnumbered four to one. And certainly Rupert's own heart filled with dread. Perhaps there was another way...but what?

Then, out of desperation, inspiration struck. It might permit them to avoid the necessary slaughter, yet allow for rescue and escape. It would require great daring, and perhaps prove impossible. But surely it was worth the risk?

Of a sudden, Rupert was alive with hope; hope for success without the necessity of a terrible bloodbath.

Chapter Twenty-Nine

Tension raced through Rupert like bolts of lightning. There was not a moment to be lost. Already the companions were hot on the trail of the soldiers and their youthful captive. Their foe would soon halt for the night, and Rupert and his friends might then overtake them. But it was what was to follow that the young prince dreaded.

Rupert spotted an orchard alongside the road. Foot traffic was almost nil. The autumn day was swiftly drawing to a close, and wise citizens had already taken shelter. Rupert came to an abrupt halt and faced his friends.

"Please, wait. I've conceived of something that could achieve our goals, and yet relieve us of the dreadful toll it would require. So let us withdraw to that grove."

They regarded him skeptically. But before anyone could comment or object, the boy was leading the way. His companions quickly formed a circle about him, surrounded by fragrant apple trees.

"Whatever you propose, Rupert, please do so quickly," said Morley with a hint of irritation. They all disliked the necessity of what was to follow, but once their course had been determined, the sooner achieved the better.

"Then hearken to my words. Perhaps it's a true inspiration!" he exclaimed. He turned swiftly to Liam. "Did you not bring all the herbs and healing plants found at my grandparents' cottage?"

"Yes, indeed," he replied, "as well as a supply from my farm. What do you have in mind, dear boy?"

"I know one thing. It's certain to be interesting!" drawled Morley.

Rupert ignored those words, again addressing Liam. "And among those plants, do we not have a goodly supply of noctura?"

"Yes indeed," replied Liam again, a light of understanding coming to his clear blue eyes. But he looked down at Rupert doubtfully.

"I know all about noctura," chimed in Lira. "It helps people be calm, and makes them go to sleep!"

"Right you are, Lira," said Rupert. "That's just it. We can find a way to slip a large quantity into the soldier's tea. They'll not taste it, and they'd sleep soundly for hours. Why, we could simply march into their camp, take the boy, and they'd know nothing till morning. We could be far away by then!" Rupert considered with growing excitement a peaceful resolution to their terrible dilemma.

But the others exchanged doubtful looks. Daniel chose to speak first.

"I'm sorry, Rupert. I understand why you'd desire such an ideal outcome. But there is no way it could work. Firstly, how would we gain access to the camp to drug their tea? Guards keep watch throughout the night."

Daniel regarded his golden-eyed liege with compassion. "Resolve yourself that if we are to free the boy and survive, this needs be a bloody encounter. We must wipe them out. There is no other choice."

Rupert looked to the others, hoping desperately for disagreement with Daniel's grim assessment. But he found no solace in their expressions.

"I'm sorry, Rupert. 'Tis a bitter truth," said Liam with sympathy. "But we may yet change course; turn about, and leave the prisoner to his fate. For this is no fairy tale. This is war."

Rupert felt as if icy water had been dashed into his face. But his counselors were right; his plan was completely impractical. This *was* truly war, and that inevitably involved blood and death.

"Yes, I understand. We must return to our original design. Forgive me for becoming distracted."

Daniel placed his hand upon Rupert's shoulder. "It is never wrong to seek a peaceful strategy. You've always been remarkably resourceful, Rupert. But this time, it simply wouldn't work. I'm so sorry. We all are."

Rupert sighed and silently turned back towards the road as the others followed. The decision had been made.

Anxiety returned to his stomach like a twisted knot. He was leading his friends into this terrible moment. Either they'd free the boy and slaughter all the guards - or else perish themselves. Rupert hoped his companions truly felt this to be the proper course, and not merely obliged to follow their king, even if ill-advised. If only Rupert believed it conceivable to leave the young stranger to his fate!

The comrades swiftly proceeded along the ever-darkening road, searching for signs of the soldier's camp. Morley decided to scout ahead, and after an hour's absence reported that their target was a mile further on. The king's men had settled in a small grove and had a bright fire going. They'd likely retire before long.

Morley led the others off the road behind the ruins of an abandoned cottage. Though no one appeared to be about, they chose to converse in whispers.

"We should wait until later, towards midnight. They'll be sleeping, except for a sentry or two. We could pick them off with bow and arrow, take care of the others, then free the boy. And head for the hills as fast as we can!"

Morley spoke with a kind of grim merriment that made Rupert's blood run cold. Because he was speaking of killing. But Rupert himself would be just as guilty as the others.

Daniel turned to Lira. He handed her a pouch. "Here darling, you must take this and keep it in your tunic. It's filled with gold. If anything happens...if we do not return before sunrise...you must flee with Raja and Majesty. Head for the village where Sarah stays with her sister. She will care for you until we come. The gold will be enough to survive for a very long time." He attempted to speak calmly but could not prevent his sapphire eyes from clouding.

Lira went into his arms, as he held her close, kissing her cheek and hair.

"Father, why can't I go with you? I can help!"

"Darling, your job is vital. You must take care of Majesty and make certain Raja does not follow Rupert. Can you control him? Make certain he stays out of trouble?"

"Yes, I can. And I will," responded Lira stoutly, comforted that she had her own mission to accomplish. It was clearly possible her family could be caught or killed. However, she had approved the action, and so it was not her place to weep or protest now.

They passed the hours till midnight in silence. There was nothing to be said, after all. Rupert spoke silently to Majesty and Raja, instructing them to guard Lira well; and sensing danger, depart with greatest speed for Sarah's village home. Lira would remain astride Majesty until they returned, so the horse and Raja could take off at a moment's warning. It took much convincing for Raja to agree. But finally, as Rupert's loyal friend, he had to obey.

At last the moment arrived. They embraced Lira, and she did her very best to maintain composure. As they disappeared into the night, she knew she was watching true heroes, and hoped with all her heart that they would return in safety.

The companions avoided the road, and with Morley leading the way through the trees, headed off. Rupert turned one last time to see Lira atop Majesty, with an already restless Raja pacing 'round them. They looked so beautiful under the moonlight, Lira's hair lit up like tendrils of silver.

But the full moon was not their friend this night when they must depend on stealth. The three men carried bows, arrows, swords, and daggers. Rupert armed himself with his dagger. His friends desired the boy be excluded from what awaited. He was so young, and practically speaking, not trained for combat. But Rupert would not be denied.

The comrades covered the distance in less than half an hour. They could already smell the campfire's smoke. They attempted to maintain utmost silence; almost not to breathe. Morley gestured for the others to remain, then moved forward to assess the situation.

Swiftly he returned. Morley took up a stick and began drawing upon the ground, the bright moon making the pattern visible. He indicated the location of two sentries, one on each side of the camp. The others slept around the fire. The boy-prisoner was also by the fire, bound hand and foot.

Daniel gestured that he and Morley would dispatch the waking guards with arrows and then move in to deal with the others. Liam would join in the task, free the boy, and return to where Rupert would remain watch. But Rupert objected with a violent shake of his head. He was determined to accompany them.

And so, Rupert would participate. They assigned him the task of cutting the boy free and heading back to where Lira awaited. The others would hopefully follow on their heels. They then set out. Rupert's heart pounded so deafeningly he feared it might awaken the guards. Now he wished Raja was by his side. For surely he would sense danger they could not.

Liam tapped Rupert's shoulder and brought the boy to a halt, nodding to Morley and his son to move ahead and eliminate the sentries. Then all would advance into the camp. But Morley and Daniel had only taken a few steps when they heard the hideous sound of booted footfalls just behind them.

"Drop your weapons this instant!" called out a familiar voice that sent a thousand chills down Rupert's spine. The comrades, aghast, turned to find they were surrounded by a dozen soldiers, all with bows raised and arrows pointed in their direction. There was no opportunity for Daniel or Morley to get off a shot. They were well and truly taken unawares. Helpless, the companions lowered their arms.

The man who had spoken was the very guard who had appeared in full armor at Wolfbridge earlier that day. He proceeded over to Rupert and the others, his sword drawn. "Drop your weapons to the ground, all of them, or I'll gladly have your throats slit!"

There was nothing to do but comply, and swords and daggers also fell. Only Rupert's own dagger still lay concealed in his tunic.

Roughly, the other guards moved in, herding their captives towards the campfire. Rupert longed to scream out his anger and frustration. He had led his friends into disaster - a deathtrap! He'd refused to heed caution and now this was the wretched result. They would all die. Lira would be alone in the world. And the hope for his kingdom, the return of golden-eyed justice and peace, would never occur.

He struggled not to tumble into despair. He'd learned of late that when things looked darkest, that there might yet be hope. Or had he consumed his share of miraculous luck?

The companions were forced down beside the fire, next to the youthful prisoner, who regarded them with bewildered eyes. It was difficult to believe that mere strangers would have attempted such a hazardous rescue.

"I do believe it's time for introductions all round," said that cold and unforgettable voice. The fellow drew back his visor and there revealed was the face of Ned, his icy eyes gleaming with triumph. He snatched back the hood of Rupert's cloak, laughing aloud at the boy's horrified expression. For Rupert realized the bitter truth.

"It was all a trap, wasn't it? A trap all along!" uttered Rupert, trembling with cold fury.

"Yes, and how very gratifying to see you fall right into it, my little snake," responded Ned with a sadistic grin. He moved to pull back the hoods of the others, while their hands were bound behind them. The comrades were truly helpless. And they now faced not a dozen soldiers, but closer to thirty by Rupert's hasty count.

"Why, all present and accounted for, just as I expected; your kindly granddad, your loyal cellmate, and my old comrade Morley, traitor to the king!" Ned kicked Morley a mighty blow to his stomach, and he keeled over, groaning.

Morley managed to look back up at Ned. "See you haven't changed a bit, Ned," he gasped.

Ned merely smirked. "But where is that beautiful little princess with the flaxen curls? I was looking forward to renewing acquaintances."

"She's dead," responded Liam flatly, "of hunger and exhaustion while fleeing from you."

"Dear me, what a pity," observed Ned, mildly annoyed. "But fear not, you'll all soon join her, and she won't be lonely."

"How did you know where to find us?" Rupert could not help but ask. "And is the boy truly your prisoner? Or was this all just a charade? For of course, you knew he was not me."

Ned laughed in genuine enjoyment. "Yes, I trailed you endlessly through the forests, but then lost your scent. I was certain you'd taken to the roads. But you'd traveled dead east, so I surmised you'd continue doing so.

"By coincidence, some of my men arrested a boy fitting your description. I was overjoyed, but then, rather vexed when I saw him face to face. A likely looking lad, but not my dear little snake Rupert!

"I was about to execute him on the spot for the inconvenience when a better plan came to mind. For surely my old friend would take any opportunity to help someone in distress! Yes, that's your true weakness, dear boy; lots of heart, but not much brain. Though I do wish to know how you managed to escape High Tower. No one has ever pulled that off before. I assume dear Morley had a hand in it. I'll have all my answers before I'm done, let me assure you.

"But I digress!" Ned continued, with a provoking air of self-congratulation. "The boy presented a lovely opportunity. For surely, if you learned of his capture, you'd idiotically but gallantly attempt a rescue, which is why he's been paraded through every village and town from here to High Tower. I had only to wait. He's been on display five days...that's all it took for the little rats to fall into my trap."

Rupert felt a surge of humiliation to realize he'd been such a fool. The possibility hadn't even *occurred* to him. And now, it was too late.

"What will you do now?" inquired Morley, still feeling the effects of the painful kick.

"Well, I won't be troubled taking you all back to High Tower. Amusing as that may be, I fear it would prove a bit tiresome. But I will return the snake and you, my old friend. I believe King Ryker would be gratified to see you justly and publicly disciplined; though not before a thorough interrogation, of course."

The comrades realized with horror that Ned meant to torture Rupert and Morley for information about the escape.

"But as for dear Granddad, your former cell mate, and the unlucky lad, I do believe their usefulness is at an end."

Ned nodded, and a dozen guardsmen surrounded the bound prisoners, dragging Liam, his son Daniel, and the boy whose name they still did not know, to their feet. They were pushed to the other side of the fire. And to Rupert's unimaginable terror, a line of archers formed across from them. They were about to be executed before his eyes! This must be a nightmare. Surely he would wake up! Surely he must!

He attempted to gain his feet, though they'd been bound as well as his hands.

"No!" he cried in agony. But Ned merely strolled to his side and struck him hard across the face. Rupert fell in a heap beside Morley. The breath had been knocked out of him, but when he regained his senses the same hideous sight greeted his eyes. His beloved Liam and Daniel, along with the stone-faced boy, were facing immediate death.

Rupert believed he must die on the spot from the agony of it. Everything was happening so horrifyingly fast! From his side came Morley's gasps of anguish, but he, too, was helpless. Rupert looked deep into Liam's eyes, then Daniel's. Father and son were staring back at Rupert and Morley with strongest affection and valor. Yet also anguish at their fate. But they would go to their death with honor, knowing they had attempted what their hearts had demanded of them.

Rupert could not look. He closed his eyes, turned his face, and wept. Then, in the next instant, came the sound of flying arrows. But he still could not bear to see. Because he knew Liam and Daniel were gone. Gone forever. Gone because of his arrogant mistake. And Rupert truly wished those deadly arrows had pierced his own heart.

Chapter Thirty

Rupert's eyes remained squeezed shut, his heart frozen in pain. His world had crashed to an end. The boy could not fathom how he could endure drawing another breath. But abruptly, something began to penetrate his being; the sound of flying arrows, the clanging of crossed swords, men's voices raised in shock and alarm, and booted footfalls racing through the soldiers' camp.

Rupert dared to look. Surely he must be dreaming! For there, before his unbelieving gaze, were men he'd never before seen, strangers, battling the king's guards. They wore no uniform, but were armed and on the attack. The stunned Rupert gasped aloud and turned to Morley, lying bound beside him. He was struggling to sit up, his eyes ablaze with grim joy.

"Not beaten yet, my boy!" Morley exulted.

A surge of hope and tremendous energy galvanized Rupert's being. He swiftly turned his gaze to Liam and Daniel. He had, only a moment before, expected to see their bodies dead upon the ground, pierced with countless arrows. But no, they had been cut free by their rescuers, and were already reaching for swords of fallen soldiers, taking them up to join the fight! The sight was so amazing and incomprehensible he could hardly imagine it was not fantasy.

An instant later, Rupert found himself released. Someone behind him cut the ropes that bound Morley and himself. Morley jumped to his feet like lightning and snatched up bow and arrow from a fallen guard. He turned to Rupert while taking aim at their foe.

"Keep down, Rupert! Let us handle this!"

But Rupert had no intention of obeying. He felt his dagger must be useless here, and looking about for a sword, grabbed one up from the weapons his captors had tossed beside the fire. It was Daniel's own sword!

Rupert took it up, aching to join the struggle. But before he could, Raja appeared by his side, howling in warning. Rupert turned and beheld a soldier, bow in hand, arrow pointed in his direction. Rupert threw himself down, and found Raja leaping atop him as the arrow flew harmlessly over his head.

Rupert looked up to see Morley's own arrow fly, killing the soldier who'd aimed at him. He attempted to stand and join the fight again, but Raja was doing his best to pin him down. In a flash, another guard, sword in hand, charged directly at the golden-eyed boy. But like lightning, Raja leapt from his master and crashed his body onto the attacker's, who was thrown off his feet by the powerful pup. Raja sank his teeth into the arm bearing the weapon.

Rupert jumped up, grasping his blade. He was terrified for Raja's safety, but the fellow looked in shock, his arm bleeding profusely. A compassionate Rupert made to call Raja off, when his victim used his other arm to reach for a concealed dagger. In one swift move, he was about to drive his weapon into Raja's side.

Rupert raised his sword knowing he had no choice but to act. But amazingly, an arrow streaked by, striking the soldier in his heart. The boy turned to see Morley's grin. He seemed truly to be relishing the combat.

"Never worry, Rupert. Not while old Morley is here!"

His friend laughed aloud, and somehow Rupert did not find it strange. He, too, was utterly euphoric; because certain death and defeat had miraculously been overthrown. And Liam and his son were alive! They were fighting side by side with dazzling skill. But abruptly, Rupert felt a terrible alarm for Morley.

Rupert turned to behold a horrifying sight. Ned had somehow circled round him and was about to strike his friend down.

Rupert shouted a desperate warning. "Morley, Ned! Behind you!"

But, even as Morley swung about, Rupert realized his bow and arrow were useless at close quarters. In a desperate move, he dashed to his comrade's side, sword in hand. Raja followed, but the boy arrived first, stepping in front of Morley, weapon raised. With great alacrity, Morley pushed Rupert aside, seizing the sword in the process. In one dizzying move, he drove it deep into Ned, piercing through a narrow opening in his armor, just as Raja crashed atop Ned as well.

Morley reached down, pulled Rupert up, and gave him a swift one-armed embrace. Rupert beckoned Raja as Morley knelt to examine his victim. Ned was dead.

Rupert stared down at his nemesis, feeling no triumph, only a vast sense of gratitude that Morley had been spared. He embraced Morley again and breathed a huge sigh of relief. And then he realized the sounds of battle had ceased. Morley grinned down at him.

"Looks like our side won," he exulted, "though I'll be much obliged knowing to whom we owe our good fortune!"

Rupert whirled about to see the encounter was indeed over. Twenty or more guardsmen lay dead. Another five had surrendered, now on their knees before the mysterious leader of the rescuers. Concealed by cloak and hood, Rupert could not behold his face. The surviving soldiers begged for clemency.

"Have mercy," pleaded one. "We never desired to serve King Ryker! We were forced to, or else forfeit our lives and those of our families. Allow us return home in peace."

The cloaked man spoke up. "Very well. You may return to your loved ones if you feel it safe. Or you may consider remaining to join our fight. In either event, we will require your presence until we are certain of your loyalty. Go with Jack, here. Do not fear; no harm will come to you."

They slowly rose, hardly believing they might be spared. The defeated men followed the man Jack and half a dozen others as they were led off. Rupert watched with approval. For indeed, many had been forced into service against their will. Why, Morley and Daniel had been victims of that very fate.

Rupert now had only one thought. He raced to Liam and Daniel. They stood blood-spattered, and Daniel had received a wound to one arm and his cheek, yet hardly seemed to notice. They held out their arms and Rupert embraced them both, one arm about Liam, the other about his son.

From deep within Rupert there came a strange cry, half horrible sob, half great laugh, for never had his feelings been in such tumult. The unutterable joy at having them safe was poisoned by the failure of the strategy which had been entirely his. They'd nearly perished before his eyes, and their rescue had been none of his doing.

"Please forgive me, I beg you! Though I can truly never forgive myself!" the boy cried with a gasping sob.

"There, my dearest Rupert," said Liam in his most soothing tone. "There's truly nothing to forgive."

But before Rupert could protest, he heard their savior instructing his men to drag the fallen deep into the forest and to bury them all, leaving no sign of their graves. The slain must disappear without a trace.

In the next instant, bodies were being dragged off, and the only ones remaining were Rupert, Daniel, Liam, Morley, and their rescuer, along with the rescued youth. It was only then that man and boy ran to each other, embraced, and wept.

"My darling son, I hope you realized I'd come!"

"Of course, Father!" he exclaimed. "I never doubted or feared. But I did not expect these courageous strangers to come to my rescue as well!"

At that moment, their reunion was disturbed by the sound of pounding hooves. The father and son were alarmed, but Rupert knew the truth.

"Never fear," he called to them, "for unless I'm very much mistaken, that is my horse come bearing my little sister!" And before he could finish his words, Lira and Majesty indeed appeared. She threw herself from the horse and raced to her family.

"You're safe! Why, you're all quite safe!" she exclaimed, and rushed to embrace each one in turn. She turned to face the man who'd rescued them. "Thank you, thank you! You kept your word that you'd save them all!"

"Well, it appears you've already met my daughter," exclaimed Daniel, moving forward with Lira in his arms.

"Yes, indeed. My men and I were tracking the soldiers and my son. We planned to attack their camp this very night when a very large hound came racing towards us. He ran about in circles until I understood he wished us to follow; he led us to your remarkable girl. She informed us of your mission and instructed Raja to lead us to you. Unfortunately, you'd walked straight into a trap. But we soon set that to rights, wouldn't you agree?"

The comrades hardly knew how to thank the man adequately. Liam walked the distance separating them and clasped his arm.

"We are forever in your debt. I am Liam. This is my son Daniel and my granddaughter Lira. And there stand Morley and Rupert, who are also members of our family. Raja and Majesty you already know."

"Please allow me to introduce myself as well." He threw back the hood of his cloak to reveal a fine-looking man a few years younger than Liam, with long shining black hair and coal black eyes. His complexion was several shades darker than Rupert's.

"My name is Rajiv, and this is my son Lalja. It is we who are forever in your debt because you risked all to rescue him - a mere stranger. It brings joy beyond measure that in these dark days such an exhibition of compassion and courage is still to be seen!"

"But we'd have perished if not for you," observed Rupert truthfully. "Your son had been mistaken for me. For you see, Daniel and I escaped High Tower Prison, and they've been trailing us relentlessly. Your son resembles me slightly, enough for our pursuers to make the mistake."

Rajiv approached Rupert. "But many would have thought only of their own safety. You were vastly outnumbered. Yet consider this! Because you walked into their trap, my men and I were able to elude it! Surely the thought hadn't occurred of *two* rescue parties in one night. Thus, if not for you, we'd have been taken by surprise, my boy. So let us rejoice in our blessings and our good luck!"

"Rupert is the king of good luck," declared Lira with a laugh.

"Indeed," agreed Liam. He'd found himself staring at Rajiv. There was something strangely familiar about him. Of course, his unusual coloring was almost identical to Rupert's, but there was something else.

Rajiv and his son joined the others. "Please allow us to bestow proper thanks!"

They stepped to Liam first, and father and son saluted him. They moved to each in turn, and when they reached Rupert's side Lalja spoke.

"May I be permitted to see the face of my rescuer? I, at least, know full well that none of you are ladies, though the only girl among you dresses as a boy...which I find most perplexing."

All broke into laughter. "It's a long story," declared Rupert, "but it was thought safer to appear to be women. Since the guardsmen had been hard upon our heels, we required every device to outwit them. But for now, I'd be more than willing to remove my hood," he finished with a grin, recalling he'd pulled it up as soon as his hands had been untied. Disguise had become force of habit.

He reached up and revealed his face. But he was in no way prepared for the response.

Rajiv and Lalja gasped in astonishment. They exchanged hasty looks to confirm that each was seeing what the other was witnessing. And without a word spoken, father and son sank to their knees.

"Your Majesty! How can this be? A golden-eyed survivor stands before us!" Father and son wept. In another moment both lay flat upon the ground, and kissed Rupert's well-worn boots.

This was more than Rupert could endure. "Please arise, my friends. I beseech you! I do not wish for such gestures. It is in no ways suitable. We are friends and equals. Please! I beg of you!"

They at last arose, but continued staring in utter disbelief, quite speechless.

"I knew it! I knew it!" exulted Lira as she ran to Rupert's side and kissed his cheek. The girl then sank into a curtsy, which looked most amusing as she was not wearing a skirt.

Rupert regarded her in surprise. "Did you truly know? For how long?"

"Oh, I've suspected for a bit, but last night I was thinking it over and became quite certain. And Father, you could see his golden eyes ever since you were in prison together, is that not so?"

Daniel and the others stared in amazement. "Why, that's true!" How could you possibly know that?"

"Oh, it wasn't so difficult! It just took a little thinking, that's all. And I *am* old enough to keep secrets! So please don't keep any from me ever again. Promise?"

Daniel smiled with awe. "Obviously, it would be a waste of time to try. For you're far more clever than the rest of us!"

Rajiv and Lalja could not join in the banter, however, for they were as yet astonished and stunned. Their world had transformed forever, knowing their true king was alive and might someday be restored to his rightful throne.

Rupert stepped forward. "Please, do not inform your men of my identity. It would be far too dangerous."

"I swear, as does my son. For this is the sweetest moment of our lifetime. Please confide as much as you dare here and now."

"We are as anxious to hear your tale," Rupert replied truthfully. "And there are yet many hours before dawn."

Abruptly, Liam spoke up with a shout, words pouring out in a rush. "I remember you now! Rajiv! You were brought up in High Tower Castle. Your mother was kin to Queen Khar-Shar-Leen! Why, we played together as children!"

Rajiv gave Liam a penetrating look, and broke out in a smile of delight.

"Yes, I too remember. I could not have been more than seven or eight. But you came often to the castle with your noble family. Your father and mine were well acquainted. Yes, it is coming back to me!"

Liam was stunned. He turned to Rupert and Daniel. "Rajiv is the boy who showed me the secret passageways of High Tower. That is how I was able to come to your rescue! Rajiv helped save your lives!"

"And now you helped save my son," finished Rajiv in awe. They regarded one another in amazement.

"And there is one more thing, my young king," Rajiv added examining Rupert in fascination. "For if your eyes be truly golden, we are of the same clan; distant relations to be sure, but kindred all the same!"

Rupert looked to Rajiv and his son with pulse pounding in joy. For these were perhaps the very first blood relations he'd ever encountered, (since he'd lately grown to doubt the identity of his grandparents). And his heart expanded in that thrilling moment to include them forever among those he loved.

Chapter Thirty-One

The spirits of all present could not have been higher. The astonishing truth of all that had occurred was beyond wildest credence or fantasy. It was quite simply miraculous! And who among them could not now believe that their destiny was being guided...though by what power they could not yet comprehend.

They agreed to remove themselves from the scene of battle. The ground was stained with the blood of the slain, and did not seem fitting for an eagerly awaited exchange of histories. They quickly moved towards the abandoned cottage where Lira had kept watch with Raja and Majesty.

The party soon reached their destination, and before long all had strong cups of tea in their hands, as well as bread and cheese to eat. Lalja had hardly been fed since his arrest days before, and the others had been too tense to eat in recent hours. So they all had appetite, both for food and information.

Rupert and his friends deeply desired to hear everything Rajiv had to recount, and though Rajiv wished to hear first from his prince, he consented to speak. All present were riveted from his very first words.

"I must begin with the story of my mother. Her name was Meera, born in Raja-Sharan. Her father was brother to the Raja, and his Grand Vizier as well."

"What's that?" interrupted Lira. "A Grand what?"

Rajiv smiled. "As I was about to explain, my impatient one, a Grand Vizier is the Raja's closest advisor. He lived in the palace, along with the rest of the royal family; a beautiful palace carved from pink stone."

"Pink stone!" cried Lira entranced. "How beautiful it must have been!"

"Please, Lira. Kindly don't interrupt," scolded Rupert, but with a smile. "I, for one, do not wish to be kept in suspense!" Lira nodded, properly chastised. But she was on fire to hear the tale, and it was difficult to maintain silence.

"Eventually, my mother Meera was born. And not a year later, the Rani gave birth to princess Khar-Shar-Leen. Being so close in age and cousins as well, they were raised together. And they looked remarkably alike, often mistaken for sisters...even twins.

"They grew up happily and more beautiful with each passing day. And when the princess turned fourteen, time to search for a proper husband, the girls felt saddened at the thought of separation.

"The Raja and Rani had several fine candidates in mind, but Khar-Shar-Leen had ideas of her own; for she'd long ago dreamed she was fated to marry a Golden-Eyed Prince, though her people had but the vaguest knowledge of such a far-off kingdom.

"When she stubbornly refused to consider other suitors, her parents grew angry. Things might have taken a truly disagreeable turn, but for a dream, shared by both the Raja and his queen; visions of a strange, hooded figure instructing that their daughter must marry the Golden-Eyed Prince who awaited her.

"Still incredulous, they consulted their favorite sooth-sayers, Kamal, and Shomila, who informed them that indeed this marriage was the Ranila's destiny.

"If it was fated, there was nothing to be done. And so the royal couple commanded their minister to make the journey, bringing gifts of great value to the distant kingdom, and to arrange the match.

"Khar-Shar-Leen was euphoric, yet could not imagine parting from her dearest friend and cousin, Meera. Thus, it was decided that Meera should accompany her.

215

"And so it happened that before even learning if the proposal had been accepted, the girls set out, along with a huge retinue, which included the soothsayers Kamal and Shomila. For the Raja had concluded that his daughter would need advice and guidance in this far-off and unpredictable land.

"The journey lasted for many months, and the two young beauties enjoyed the freedom of daily gallops on camelback, then horseback, through strange territory. They saw worlds never dreamed of and were young and adventurous and eager to face the future.

"They finally arrived, bringing about the long-awaited meeting with Prince Marco; as handsome as a god, and like no man the girls had ever seen.

"The marriage took place that very day, the celebration lasted for a week - feasting, rejoicing and dancing. Meera and the princess had never seen men and women dance together, and they were shocked and fascinated. Everything about this new land was strange, especially the eating of meat, which repelled them both. When Prince Marco learned of this, he ordered that none be served at the royal table, for which his new bride was grateful. But she hoped to adopt some of the other customs of her new land.

"At the wedding itself, she agreed to wear the simple white gown of her new kingdom's tradition. But half-way through the feasting, she changed into the royal wedding garb of Raja-Sharan. When Khar-shar-leen returned, all were awestruck at the sight. She wore a turquoise tunic embroidered with gold, and a billowing skirt of red silk. She glittered with necklaces, bracelets, rings, and even anklets of sapphires and rubies, surrounded by gold. Her black silken hair hung almost to her knees. She was a vision of perfect beauty.

"The princess was not the only one who found her destiny that day, for my mother Meera also met her future husband. His name was Danforth, one of the king's finest knights. Upon beholding Meera he was smitten at once and determined to win her love. According to my mother that did not take long; for the moment he boldly asked for her to dance with him, her heart spoke that this man would be her husband.

"And so, within a month of their first meeting, another wedding was required. And the two young girls from Raja-Sharan lived most happily. Meera resided at her husband's estate, not far from the castle, and seldom did several days go by without a visit to the princess. They remained as close as sisters, and when their children began to arrive, they were as one family.

"Years passed, and while their personal happiness remained unbroken, these were troubling days for the kingdom. Attacks from the south were growing in frequency, and villages that lay near the border were under constant harassment.

"By now Prince Marco had become king, and after several years of skirmishes, full-scale battles erupted. The dazzling young monarch maintained the full support of his people. He could hardly imagine there was real danger. The reputation of King Marco as a fierce and clever warrior, as well as a just and compassionate ruler, brought admiration from the surrounding world. But this foe 'Zorin' had no respect for reputations. And it seemed that a dark shadow was cast over the land.

"It was about this time that I met you, my friend Liam. Your father, the Baron Brax, was often called to the castle for consultation. And while they spoke of serious matters, we played together, exploring the forbidden secret passages under the fortress. And how miraculous that the knowledge provided proved so life-saving many years later!

"But I digress! King Marco and his advisors were startled when, after one particularly brutal attack on a border village, Zorin appealed for a parlay of peace. After much debate, King Marco agreed. Despite the warnings from Kamal and Shomila, he allowed his royal children to accompany him.

"His beloved queen, however, remained behind. This was to protect a precious secret. She was expecting a child. She preserved the tradition of Raja-Sharan to make no mention of a royal pregnancy until the baby was safely born. For it was considered ill-luck to let the matter be known to any but their closest family.

"At this same time, my father, at King Marco's behest, was ordered to the Northern Lands to confirm our alliance with their king. I was but eight years old, and proud to be allowed to go with him.

"As I'm certain you've already learned, Zorin's peace talk was a trap. King Marco, his children, and his entire retinue were poisoned at what was to be a feast of friendship. And before resistance could be mounted, the murderers were on the march to High Tower Castle to destroy what remained of the royal family.

"When word reached the queen's ear, she collapsed in grief. My mother roused herself to convince Her Majesty and several loyal servants to flee by hidden ways and run for their lives!

"Soon, word of the catastrophe reached my father. He begged the Northern King to come to our aid, but he refused, knowing King Marco and his heirs had been slain.

"Bitterly disappointed, my father and I raced homeward. It was a perilous journey, for most of King Marco's army had been defeated or scattered. None knew of the queen's pregnancy, and they feared the royal line must be at an end.

"Our task seemed hopeless. Already hordes of Zorin's men were flooding in. The populace was terrified, helpless, and grieving. Father and I were marked targets, and we took up disguise, attempting to appear as poor farmers. And at last, we reached home.

"We were sick at heart at what we saw. High Tower was half-burnt, and what remained turned into a prison for Zorin's enemies, which were many. We were homeless and helpless. But nothing compared to our dread concerning the fate of my mother and the queen. Rumors that she had escaped were swirling, but we doubted she could have traveled far. We feared the worst, and later, those fears were confirmed.

"It was announced that Queen Khar-Shar-Leen had been discovered. She and her royal guards were dead: by suicide, when surrounded by their enemy. Her corpse was to be exhibited for all to see.

"And the very next day, her body was on display amidst the ruins of her former home. She was clad in her finest Raja-Sharani royal garb, taken when she'd fled. Beautiful even in death, she sparkled in blue and red and gold. But what a horrid and pathetic sight it was.

"My father and I joined the mournful citizens parading slowly by. But as we drew nearer, we observed what the others did not. Firstly, she was not pregnant, which meant that perhaps the baby had been safely born. But as we gazed closer at the fading beauty, my father nudged me until I observed her left hand. There was a faint scar upon it, one that occurred when she'd been bitten by a pet monkey as a girl.

"But the one who had been bitten was my mother, not Queen Khar-Shar-Leen! They'd obviously traded places; my mother disguising herself, allowing the queen to escape. They'd so closely resembled each other, that now, no one could know the truth...no one except for my father and myself.

"We mourned and wept. But despite our grief, we felt a surge of hope; perhaps Her Majesty had indeed eluded Zorin. And by some miracle, the child of King Marco and his wife may have indeed survived!"

Rajiv brushed tears from his eyes, the memory still painful after so very long. "I'll conclude by reporting that my father and I took to the forests, eluding the black-hearted Zorin, who dared to call himself king. From time to time we encountered other fugitives and bonded together, attempting to survive, constantly facing capture or death.

"Of course, we might have thought to flee. But my father had a strange dream in which a mysterious lady foretold that it was his duty to remain until a Golden-Eyed King might return.

"How I longed to believe in those words! And though my father has been gone these ten years, I chose to carry on his cause. I'd often despaired, believing it my poor father's fantasy.

"But now I've lived to see his prophecy fulfilled! And my son as well. All our hopes and sacrifice have not been in vain. Because a boy with golden eyes called Rupert has returned as from the dead. And we are yours to command until our own dying day!"

Chapter Thirty-Two

The hearts of Rajiv's listeners were in tumult, and myriad inquiries flooded their minds. They had learned much, yet much remained unknown. But Rajiv first begged for Rupert's words; for he was their Golden-Eyed King, and father and son longed to know how this marvel had come to be. And so Rupert was forced to put his own raging curiosity aside. His narration began with earliest memories of the forest and his enigmatic grandparents, until the day he discovered the royal treasure, along with his family's baffling abandonment.

Before continuing his tale, Rupert rose and went to Majesty's side, unloading some of their belongings until finding what he sought. The boy carried something wrapped in his old cloak to the fireside and slowly opened the folds until the treasure in all its glory was revealed.

Rajiv and Lalja gasped. It made everything seem even more real, more true. For here was the sword, the mirror, the necklace, and the ring, before their stunned gaze. Rupert encouraged them to examine each freely. Rajiv did so, his handsome features shattered with profound emotion.

"I recognize them from so long ago," he pronounced with difficulty. "I witnessed King Marco wearing this sword and ring on many occasions, and Queen Khar-shar-leen wear this... a wedding gift from His Majesty. The mirror, too, I know, for as a child I was often in the queen's private chambers. These treasures belonged to Their Majesties, no doubt. I swear it!"

That said, he kissed each item, as did his son, and then begged Rupert to continue with his saga. He did so. Even his companions, who knew the tale, and indeed had lived recent events at Rupert's side, were filled with wonder by the telling.

Lira listened, enchanted, reflecting that a hundred years from now, or even a thousand, people would repeat this chronicle to their children. She wondered if they'd believe it to be true or mere fanciful long-ago legends. For the facts seemed almost too marvelous to be real.

At length, Rupert concluded, and his comrades had details to add, praising Rupert's resourcefulness and bravery, yet admitting he could be stubborn and heedless as well. But finally, the moment for inquiry and reflection had come.

"Well, it is obvious that King Marco's and Queen Khar-Shar-Leen's son must have grown to manhood, married and had a son of his own," concluded Rupert. "For these events happened more than thirty years since, thus I could hardly be that child.

"Yes, that is the logical conclusion," observed Liam. "But if your father lives, where is he? And why were you brought up in isolation, with no knowledge of your true heritage? It is extremely vexing and puzzles me still."

"Indeed," agreed Rajiv. "Or is it somehow possible that *Rupert* was the child born so long ago? For perhaps an evil spell prevented him from growing up in the usual manner?"

The others regarded their new friend strangely. They had never heard of such a thing.

Rajiv laughed. "I confess it sounds most absurd. But my mother told me of the powerful soothsayers and magicians of Raja-Sharan, with ability to cast the darkest of spells. However, upon reflection, I suppose this is not a reasonable theory.

Lira had a sudden thought. "But where is the crown?" They turned to look at her. "King Marco's crown," she continued with excitement. "Why is it not here with the other royal treasures? Surely, the crown is the most important of all! For without it, one cannot be truly a king!"

Rupert could not help but smile. "Lira, as usual, you have the most pertinent comment to make. I had not thought of it, I must admit. But where *is* the royal crown?"

Liam spoke up thoughtfully. "One would suppose King Marco wore it to the peace talks where he was ultimately murdered. That would mean that Zorin must have taken possession of it."

"I cannot agree," objected Morley, "because if Zorin had it, he would have most certainly flaunted it before the populace. And his son King Ryker, our present tyrant, would have made use of it also. But to my knowledge, the true crown has not been seen from the day of King Marco's murder to this."

"It was most beautiful and unique, made of heavy gold and studded with rubies and sapphires. Anyone beholding it would be certain never to forget it. So young Lira is quite correct. The true crown is indeed missing," concluded Rajiv.

"I wonder why it wasn't hidden in the forest so that Rupert could find it?" she wondered again. "If Rupert is to be king, he'll certainly need a crown!"

"Perhaps I am not yet worthy," said Rupert sagely.

"Unless there is another who wears it," whispered Daniel.

"Then you believe my father still lives?" demanded Rupert, stunned.

"Could another miracle be possible?" wondered Rajiv. "But if so, why leave you to those strange 'grandparents', knowing nothing of your duties or heritage?"

"To keep Rupert safe," suggested Morley. "For any hint of his existence would have been a death sentence."

"True," agreed Rupert. "But what joy to even speculate that my father may yet live!"

"I hope it's true!" declared Lira. "Wouldn't that be a most wonderful thing? And you and your father could rule the land together someday!"

"Let us pray you are right, Lira," said Lalja. "But for now it is already beyond my wildest dreams that Rupert exists in the world, and is preparing to be king someday."

"But isn't Rupert king already?" Lira demanded. "Why wait?"

They exchanged looks and sighed. 'Why wait' indeed! If only this were the moment to stage a rebellion and drive out the ghastly cold-blooded usurpers from the land forever!

"Lira, the people are not prepared," observed Rupert stoically. "There is no army but King Ryker's savage men, and the populace is frightened and weak. I do not believe they would fight. Not yet."

"Even for a Golden-Eyed King?" Lalja demanded.

Liam looked long and hard at Rupert before responding. He had been thrilled beyond measure to know that Rajiv and his son could testify to Rupert's golden eyes. It put all doubts to rest. And what an astonishing ruler he would make someday. So Liam truly believed. But the time was not yet.

"I cannot imagine the populace, who are now so very frightened and cowed, would risk all to follow a child, even one with golden eyes."

"Let us not get ahead of ourselves," said Morley, "for surely our first duty is the journey to Raja-Sharan. That is where your vision leads, unless things have changed, Rupert?"

"No, I feel more than ever that we need make haste; for the land calls out to me. But Rajiv, you and Lalja must come. You belong with us now."

Father and son exchanged looks, comprehending each other without words. Both regarded their extraordinary young prince with sorrow.

"If you command us, we shall certainly obey. But I believe our duty lies here. All my visions tell me this. My son and I must prepare the people for your homecoming. There will be a war, do not doubt! We give courage and hope that there exists a hidden band of rebels ready to come to their aid. We serve you best by remaining to defend your people and your interests. But only with your blessing, my Lord Rupert."

Rupert realized that Rajiv spoke true. He felt shame that he himself was fleeing. But he bit his tongue before he could blurt out that he must remain as well. His duty was to proceed to Raja-Sharan, for his path was guided, as was Rajiv's. He so greatly wished those two paths led to the same destination, but that was a false hope.

Rupert rose and walked to Rajiv's side. He and his son stood and Rupert embraced them. "You do not offend me. You stay to help our people, and there is no greater wish of my heart. And someday we shall be reunited; when the moment comes for our land to be free."

"Oh, it's too sad that you can't come with us!" exclaimed Lira, "for you could then see Lady Meera's homeland. And you could speak for us, for we don't know the language. So no one will understand us!"

Daniel lifted his daughter and kissed her cheek.

"Very true, though we'd desire your company for other reasons: being Rupert's blood kin and having saved our lives are other very agreeable factors in your favor."

"Yes, I do speak the language, as does my son. But I have several books from which my mother instructed me. I will happily present them to you."

By now it was dawn and the party had to rouse themselves. They hoped the graves of Ned and the other soldiers would not be discovered for many a day, if ever. But it was not wise to tarry. The companions must proceed towards the eastern border with all due haste.

They conversed with great animation while making their way to Rajiv's camp. Lalja recounted how the guards had come to capture him when he'd insisted on going to a village market, and then found himself alone, helpless, and caught.

By the time he'd told of his days in captivity, Rajiv's men had returned from their burial duties. The companions immediately put up their hoods. But Rupert and his friends, faces concealed, did thank them for saving their lives. There were about thirty in number, as well as a dozen women and children. All had fled the king's oppression, surviving as best they could, while coming to the aid of those in need.

Rajiv and his son led the comrades into a secluded grove where he kept his few belongings, and produced two books about Raja-Sharan and its language. He held them to his heart before presenting them to Rupert.

"There you are, my young liege. I retrieved them from the ruins of my home and carried them always. And now they are yours. My son and I wish you a swift and safe journey. Our hearts go with you each step."

Rupert took the books, then embraced Rajiv and Lalja. "But how shall we meet again? For the time of my return is uncertain, and the kingdom is wide."

Rajiv laughed with exhilaration. "I have every confidence that, when the time comes, we will be shown by dream or vision exactly where to find each other. I doubt it not!"

Rupert felt suddenly certain that this prediction would indeed come to pass. "Very well, we will await the moment of our reunion. For you have spoken true; we have our separate duties and destinies to accomplish."

Liam produced a pouch retrieved from Majesty's back. "Here, take this. It will help our people in their cause. Use it wisely, my dear old friend. And I, too, will count the days until fate reunites us."

Rajiv received the purse heavy with gold coins and embraced his childhood companion. "You must go quickly now, before parting becomes too painful to bear."

"Yes," agreed Rupert, "though the events of the past day are almost too glorious to comprehend. Our lives are linked forever, doubt that not."

They embraced, and with only one backward glance, Rupert and his friends began their way east, leaving family and comrades behind. And how he already yearned for their reunion, and the liberation of their kingdom from the hideous force that blackened its existence!

Chapter Thirty-Three

Rupert's heart was singing as their morning march began. They had faced almost certain death, and the destruction of all their hopes. Yet now there existed so much reason to rejoice. Rupert had discovered blood relations who had not only delivered them all, but were able to testify to his Golden-Eyed Kingship. Moreover, Rajiv's boyhood friendship with Liam had led to the rescue of Daniel and himself when doomed at High Tower Prison!

Rupert felt an overwhelming desire to reverse course. Why could they not be permitted a few days together? It was painfully difficult to part so soon after discovering their existence; a discovery made under the most dramatic circumstances possible.

But Rupert was aware of another instinct - a compulsion - that his party must cross the eastern border without delay. Each time he harkened to it, it had served him well, though the source of these intuitions continued to remain a mystery.

None had slept the two previous nights, but for a while the exhilaration of miraculous events buoyed them up. By early afternoon fatigue crept in and they sought a roadside haven. There were dark clouds gathering and a chilly wind began to blow. None felt eager to face another storm out of doors.

As they ate a hasty repast of slightly stale bread and cheese, Lira spoke up. "Do you think it safe to stay at an inn this night? It's cold and I just know it will rain."

"We should have opportunity once we cross the border," observed Liam. "Let us consult the map, for we should be certainly nearing Zurland."

Rupert snatched it from his tunic pocket with eagerness. "Oh, yes, we must be close indeed. Though danger might have decreased by eliminating Ned, the need for haste seems more pressing than ever."

"Well, your 'strange feelings' possess more worth than our deepest thought-out schemes," observed Morley with a grin. "So let us examine that mysterious map of yours and see where things lie." What they saw encouraged them.

"I would calculate the border is not three or four days distant," Liam declared. "I find it most incomprehensible that we have survived and soon may have reason to proclaim a measure of safety."

Rupert smiled. "Let us proceed by day as swiftly as we may. For on our speed, all depends."

That said, the party immediately took to the road. The wind picked up and a light but steady rain commenced. But luck was with them, because just before darkness, they happened upon the ruins of a small farm several hundred yards from the roadside. A sharp-eyed Raja had discovered it. The farmhouse had been burned to the ground, but a very rickety barn remained. It would serve their purpose well enough for one night.

By the time they'd built a warm fire under the barn's sheltering roof, the rain had turned to downpour and all were grateful to be out of the elements. And very soon, Liam had prepared a dinner of potatoes seasoned with fragrant garlic, with cups of hot, honey-flavored tea to follow. And so, they felt lucky and content.

The events of the preceding day dominated their thoughts.

"I do wish Rajiv and Lalja had been able to join us," said Lira with a sigh. "They were so nice! And Rupert's true family as well."

"And handy indeed in a fight," added Morley with a slanted smile.

"To be sure," said Rupert. "I've been thinking the very same all day long. It was a great pity we could not spend a few days together.

But the instinct to cross the border drove me on. I'm certain they understood."

"I doubt it not," said Liam. "And we remain united in our hearts."

"I've been thinking about so many things," said Lira. "I must guess that the baby of King Marco and Queen Khar-shar-leen was your father, Rupert. So they were your grandparents. But who are your other grandparents? Who was your mother?"

"Of course, we cannot know," said Rupert. "That baby clearly grew up and married *somebody*...and the lady would have been my mother. But who she was or from where she came, we can hardly guess."

"But do you believe that your grandparents from the forest were your mother's parents? If so, why wouldn't they reveal anything about her?"

"Lira has a good point, as usual," observed Morley. "For your father was a king, even if in hiding or exile. Would he still not seek a princess for a wife? And if so, would it be seen fit for a royal child to be raised in such circumstances?"

"Indeed," agreed Liam. "Why would they not speak of their own child, your mother? I certainly did not hesitate to tell Lira of her absent parents. I desired their memories to be alive in her heart forever. Surely your true grandparents would have done the same."

"Well, I can only hope to meet them again that I may address those very topics," said Rupert with a determined expression. "But for the moment, let us occupy our evening in study of the language of Raja-Sharan. I am eager to learn!"

Lira turned a beautiful pink at the thought of this new and mysterious tongue. Before another moment passed, they were examining the books, which appeared intriguing as well as challenging.

There were long lists of vocabulary, the words in the language of Raja-Sharan on one side of the page, the equivalent in their own on the other. The writing was completely unfamiliar, but luckily, a pronunciation guide was provided. The companions soon sat riveted, attempting to make sense of it.

"My goodness, this won't be easy without a teacher," sighed Lira.

"Oh, but it will be great fun," exclaimed Rupert. "Let us begin to puzzle it out. We should determine to spend at least an hour each day in study. Agreed?"

They did agree, though Morley was less than enthusiastic, having little opportunity for schooling as a youth. He felt some shame at his scant reading skills.

Lira continued to flip through the pages, overjoyed at the colorful illustrations. There were glorious scenes of royal travelers mounted on camel back, garbed in gorgeous robes. Another featured a camel caravan, the beasts loaded down with spices, silks, and gold. Exquisite women and dashing men were featured, all with black hair and eyes. Lira's heart beat faster knowing their journey would take them to this exotically beautiful destination.

But study came first, and before the hour was up, they had acquired some vocabulary and had an enjoyable time quizzing one another; the adults proving somewhat less adept than their juniors. Lira and Rupert possessed amazing memories. It seemed they'd leave the grown-ups far behind before long.

Finally it was time for sleep, and after two nights with no rest, all welcomed it. But Rupert's night was not uneventful. The mysterious, hooded lady made yet another appearance. She warned in the most urgent of tones to display greatest caution, yet make utmost haste to the eastern border.

She repeated her counsel again, in clear yet dream-like tones. 'Take to the hills. Avoid the road. Proceed with dispatch!' And Rupert, waking well before dawn, realized as when the soldiers had been hot on their trail, that again there was not a moment to lose.

He leapt to his feet and lit a fire. And as the porridge and tea were prepared, he woke his soundly sleeping companions, who looked up with momentary alarm. For the expression on Rupert's face was filled with urgency. As they hurriedly downed their repast, Rupert recounted his dream. There was clearly some danger lurking, but of the details Rupert knew nothing.

"It is as if we're regarding an enormous, complex *tapestry of life*," reflected Liam. "We are permitted to observe but one small portion at a time. It is only by standing back and taking in the whole that we will ultimately comprehend what is truly unfolding."

They were swiftly on their way. Despite the warning, Rupert believed they might continue along the main route for another day. After that, they should take to the hills and look for safe passage across the border.

Following Rupert's lead they did not pause until well after dark. They camped, ate hastily, managed to study their language books, and snatched a few hours sleep, rising again before daybreak. All were reminded of their flight through the forest. Yet this was so much better in comparison. They had enough to eat, some opportunity to rest, and could now dare to travel openly due to their masquerade.

From tomorrow, their journey would become more challenging. The comrades were so tantalizingly close to the frontier - only another day or two. Nothing could be allowed to hinder them now.

By early afternoon, the companions reached another crossroads. A soldier nailed a notice to a tree, made an announcement, then mounted his horse and departed. The citizens buzzed about, appearing confused and confounded.

The comrades approached. But before they could examine the proclamation, words of the citizens reached their ears.

"What could this mean?" asked one farmer in indignation. "Why would His Majesty close the border? It's most unjust. My daughter resides in Zurland and is soon to be married. Why should I be forbidden to go?"

"Shh!" hissed his wife. "Do you want someone to report you? It's not for us to question the king's actions."

"Is the border to be closed?" inquired Morley, remembering to use his feminine voice.

"Indeed," replied another passerby, "without rhyme or reason, if you ask me. It's always an ordeal to get across, mind you, and I seldom make the attempt. But suddenly, it's forbidden. Could this mean a war?"

"War!" cried a ragged woman, aghast. "That's all we need to add to our miseries."

"No war," said another fellow. "It appears many suspicious types are trying to leave. I doubt many are planning to sneak in! For why would anyone wish to visit this hellhole?"

There was a bit of grim laughter at that.

"There's a rumor that a detachment of guards has disappeared. Maybe the king thinks they'll flee into Zurland. It's common knowledge that most soldiers don't serve His Highness with a whole heart!"

"How long is the border to remain closed?" inquired Rupert, struggling for calm.

"Who can say? But it's not likely to be opened again any time soon," remarked one woodcutter with a shrug.

With that, the gathering broke up. Rupert and the others surreptitiously examined the posted notice. It did not give much information, only that all borders would be closed indefinitely. Rupert fought against becoming overwhelmed with alarm.

"At least now it is clear why you felt such need for haste," remarked Liam with irony. "We're but a day or so too late."

"We must find another way," proclaimed Rupert. "And we shall! I know it! Nothing will be permitted to keep us from our journey."

With that, the golden-eyed boy proceeded towards the east without another word. His comrades followed with admiration in their hearts. For they knew their boy-king well enough to suppose that, with luck, he'd find yet another improbable solution to their seemingly impossible dilemma.

Chapter Thirty-Four

The comrades continued their rapid march. These were the very last hours of easy travel. As soon as darkness fell, they'd take to the hills and whatever perils awaited.

Rupert, with each step, wondered if he'd erred in permitting delay in their flight. He'd known for days haste was vital, yet could hardly regret pausing to aid Sarah and her baby, or going to the rescue of the unknown boy arrested in his place. For what marvels had been the outcome!

It was foolish to reexamine the decisions which had brought them to this pass. It made no matter now. But along with anxiety about the border closing was a growing certainty they *would* somehow succeed, come what may. Yet Rupert was wary of overconfidence - when one false step could lead to disaster.

They continued in silence until darkness approached, then bid farewell to the road, and moved off toward a grove of trees. No one traveled by night without drawing suspicion.

They prepared a hot supper, keeping warm by their fire, which later provided illumination for their language lesson. But foremost in their thoughts was the challenge that loomed before them.

"Let us look at your map again, Rupert," said Daniel, "for there must be alternate routes across the frontier."

Rupert unfolded it before the firelight. "I see two small paths that head in an easterly direction. They seem to meander through the hills. I'm wondering if they will be patrolled."

"We must assume we'll encounter guards," declared Morley. "It would be just too lucky otherwise."

"Let us decide in the morning," said Daniel. "For it would not surprise me if Rupert received a fresh set of orders from that lady who frequents his dreams!"

But Rupert's slumber was without incident, to his disappointment.

He arose before first light and took an invigorating ride upon Majesty, with Raja chasing their every step. Strangely, he felt exhilarated rather than concerned. The young prince had come to look forward to challenges and obstacles, rather than dreading them.

He greeted his companions as he returned to find breakfast awaiting. "I had a fine sleep, but nothing new to declare," he reported. "I hope that doesn't disappoint."

"Not at all," replied Liam. "It is sufficient to see you looking so cheerful. It makes me suppose that all will be well."

"We will obey you, King Rupert," said Lira with joy. For it was astonishing and wonderful to realize that he was their king, and the fact could be acknowledged - though only in secret, of course.

And with that, the comrades set out. It was not long before they came upon the narrow path indicated on the map. It was seriously overgrown with brush and bramble. They hoped the soldiers were not aware of its existence.

Progress was slow. The way led up and down many a hill, and as they could never be absolutely certain no one was about, they proceeded as silently as possible. Rupert, however, had confidence Raja or Majesty would warn of danger, whether animal or human.

As always, the boy was joyful to be back in the forest. He delighted in the bewitching fragrance of the trees. And the sound of the wind blowing through their branches was one of the most intoxicating melodies in all the world. It aroused in him a trance-like state; as if the harmony created by that music blew through his own self, penetrating his very being.

The party journeyed till dusk and then found an appropriate place to camp. They hoped to reach the border the very next day, and they were obsessed with the prospect.

"Do any of you have knowledge of Zurland?" Rupert wanted to know. "For I know nothing other than its name."

"We have been cut off from report of the outside world since the death of King Marco," said Liam with a frustrated sigh. "From my childhood days, I recall the land as a firm ally of the Golden-Eyed Kings. I believe years ago one of their princesses married into our royal family. I journeyed there with my father when I was a lad."

"Oh, what do you recall?" cried Lira. Her imagination was already afire about a country she'd never seen.

"It was mountainous compared to our land," he reflected. "The people were fond of celebrations. I do recollect that my father and I attended a village wedding. I was only six or seven at the time. But I remember a delicious dessert - chocolate with some sort of mint cream."

"Well, that convinces me that nothing will keep Rupert from getting us there in safety," declared Morley. "For nothing must separate our sovereign from his chocolate!"

They broke into laughter while Rupert blushed.

Unfortunately, none of the others had any experience of Zurland. And so they'd be traveling blind. For all they knew conditions there might have changed as drastically as those in their own kingdom, and they might be facing anything but a friendly welcome.

Dawn was magnificent, and Rupert, as usual, was there to greet it. As the purple and pink masterpiece spread its way across the sky, Rupert spread out his arms in welcome. He felt the sun's radiance penetrate his being. The boy perceived joy, energy, and a sense that he was on his true path.

"Let us set off as soon as we may," he urged.

"Do you fear danger is upon us?" inquired Daniel with concern.

"By no means - somehow I feel that all shall be well."

And with that, the party packed their few belongings and set off. Zurland's border lay no more than ten miles distant. The weather was clear, crisp, and glorious, adding to Rupert's sense of well-being. He wanted to shout and sing. They were so close to escape! It was regrettable that flight from his homeland was essential. He was ruler here, and wished to declare the truth and begin his battle against the loathsome usurper. But fleeing his kingdom was the first step in reclaiming his throne.

They would not pause. The border and freedom lay closer with every step, with the sound of every twig and branch crunched beneath their boots. The men wished they were not forced to travel in heavy skirts, but disguise was still essential to their purpose. But in perhaps just another day they could don masculine garb and stride about openly as men. Rupert thought of that moment with relief, and assumed his male companions would feel the same; especially Morley. How his friend would rejoice!

Abruptly his reverie was broken by Raja, coming to a halt before him. The hound looked meaningfully into his master's eyes, and Rupert instantly understood. Majesty too, had come to stand stock-still.

There must be soldiers about, or at least other people. Daniel indicated he would move forward. Rupert signaled Raja to accompany him, and the two left the path and circled ahead. The others froze in place, Rupert's heart beginning to pound. Some of his easy confidence wavered with the realization that danger might well be at hand.

Very soon, Raja and Daniel returned. He signaled that there were at least a dozen soldiers guarding the border. The comrades were taken aback, somehow believing that avoiding the main road would avoid a challenge to their crossing. Daniel whispered to Rupert, wondering if they should circle around to bypass the king's men.

But Rupert believed it would not be wise. For if discovered, it would be apparent they were attempting to cross in stealth. They must by all means continue to appear as innocent travelers.

So Rupert, after taking a calming breath, closed his eyes to think. And most mysteriously, he felt a disembodied hand upon his shoulder, a hand that wordlessly conveyed warmest assurance. And in a rush, tranquility and certainty returned. He smiled.

"All will be well," he whispered. "Follow me."

Though the others wished to form a more coherent plan, Rupert was already heading towards the border. And the companions soon found themselves confronting the guardsmen, who had targeted them the moment they'd emerged into the clearing.

"Halt, who goes there?" demanded their leader. He was a hard though weary-looking man about Liam's age.

Morley moved himself forward, being the most convincing 'lady' of the group. "Why, we're a family bound for Zurland," he improvised with sudden inspiration. "Is there a problem, dear sir?"

"A problem for *you*," he responded with a smirk. "The border is closed as of yesterday. You ladies are a bit late!"

"My goodness, we've been gathering herbs in the forest. We've heard nothing of this. May we not proceed? We can mean strong soldiers like you no harm."

Morley's response drew rude laughter. "Not unless you mean to attack us with your plants. But we're forbidden to let anyone cross. You'll have to turn back."

"But my dear sister is to be married in two days' time. We must attend, or it will be ill- luck for the couple indeed!" proclaimed Morley.

"Well, they'll just have to carry on without you," said the lead guard, no longer amused.

"Is there not some way we could persuade you?" inquired Morley demurely. "For I'm certain you are all honest gentlemen who would not keep ladies from a family gathering."

The guard was growing weary of them. "Turn back now, I say. Or do you seek trouble? For if so, I'll not hesitate to give it!"

Rupert sensed his friends silently preparing to reach for their concealed weapons. But the comrades stood no chance in an open fight, being far outnumbered. Rupert stepped forward.

"Please, sir, do let us pass. For it would be most unwise indeed to impede our way."

Now the fellow was growing truly vexed, and Rupert's friends attempted to conceal alarm at their prince's hasty action.

"Who dares speak to King Ryker's man like this? Why, you little brat..."

"I mean no disrespect," proclaimed Rupert. "But we are fortune-tellers and thus know the future. I can only warn that ill-luck will descend upon any who hinder our journey. It would not be *our* doing, good sir, but rather forces beyond our control!"

Rupert did not know what madness inspired him to invoke fortune-telling ability. The words seemed to have popped from his mouth without conscious thought.

The claim of being soothsayers produced a ripple of concern from the soldiers. Many were deeply superstitious and feared bringing curses upon themselves. Their bitter lives seemed cursed enough already! The leader, however, appeared unimpressed.

"Oh, so you're all seers and prophets, are you? Well, we could do with a bit of amusement. Go ahead, girl, and read my fortune!" He poked Rupert rudely in the shoulder with his bow, daring him to comply.

Rupert felt a bolt of fear course through him. For he knew well enough he had no such powers. But out of nowhere, some peculiar instinct made him turn his head to the left. It was as if an outside force was controlling the movement. From the corner of his eye, he perceived something clearly - and it convinced him to take a wild chance.

"Why of course, I'll be honored to oblige. But you, sir, are a leader of your men, and your feats and exploits may be only too well known. Do truly put me to the test! Permit me to read the fortune of the least among you."

That produced a general guffaw. "That would be easy enough!" one of the troop declared. "The least among us must be that ridiculous fool there!"

And the ruffian indicated the very man that had caught Rupert's eye. The other guardsmen sneered and shoved the poor fellow towards Rupert. The scrawny soldier had obviously many a time been the butt of their jests and taunting.

The frightened young man hobbled forward. He looked ragged and thin in his tattered uniform. He limped badly. He had a crooked leg. And Rupert felt this could be no coincidence, and gambled that his wild luck would continue.

"Come sir, do not fear us," began Rupert. He took the man's dirty, scarred hand in his and stared at its palm. "I can see you have not been in His Majesty's service long. And I believe your name is Micah," ventured Rupert, attempting to appear without doubt. For on this, all depended.

The others gasped. "Why, yes indeed," whispered the man almost in alarm. "How could you know that?"

"I know many things," continued Rupert now with total assurance. "You have a wife, and a baby girl named...Zelah. Your wife is known as Sarah. And you grow potatoes, when luck is with you."

Poor Micah almost burst into tears. He loved and missed his family so. To hear their names spoken amazed him, though he feared he'd never live to see them again.

Rupert turned to the head man. "Sir, I must warn you that this knave is a danger to you all! He brings dark misfortune to any who cross his path. For your own safety, I urge you to send him home at once! And no harm must befall him along the way, or you will pay the consequences. I fear his mother was a witch who cast dark spells upon any who might interfere with him!"

The soldiers were aghast. "Why, that's true enough," proclaimed their leader. "Ever since he joined us, men have fallen ill. And then, we were assigned to this forsaken post in the middle of nowhere. Besides, he's useless in a fight. I'll be happy enough to see the back of him, let me assure you!"

"Your wife is no longer at home I see," continued Rupert staring at Micah's palm in concentration. "She stays with her sister in a village called Crossly. Go to her at once, and relieve these honest men of their curse!"

Micah looked into Rupert's eyes with disbelief. How could this be? But Rupert smiled reassuringly. And Micah noticed something else at close quarters. The young 'girl' reading his palm was, in fact, an amazingly handsome lad. But he knew enough to maintain silence. And almost staggered at his luck!

Micah looked to the guard for permission to leave.

"Go indeed, and good riddance!" The other soldiers nodded, jeering their own farewells. But before Micah could depart, Rupert spoke again.

"Do not forget to give him means for a safe journey home. For remember, no harm must come to him along the way."

And so, grudgingly, the soldier reached into his tunic, produced a few gold coins, and tossed them onto the ground. "Get on with you. You've brought us nothing but travail. At least we now know the cause!"

And before the soldiers could rethink the matter, Micah retrieved the coins and took off as fast as his crooked leg would allow. And Rupert's friends were dizzy with admiration at their prince's brilliant stratagem.

"I do hope you'll return the favor, kind sir, and allow us to pass into Zurland. For powerful forces protect us as well. We wish no harm to come to brave and gallant servants of your king!"

The leader looked askance, but then shrugged. "They don't pay us enough to take upon ourselves omens and curses. Get along with you then, and let it be known you crossed the border a few days past. And we'll call it even. For you've done us a good turn relieving us of our cursed one."

"Oh, you are kindness itself, dear Captain," said Rupert, giving the man an instant promotion.

And before anything more could be said, Rupert and his party stepped around the barrier that guarded the border and took their first steps into Zurland. And freedom! And Rupert, with his whole heart, blessed whatever had guided them so faithfully.

Chapter Thirty-Five

The boy with golden eyes and his band strode into the Kingdom of Zurland in a euphoric daze. It seemed they were existing in a dream; slow to comprehend their miraculous triumph. They proceeded in stunned silence. After traversing a hillside for several miles, they arrived at the summit, and below spread a magnificent vista; a lovely verdant valley with snowy mountain peaks dazzling in the distance.

Rupert came to a halt. Something enveloped his soul - something he had merely glimpsed before. But now this new sensation flooded his very being: a sense of glorious euphoria, peace, joy, unity with all things. He perceived perfection in all existence. Even the darkest occurrences now found their place in that fabulous and mysterious 'tapestry of life' Liam had spoken of.

His steps were guided, guided from something afar, yet ultimately part of his very being. All of life, of creation itself, seemed spread before him, and never had it all seemed so comprehensible, so certain, so wondrous!

So many rich feelings overwhelmed his heart. Overcome with the glory of the moment, the prince sank to his knees; the sensation as if a magnificent flower within was at last coming to perfect bloom. There were no words to convey this experience. It was beyond words. But the awareness of peace and perfection prevailed in his spirit.

And though this moment would forever remain encased in memory, the splendor of this revelation could not endure. It was something Rupert could not hope to grasp and own, only to treasure forever. For life was not to be lived at this summit of clarity, but instead in the every-day world, and that world was fraught with peril, triumph, and testing.

Tears of wonder and gratitude spilled upon his cheeks. Rupert at last opened his eyes to behold his beloved friends kneeling before him. Joyous rapture was upon their features as they paid him kingly homage and heart-felt fidelity.

But for the first time, Rupert did not blush or stammer in protest. For in truth, *their king he was!* And he had come, in this splendid moment, to fully accept this reality. Yes, he had yet so very much to learn, and would doubtless not always act wisely. Yet wise or foolish, *he was a Golden-Eyed King!* And to deny what that entailed would be absurd and futile.

At last prepared to truly embrace his destiny, Rupert knew generations of Golden-Eyed Sovereigns were with him. And yet there was something else; guiding, supporting, and preparing his true path. What or who this might be remained a mystery. But surely, he would discover it in time.

The young prince finally rose, and gestured that his companions arise as well. He moved to embrace each one. How he treasured them! And how very much he owed them.

"*We can see your golden eyes!*" uttered Liam finally, voice choked with emotion. "All of us can truly see you at last!"

Rupert turned to Morley and Lira for confirmation. Yes, it was true. At last, the moment had come to pass. And they joined Daniel in testifying to those impossibly magnificent eyes and Rupert's royal destiny.

"Nothing could bring me greater happiness. For this moment, I truly know myself for the first time. The joy that fills my being is beyond my capacities to express. But how wondrous that we are joined even more perfectly than before, and truly united in our quest."

Rupert spread out his arms and gave a glorious laugh. The vision of their coming journey filled him with exhilaration and overwhelming anticipation. For certainly, the answer to so many mysteries lay upon their path.

And so Rupert embraced his loved ones, including Raja and Majesty, with a heart bursting with gladness.

"Come, let us truly commence our journey anew. For now we start to Raja-Sharan, breathing freedom for the first time. And let us welcome with courage and gratitude whatever awaits!"

And the companions began their way down the mountain and towards the unknown.

LaVergne, TN USA
17 August 2010
193578LV00001B/5/P